P9-DFS-361

THE ACCOMPLICE

ALSO BY JOSEPH KANON

Defectors

Leaving Berlin

Istanbul Passage

Stardust

Alibi

The Good German

The Prodigal Spy

Los Alamos

JOSEPH KANON

THE ACCOMPLICE

London · New York · Sydney · Toronto · New Delhi

A CBS COMPANY

First published in Great Britain by Simon & Schuster UK Ltd, 2019
A CBS COMPANY

3 5 7 9 10 8 6 4 2

Simon & Schuster UK Ltd
1st Floor
222 Gray's Inn Road
London WC1X 8HB

Simon & Schuster Australia, Sydney
Simon & Schuster India, New Delhi

www.simonandschuster.co.uk
www.simonandschuster.com.au
www.simonandschuster.co.in

A CIP catalogue record for this book is
available from the British Library

Hardback ISBN: 978-1-4711-6265-7
Trade Paperback ISBN: 978-1-4711-6266-4
eBook ISBN: 978-1-4711-6267-1
Audio ISBN: 978-1-4711-9108-4

Printed and bound in Great Britain by CPI Group (UK) Ltd, Croydon, CR0 4YY

For

Peter Stansky

and

William Abrahams (in memoriam)

I

HAMBURG

1

HAMBURG, 1962

IT WAS LATE IN the season to put tables outside, but the unexpected sun had drawn crowds to the Alsterpavillon, all asking for the terrace, so that by noon the entire promenade had become one long outdoor café, people sipping coffee, wrapped in coats and mufflers against the wind coming off the lake, their faces tilted up to the sun.

"You look like a turtle," Aaron said, glancing at his uncle sitting with his chin down in his coat, his great nose sticking out like a beak.

"Idiots, they think it's summer." He drew on his cigarette, a small shrug. "I'm cold all the time now."

"Go to Israel."

"Israel. What's in Israel?"

"Sun at least."

"And then you're even farther away. Another ocean. So maybe that's the idea."

Aaron moved his hand, brushing this away. "Then come back with me."

"To America. To sit around and argue with you." He shook his head. "My work is here."

Aaron looked up at him. "You can't keep doing this. Your heart—"

"So then it's something else. How can I stop? We got Pidulski. All these years and we got him. What is that worth? A man who kicked children to death. In the head, like a football."

"Max—"

"So what is that worth?" he said, his voice rising. "To get him. On trial, so everybody sees. A little heart trouble? OK. I'll take it."

Aaron sipped his coffee, a second of calm. "Max, we need to talk about this. The doctor said—"

"Give up smoking," Max said. "I'm not going to do that either." Taking a noisy puff, illustrating.

"I have to go back."

"You just got here."

"Max."

"You're a big shot. You can take the time off."

"Compassionate leave. It's usually a few days."

"What, to bury somebody? So hang around, it won't be long."

"You told me you were dying. You're not dying."

Max shrugged again. "Anyway, it's cheaper for you to come

here than talk on the phone. Calls to America. Who can afford that?" He paused. "I wanted to talk to you."

"I know. I'm here, aren't I?"

"But you don't talk back. Days now and you don't answer. Who else is there? You're a son to me." He looked toward the bright lake, taking a breath, a theatrical gesture, overcome.

"Max, we've been over this."

"But you haven't agreed yet."

Aaron smiled and Max, catching it, smiled back.

"You want me to retire. Whatever that is. This is something you don't walk away from, what we do. It's not possible. For you either. We're the only ones left in the family. Everyone else— Think about that. Everyone else. You don't turn your back on that."

"Twenty years."

"And still guilty. Still."

"It's different for me. I never knew them."

"You knew your mother. You remember her."

"Of course."

But what exactly? The way she smelled when she leaned down to kiss him good night, the day's last trace of perfume. Sitting in her lap on the train. The voice, wrapping around him like a blanket. But her face was a face in photographs now, no longer someone he knew.

Max was shaking his head. "She waited too long. Herschel was right—get out now. And she says, 'You go, I'll come after.' You know she wanted to keep you here with her? So think, if Herschel had agreed. You would have been killed too, like everybody else. And you think it's not personal with you?"

"Why did she stay?" Aaron said quietly, as if it were a casual interest, the question he'd been asking all his life.

"She was helping people here. You know this. Herschel said, 'Save yourself. Think of the child,'" he said, nodding to Aaron. "But he'll be safe with you, she says. I can't leave now—" He stopped, the story still painful. "She thought she had more time. We all thought that. Except Herschel. The smart one. So you can thank God he didn't wait. You'd be a statistic. A number. Like Minna." He looked over. "She was tall, like you. That's where you get it. And the hair." He touched his own, a few wisps. "Not from our side." He took a breath. "Did he talk about her? Herschel?"

"When the letters came." The ones that meant she hadn't abandoned them, however it felt. "She was always on her way. Soon. Any day. And then they stopped." He looked up, answering the question. "He didn't talk about her after that. He didn't want to talk about—what happened. He said people didn't want to hear about that."

"People there. And by this time he's Wiley. Weill isn't good enough. More American than the Americans. As if it would make any difference—that they wouldn't know what he was."

"He blamed himself. Leaving her behind."

"*Ach*," Max said, a sound of dismissal. "And what good did that do?" He shook his head. "She didn't die because she stayed. She died because they killed her. Don't forget that. That's what this is all about. They killed her. Everybody. That's who we do this for. Your family."

"Max, I never knew them."

"Listen to them now, then. You can hear them if you listen." He moved his hand, taking in the crowd, as if all the Weills, all the dead, were here in the crowd on the Binnenalster. "I hear them all the time. You don't retire from that." He moved his hand toward Aaron's. "I'll teach you what you don't know. The archives. It's all about the documents. Not all that cloak-and-dagger stuff Wiesenthal talks about. Liar. You listen to him, he found Eichmann himself. Shoved him in the car. Oh, the Mossad was there? Who would know, with Wiesenthal playing Superman?"

Aaron looked over. "Max." The old rivalry, Max and Wiesenthal even sharing a *Time* cover. The Nazi Hunters. As if the feud were a Macy's and Gimbel's rivalry, with discount sales.

"All right. So it helps him raise money. Eichmann. Who cares about Pidulski? Except the children he murdered. Maybe I should do it too. Say I'm this close to Mengele," he said, pinching his fingers. "To Schramm. You could always raise a few donations if you said you had a lead on him. Which I did once." His voice went lower, private. "Imagine, to get him. After everything. But he got away. And then he cheated me. Dead. But no trial. No—" He caught himself drifting. "So now it's Mengele if you want to raise money. Wiesenthal says he's in Paraguay. No, Brazil. No, somewhere else. So here's a check. Go find him." He stopped. "We all do it. How else to keep going? Think how useful you would be. An American. The money's in America. And maybe a little guilt too. A nice young American. Not some *altekaka* who talks with an accent. An FBI man—"

"I'm not FBI."

"So whatever it is. Which you don't say. You think I can't guess? 'For the government,' except you don't say what. So what else could it be?" He shook his head. "Herschel's boy. Who can't tell me what he does."

"I did tell you. I'm an intelligence analyst."

"Herschel said you were thinking of leaving the job. Before he died. That's what gave me the idea."

"What idea?"

"You taking over the business."

Aaron smiled. "The business." As if it were real estate. Linen supply.

"Laugh if you want. OK, not a business. But not a charity either. I have to pay my people. Elena. The office rent. Nothing grows on trees. The World Jewish Council gives something. Then, donors. Maybe you could raise more. I don't take for myself. A little. Not like Wiesenthal. And then pleading poverty. He puts the office in the living room. What next, a hair shirt?" He looked over. "But he gets the donations. And after Eichmann, even more. An impresario. Show business. Not justice. That's what we gave Pidulski, justice."

"And the children are still dead."

Max said nothing, squinting against the glare on the water. "Yes, still dead."

"I'm sorry. I didn't—"

Max waved his hand. "You think I don't think about that too? What good?" He took out another cigarette. "You know what Confucius said?"

Aaron looked over, surprised.

"'Before you embark on a journey of revenge, dig two graves.'" Blowing a little smoke for effect. "So maybe I'm digging mine too, I don't know." He looked at Aaron. "But it's worth it. Even if it's that. My grave too. What else am I living for?"

Aaron said nothing, watching him smoke. Like his father, the same gestures, all three of them marked by some shadow on a gene.

"It'll be like when you used to come in the summer. We'll do things."

Summers with Max. Sometimes just a few weeks, once a whole month, Herschel's gift, Aaron passed from one brother to the other like a family heirloom that had to be shared. Max eager and then overwhelmed, his routine disrupted. Day trips to Lübeck, Max fully clothed on the beach, Aaron playing in the sand. A visit to the Buddenbrooks house, which Max insisted was a holy site of German literature, and which Aaron found stuffy and old. A borrowed cottage on a lake, Max reading files on the porch, Aaron trying to fish, make friends with the neighbors. Awkward, well-meaning summers. But what Aaron remembered were the good-byes, Max teary and fussing over the luggage, turning him over to the stewardess, his hands almost clutching at Aaron's clothes, holding him back, as if he were asking for another chance. Then a kiss on the forehead, Aaron embarrassed without knowing why, the love so desperate.

"Tell me something," Max said now. "This government work you do. That we don't talk about. This analysis. Why do you do it?"

"Why?" He pretended to think. "Because I want the good guys to win."

"Ah. And you know who they are?"

"I know who the bad guys are."

Max looked over, his eyes almost impish. "Then you're perfect for this job."

Aaron looked away. A fountain in the lake was shooting water into the air. Beyond, on the larger Aussenalster, there were sails. The air around them was noisy with German, a soft buzzing, no one barking orders, just enjoying pastry in the sun, the war a long time ago.

"I have a job, Max."

"Chasing Communists." He put up his hand before Aaron could say anything. "Don't bother. That's what they do over there. A Red under every bed. Herschel was a Communist. You knew that, yes? Your own father. That's why he had to leave. The Nazis went after the Communists first. And now here you—"

"He didn't stay a Communist."

"What would you have done? Round him up with the others?" He stopped. "All right. Never mind. We didn't come here to argue. Just to warm me up before you pack me off to Israel. Some old people's home there. All Jews. Talk about peaceful. But that's why you're thinking about leaving? You don't want to be a part of that." His voice softer, reeling him in. "Am I right?"

Aaron turned back to face him. "Always," he said with a small smile. "Another Confucius. Did he really say that, by the way? About the two graves?"

"Who the hell knows? What do you think? They had a steno right there to take things down? Maybe it was Charlie Chan, I don't know." He looked over at him. "You wouldn't have to move here. Just some of the time, because the documents—we could work something out. You could get the Americans involved again. It's funny, when you think that's how I started. With the Americans. All the DPs, all of them with stories, with testimony, and the Americans didn't know what to do with it. Even the ones who could speak German. And I was a doctor, so I would take the medical histories. Then the rest. They would talk to me. What they saw, what happened to them, who did it. I realized this was *evidence*. So I got a job with the CIC. Collecting all this, making files. Documents. It's all there. Everyone had to have a card, some record, in the DP camps. Sometimes they lied, but that becomes interesting too—why? But mostly they would tell you what happened. So I had the evidence before I had the Nazis. They could hide, you had to find them, but once I did, I had them. It was all in the documents. Witnesses. Dates. Everything."

"Max—"

"I'll show you." He put up his hand again. "All right. Just think about it. No one's pushing you. You know, the documents, they're your inheritance. It's like a house somebody leaves you, you have to take care of it. What are you going to do with them after I'm gone?"

"The German government has a department to handle war crimes."

"And how many Nazis have they caught? Unless you drop one right in their laps. Shame them into it. You give them the documents, they'll file them away, until everybody in the file is dead. This is your inheritance. You've got to think, take care of it. There are papers going all the way back to '45, DP records, Red

Cross travel permits, *Fragebogen*. This is a *treasure*. You don't give this to the Germans."

Aaron imagined the dusty files, ragged index cards once carried camp to camp, release forms, Max's collected stories, typed up on an old Underwood with a fading ribbon. A treasure.

"And now, after the divorce, there's no one— I mean, you do as you like. You don't have to think about—" He took out another cigarette. "Maybe it's a good time to make a change. Something new. What happened there anyway? If I can ask. Without getting my head snapped off."

Aaron waited a second, then reached over and lit Max's cigarette. "She said I was married to my job. The one you think I'm so anxious to leave."

"Huh," Max said, a grunt. "All right, so it's none of my business. Who knows what goes on between people? Not even them sometimes. Things change."

But not Claire, helpless as he drifted away from her into the Agency, the work he couldn't talk about, until there was nothing to talk about.

Max moved away from it, looking around, up toward the busy Jungfernstieg behind them, the department stores and shopping arcades. "Look at this place. You should have seen it after the war. Everything gone, from the bombs. Everything. And now look."

"Why Hamburg? I always wondered. Why didn't you go back to Berlin?"

"I did. But everything there reminded me of before. And you could never get anything out of the Russians. Documents, any help. The Americans, yes, but not the Russians. And here in the

British Zone things were much looser. You could get your hands on files quickly, no red tape—you just took. The truth was, they didn't care. They thought the Americans were crazy, with all their trials. A little naïve. And they didn't have the money, so it was all loose, you could just scoop things up. Perfect for me. Besides, Hamburg was never a Nazi city."

"Neither was Berlin."

"No. But here—it's something new for me. No memories. And—" Looking up, almost twinkling. "It was good for the business. The press is here. *Stern* and *Der Spiegel* and *Die Zeit*—all here. More. So it's good for contacts. Anyway, I came. I like the water, the boats. It's pleasant." He waved his hand toward the Binnenalster.

"But Germany. To stay after—"

"So I don't buy a Volkswagen. Like the American Jews. No Volkswagens. No Mercedes. And they think that does it." He looked up again to the Jungfernstieg. "So who's hurting? Anyway, the people I want to find are here. Why go somewhere else if they're here?"

"Or Brazil. Argentina."

Max shrugged. "The big fish. Who else could afford to go so far? So let Wiesenthal waste his money and catch them. Paraguay. In the jungle yet." A kind of verbal shudder. "And meanwhile there's a man down in Altona. Like Pidulski. Keeps to himself. Polite to the neighbors. You'd never think to look there was blood on his hands. No one knows. A quiet life. Like it never happened. All those things—all in the past. We don't talk about that. Until I find him. And then, we do. My present to the Germans. A mirror. Look at yourselves."

His voice had gotten lower, as if he were talking to himself, and now he looked up, slightly embarrassed, overheard.

For a minute neither of them said anything, not sure where to go.

"Herschel was like that," Aaron said finally. "He wouldn't buy German cars, anything. Not even Bayer aspirin."

Max looked down at his cigarette, still brooding. "How was it with him? At the end. He was in pain?"

"They gave him drugs."

"Did they help?"

Aaron nodded. "Toward the end, I don't think he felt anything. He was out most of the time."

"Herschel." He stubbed out the cigarette. "I hope it's quick, when it's me."

"Don't talk like that. Plenty of mileage left," Aaron said, trying for a smile.

Max made a face. "The truth? I don't see like I used to. That water? It's like a flashbulb in my eyes. I have trouble with buttons. You think, what the hell is this? I can't button a shirt? I watch television, sometimes I fall asleep. I'm watching the show, I'm interested, and the next thing I know I'm asleep. Stairs?" He waved his hand. "So when did this happen? Overnight, you're an old man."

"You don't take care of yourself."

"It ages you."

"What?"

"This business. Everything. I came out of the camp, my hair was white. What was left," he said, touching his head. "But you know what's happening now? I'm seeing people from that time. Years, you put it out of your mind, then all the sudden they're there. I don't mean I really see them, don't worry, I'm not crazy yet, just that I think about them. Like Herschel, that's what reminded me. You picture them in your mind. Daniel. I see Daniel all the time now. I never thought we'd have children. Too old. And then—Daniel. What does it mean, I'm seeing them? They're all dead." He cleared his throat, the thickness in his voice. "So, what? They're waiting for me?"

"Max. It's a way of holding on to them, that's all."

"I see the other ones too. The ones you don't love. Even some of the guards. Not fuzzy, clear, the way they looked. Why would I want to hold on to them? Murderers."

"Maybe we don't get to pick. You remember things or you don't. All of it."

"But that time—"

"Max," Aaron said, his voice soft. "It's always going to be there if you keep it alive, the way you do. This work."

"You think I should forget it?"

"No."

"Even if I wanted to—"

"I know."

"You think I could let Daniel go? My own son?"

"No."

Max turned away, disturbed, then sat up straighter, gathering himself. "You just think I should let the rest of it go. Close the files. Let them get away with—"

"I'm just saying let someone else do it. It's time."

"So for once we agree," Max said, looking at him.

Aaron shook his head. "I can't be you."

"Who else, then? Elena? She's a typist."

"You'll kill yourself if you keep—"

"Digging my grave. Confucius says. I wish I'd never mentioned it. You know he never says how long it takes. Maybe I have time we don't know about."

"I hope so."

Max met his eyes, then looked away. "We should go. I'm freezing out here. I won't have to dig anything. Where's the waiter?" He turned, shading his eyes against the sun. "Fritz."

Not a waiter, a man with a newspaper under his arm coming down the steps from the street, his bulky form now throwing a shadow across the table.

"Max, it's you? I thought you never went out."

Young, somewhere in his thirties, not fat but thick, his clothes slightly disheveled, as if he had thrown them on without looking.

"It's for him," Max said, pointing to Aaron. "My nephew. From America. He's come to work with me. My new partner. Aaron, Fritz Gruber."

Fritz extended his hand. "Partner? For the *Einzelgänger*? What's the English? Lone wolf. Now he runs with a pack?" he said, enjoying his own wordplay.

"Just one," Aaron said easily, going with it.

"Join us," Max said, starting to pull out a chair.

"Can't. Work," Fritz said, touching the newspaper.

"The man of letters," Max said.

"You're a writer?" Aaron said.

"Only this kind," Fritz said, holding out the newspaper now. "Journalist."

"A real journalist," Max said. "Someone gets the facts straight."

"I spelled his name right once," Fritz said pleasantly. "He never got over it. So, you have anything for me?" he said to Max.

"If I did, you'd already have it."

"I'm glad I ran into you. I was going to call. You know how to reach Pidulski's son?"

"What, on the phone?"

Gruber nodded.

"Somewhere. Why?"

"I want to talk to him. I had an idea. A series, Sons of the Reich. Growing up Nazi. What's it like for the children now? What did they know? What do they remember? Here, take a look. I started with Horcher's son."

"He'll never talk to you. Pidulski."

"You'd be surprised. Anyway, I can try. You tell them one of the others talked and that makes it all right. It's in the air now." He turned to Aaron. "You picked a good time for this work. Since Eichmann, people are interested. Before, nobody wanted to know."

"And what does Horcher's son say?" Max said.

"What they all say at first. The good father. Always kind. Every Nazi, it turns out, had a child on his knee at home. What did they do at the office? No one knew. Desk work. But now, since Eichmann, we know what work. *Schreibtischtäter*. Desk murderers," he translated for Aaron. "All the good fathers. So it's difficult for them. To know what to feel now. You know how I got the idea? Eichmann's son. He never changed his name. Eichmann did, but none of the children. They must have felt safe enough not to bother. And then the son starts dating a young woman and her father—so the rest you know. One thing leads to another and then to Eichmann. Because the son never changed his name. So what did he know?"

"And what did he?" Max said, curious.

"I don't know. He's in Argentina. I can only talk to the children here. The paper's not so rich. So Pidulski's number, yes? You won't forget?"

"It's still working," Max said, tapping a finger against his temple.

"Yes? And how's the rest? I heard you were in the hospital," he said, playful but concerned.

"A checkup. Don't get excited."

"He does too much," Fritz said to Aaron.

"And you with the coffee all day, all night?" Max said. "Let's see who goes first. I'm writing the eulogy now."

"You won't be asked," Fritz said, having fun with it. "Ilse thinks you're a bad influence."

"Huh," Max said. "On such a blameless life."

He started to get up to say good-bye and stopped halfway, an old man's crouch, then froze. Aaron looked up. Max was blinking now, the blink a kind of windshield wiper, trying to see more clearly, his face white, staring past Fritz down the promenade. Aaron followed his glance—nothing, people at tables, a man in a coat walking past—then looked back at Max, alarmed now, feeling a rush of dread. It was happening. A sound in Max's throat, indistinct, a stroke victim struggling to talk.

"Max," he said, getting up, taking Max's elbow.

But now Max rose a little, not paralyzed, lifting his arm, as if he were starting to point.

"It's him." Barely a whisper, his voice an odd croak, so that Fritz looked alarmed now too.

"Max, sit," he said, moving to help Aaron.

"It's him." His face twisting, an involuntary tic.

"Who?"

"Stop him," Max said, another hoarse whisper. "It's him." Lifting his hand higher and then suddenly clutching it to his chest, his body in spasm, falling.

Aaron grabbed his arm to break the fall, but Max pitched forward, knocking the coffee cups off the table, then the table itself, Fritz grabbing his other side as he went down, the table falling, a crash, people around them turning, too startled to respond, then getting up, moving back, a first instinct. He was down now, Aaron leaning over him.

"Max." He looked up at the small crowd. "Somebody get a doctor."

But Max was moving his head, a "no no" gesture. "It's him. Otto. Go after—"

"Otto?"

"Schramm." Seeing the dead now, maybe all the other visions a getting-ready exercise.

"What did he say?" Fritz said.

"Nothing," Aaron said quickly, covering. "A doctor?"

But now Max had rolled over onto his side, pointing arm still outstretched, looking again past Fritz down the terrace. A gasping sound, which only Aaron heard as "stop him." Then a scraping of chairs as people cleared a space around him. Aaron looked up, following Max's gaze. The man in a coat still walking.

"Please. Please." Max's voice still faint, but frantic now.

"He's having an attack." A voice behind them. "Somebody do something."

"Stop him," Max grunted.

The man passed a few more tables, then turned for a second, hearing the commotion. A winter coat, a hat, the face almost hidden by the brim, features blurred, as if the camera catching them had been shaking. He looked down the promenade, a quick scan, then turned to them, his face still for an instant, a snapshot, just one, and then turned again, walking on, everyone else now coming toward Max, only one walking away, beginning to hurry, late for something.

"See. See," Max said to Aaron.

But what had he seen? An ordinary face, already forgotten. And now Max was clutching at his chest again, clearly in trouble.

"My god," Fritz said, for something to say. "Should we move him—"

"No, don't move him." Someone in the crowd. "Let the ambulance people do it. That's the first thing."

Max had grabbed Aaron's lapel. "Aaron. Don't lose him."

"Shh. Nobody's losing anything. Be quiet. The ambulance is coming."

He looked up, past the crowd. Maybe the man would turn

again, another look at his face. But he was gone, through the doors of the Nivea Building or swallowed up by the crowds in the Gänsemarkt.

Another clutch at his lapel. "I can't die. Not now."

"Nobody's dying." His stomach falling as he said it. The only one left, the last part of him, and suddenly he felt a helpless panic. Do something.

"Can you breathe?" He loosened Max's tie. What else? "Where's your medicine?" he said, starting to go through Max's pockets.

A half smile. "At home."

"At home. You're supposed to carry it." Don't scold. Not now. What was the point? "Is there pain?" Nodding to the heart, just filling time until a stretcher arrived, someone who knew what to do. Was that a siren coming from the Jungfernstieg?

"You saw?" Max said. "You saw?"

Aaron nodded, brushing it aside.

"What's he saying?" Fritz said.

Aaron looked up. How to explain? Maybe what it would be like now, seeing people for real, not just in a confused mind's eye.

"He's agitated, that's all."

"Did you see the look on his face? I've never seen him like that."

"A heart attack. They say it grabs you like a fist. The shock of it. Oh, here—"

Some waiters had come to clear away the tables for the emergency unit, sweep up the shards of broken water glasses, the other customers forming a ring around them. Aaron thought of an operating theater, people staring down at the body. And then two men in uniforms were putting Max onto a stretcher, lifting him. He grabbed Aaron's hand.

"I can't die now. After."

"After—"

"After we get him."

"Shh. You'll be fine. We're going to the hospital."

A paramedic placed an oxygen mask over Max's face.

"Get him? Get who?" Fritz said.

"It's nothing. He thought he saw somebody."

"And he has an attack? Who, the devil?"

"Schramm," Aaron said, preoccupied, feeling Max's hand.

Fritz looked at him. "Schramm? Somebody dead? He's seeing a dead man?"

"He's—having an attack. He doesn't know what he's saying."

"To think, if that's the last person he sees. To end like that."

"He's not ending," Aaron said, starting to follow the men to the ambulance.

"I didn't mean— I'll come with you," Fritz said. Then, before Aaron could object, "You may need the German. Anyway, I'm fond of him."

"Yes," Aaron said, looking at Max, small even on the narrow stretcher. The only one left.

2

THEY TOOK HIM TO the big hospital in St. Georg, tearing along the Aussenalster in the cramped ambulance, the attendants talking to each other, everyone busy with Max. Fritz had been right: Aaron was grateful for his German. His own was good enough to get around, but not to grasp the medical terms flying past him like darts as he sat half-numb, staring at Max's oxygen mask.

"They want to know who his doctor is," Fritz said.

"Bachmann. I don't know his first name. In the Neustadt."

A salvo of rapid-fire German, back and forth, an IV, a drip bag being hung.

"They know him. Jakob, by the way. Does Max take nitroglycerine?"

"Something. I don't know what. Pills. He left them at home."

A paramedic glanced at him, trying not to look impatient.

"History," he said abruptly. "Has this happened before?"

Aaron nodded. "This summer. I don't know how severe. Bachmann would know."

The paramedic looked up. "So soon."

"Don't worry," Fritz said to Aaron. "He survived Auschwitz. He's an ox."

Aaron looked at Max, somehow even smaller in the ambulance, as if he had shrunk on the stretcher, birdlike under the IVs, only his beak nose sticking up. "Thank god you got Herschel's nose," he used to say, "not Groucho's," pointing to his own, a family joke. Blood.

Now he was moving, gesturing with his free hand.

"He's trying to say something."

Aaron heard a sound through the oxygen mask, then noticed the tear, just one, running down to his ear. The paramedic moved the mask, holding it, a second only.

"I let him go. Daniel. Like this," he said, opening his hand.

Aaron looked at him, dismayed.

"Gone." Max moved his head. "I let him go."

Then the medic put the oxygen back, hearing the screech of tires, bracing the stretcher to stop it from shooting forward. The back doors were flung open and attendants swarmed around the stretcher, moving it out, as precise as a military drill, everyone hurrying, Aaron and Fritz just observers now, in the way.

"Wait in there, please," the medic said. "It's not allowed here. I'll be back."

And then he was gone too, the rest of the hospital staff still going about their work, nurses in white with clipboards, aides moving wheelchairs, pieces of machinery, indifferent. Beyond the other doors, Max was being poked with needles, refusing to die, not now, not before— His life hanging, Aaron thought, on something he hadn't really seen.

The waiting room was empty, just a few faux leather chairs and standing ashtrays, some nature watercolors on the walls and a coffee machine. Fritz brought two cups over and settled into one of the chairs.

"*Der Alte*," he said, nodding to the picture of Adenauer by the coffee. "Do you think it's for praying? Maybe to remind us how old. Cheer up, you can be as old as me." He paused, sipping the coffee. "Who's Daniel?"

"His son."

"Who died at Auschwitz? So, 'I let him go.' He can't blame himself for that, for Auschwitz. It's like that sometimes, with the survivors."

"I don't think it's that."

"Does he talk to you about it? That time."

"No. Not about himself."

"No. I used to ask him sometimes and he'd say, 'Read the stories, they're all true, read the transcripts, from the trials, it's all there.' But not his. That he kept private. So what happened, I wondered. A doctor and then not a doctor. So why? He never says. How often does that happen, a doctor stops?"

"Maybe he lost the stomach for it, after so much—"

Fritz nodded. "Maybe the son is the clue. Maybe after that, he lost interest. In life, even. Just the hunt. Now it's just the hunt."

Aaron looked over at him. "Is that what you're going to say in the obit?"

Fritz held up his hand. "Thinking out loud. I don't write the obituaries. They have a man for that. Maybe it's already done. Max Weill. You want something on hand."

"Well, let's hope he's early." He glanced toward the door. "You don't have to stay. I know you have things—"

"Let's hear what they have to say. Then I'll go."

"It's nice of you to do this."

"No, I owe him something. He's a friend." He looked up. "And a good source. So, it's true? You're going to work with him?"

"He seems to think so. I think he should stop. Maybe after today he'll—"

"He'll never stop. Feet first. Only then."

"He may have to. Seeing dead people. Then what?"

Fritz lit a cigarette, buying a minute. "Maybe it's somebody who looked—" He stopped. "I don't like to think that. That he's losing his mind. Have you noticed any—?"

"No, nothing. He's the same. Except he says he's been thinking about it, the camps. They say that happens, near the end."

"That's when you're drowning," Fritz said, waving this off. "It's more likely there's a resemblance, with this man today."

"But he knows Schramm's dead. Everybody does. There was never any question, was there?"

Fritz shook his head. "They had the dental records. The body was identified. I know, I wrote the story. Even in Argentina, when you're dead, you're dead. People have to sign off on it. Even the insurance paid."

"He had insurance, a man in hiding?"

"He wasn't hiding there. Only from us. From Max. But nobody

was looking. He had a life there. A new name. And then the accident. So maybe a disappointing end, a car crash—hanging would have been better—but what's the difference if you're dead?"

They were on the second cup of coffee when the doctor came in.

"He's stable."

"So he'll live?"

"There's no cure for this, you know," he said, seeing Aaron's face. "All these years and all we can say is 'rest.' The nitroglycerine opens the arteries, keeps the blood moving. Aspirin is good—no one knows why. But all we really can do is keep him calm, let it pass."

"Can I see him?"

"You're Aaron? He asked for you." He nodded. "Yes, it's good, someone with them. It keeps them peaceful. But wait a little. We're moving him to a room. We'll have to keep him for a few days, to be safe. I'll be back after we move him." He raised a finger. "If he's sleeping, don't wake him."

"But he'll live," Fritz said to the doctor, a reporter confirming a story.

"Until the next one," the doctor said, leaving. "A few minutes only," he said to Aaron.

Fritz put on his coat. "I'm sorry, I would stay but my editor—"

"No, no, please. I can't thank you enough."

Fritz handed him a card. "Let me know how he is. If there's any change."

Aaron looked at him, a new thought. "You're not putting this in the paper, are you?"

Fritz shook his head. "Don't worry. It's not such a big story. The *Time* cover? How long ago was that?" Then, hearing himself, slightly embarrassed, "Maybe you can get him to slow down a little now. You can't get all the Nazis. Too many. Or none, if you believe them." He nodded again to his card. "Call if there's a change. Then it's news."

When Fritz had gone, Aaron walked across the room, jittery, an expectant father pacing, then stood at the window watching clouds move in and cover the sky. Real Hamburg weather, gray as the Elbe, turning cold and raw, as if some door were closing on the Indian summer afternoon, closing on him, stuck here now.

Max's room faced the city, not the lake, a window framing rooftops and a steeple, dimmed by the cloud cover and the sheer curtains the nurse had pulled across.

"Let him sleep," the doctor said, almost a whisper. "You're the son?"

"Nephew."

"It's just—someone has to sign papers."

Aaron nodded. Back with Herschel, the stifling room, the one responsible.

He sat in a chair by the bed listening to Max breathe, a steady rhythm, a child sleeping. Maybe you can get him to slow down a little. The *Time* cover? How long ago was that?

"Is he gone?" Max, clearing his throat but audible, not weak.

"Yes."

"Good. We can talk."

"You need to sleep."

"I'm dying and you're quarreling."

"How do you feel?" Aaron said, a step back.

"How do I feel."

"The doctor said you'd be here a few days."

Max nodded, accepting this, then waved his hand. "Is there a little water?"

Aaron poured some, then held the glass to Max's mouth.

"Thank you," Max said. "That's better. You get dry. Now listen to me. It's important. I know what you're thinking—he's over the deep end, delirium, something worse. But I'm fine—that part anyway. And I know what I'm talking about. So listen."

"Max—"

"I don't see ghosts, I'm not crazy. It was Otto."

"He's dead," Aaron said quietly.

"It's a mistake. Somebody made a mistake. It was him."

"You thought he was dead."

"So I can make a mistake too."

Aaron raised his eyebrows.

"But not this. Not about him."

"You didn't even see his face."

"I saw enough."

"After how many years, for one second. Not even. And that was enough."

Max paused, regrouping. "I don't need to see his face. I saw him walk. In front of me. Do you know how many times I walked behind him? While he made the selection? He would make me come, walk behind him while he did it. Left to the gas, right to the barracks. For work. Over and over. Do you think I could ever forget that? How he walked? And then today—" He put up his hand. "All right. I'm not getting excited. I'm just telling you something. I would put my life on it. My life."

Aaron looked away. Defuse it. "I thought Mengele made the selections."

"He did. He enjoyed it. Humming sometimes. Looking for his twins. All those poor children. Barrack 14. The Zoo, they called it. And then they'd move them to the Gypsy camp for the experiments." He caught himself. "But he couldn't be there all the time. For the selection. So sometimes Schramm did it. Schumann too, or one of the other doctors, always a doctor. A medical decision if they could work. But mostly Schramm. He was under Mengele. Even though he was older, my age. So a little friction there. They didn't like each other—it was always formal with them. But Otto did the sterilization tests, and they were interested in that in Dahlem, at the Institute, so Mengele never interfered. And if he couldn't do the selection, then Otto. His second in command. That's how everything happened. Because he was making the selection the day I arrived. What should we call it, fate? Not luck. Not luck." He broke off, upset.

"Max, don't—"

"I'm all right. You have to know. What he is to me. Then tell me if I could make a mistake. Not know him. Just the walk. Out for a stroll. While he was sending people to their deaths." He stopped and swallowed, then picked up the thread again, his voice steady now, a willed calm, pacing himself.

"So. That day. You read about it, you think you know. But you don't know the smell. The noise. Shouting. The dogs. They unlocked the doors. Finally. Days on that train. No water. And

Daniel is with me. Ruth, you know, was already dead a year by then. A nervous temperament, always. I think the fear killed her. Not a very scientific diagnosis but science doesn't know everything. Not Ruth. So the two of us. Holding on to me. And the doors open and people are yelling, and you have to jump. The train, it's high for a little boy, so I jump and then lift him down. And his eyes, watching everything. The size of it. Barracks and then more barracks, you couldn't see to the end. All the chimneys. Guards with clubs. The dogs, he was afraid of the dogs. So he held on to me like this." He clutched Aaron's hand. "The children, they're mostly with their mothers, not in the men's line, but he's with me. And Otto comes to the platform. For his stroll. And he sees me. He knows me, from university. "Max, it's you?" Then he shouts, 'Any doctors, stand out of line. Over here.' And I thought, he's trying to save me, a special work detail, not hard labor. We studied medicine together. He's helping me, without showing the others. So of course I stand out of line. With Daniel. Still holding me." He clutched again. "And Otto points with his stick—go with the other children. And he says to me, 'Don't worry, you'll see him later. After the delousing.' So what could I do?" He opened his hand, letting Aaron's fall away. "I nod, it's OK, and he goes to the other line. To the gas, I learned later. I didn't know then. And Otto doesn't say a word. He watches him go and he turns to me. 'You'll work with me. We need doctors.' A smile. Knowing Daniel is walking to— A child. Imagine how frightened, to see everyone naked. Grown-ups. He's never seen this before. Alone. But maybe some mother looked after him. And then of course the doors closing and the screaming—"

He stopped again. "But we're walking, the doctors, and Otto is with us and while we're walking he must have known Daniel was dying, how he was dying, and—what? There's some pleasure in this? Talking to me while he's killing my son. Don't worry, you'll see him later. And when I don't, what do I say? Because by that time I know if I say anything, I'll be gassed too. So we pretend to be colleagues. The other doctors, they mostly worked with the prisoners. Prisoners with prisoners. To keep them alive, so they could work. Try to stop the typhus. They were afraid the guards would catch it. What doctors do. But me, I work with him. He tells me to do things. I do them. Never an actual killing. He's clever. Never a situation where you break and you can't do it. But look what you are doing. We worked with X-rays. They had the idea to sterilize people with them. It was a question of when, how long an exposure. The women they worked on in Block 10. Auschwitz 1. Terrible things. Tumors in the fallopian tubes. The pain. Burns in the uterus. We were in Birkenau, the men. Boys, really. Pubescent. The genitals placed on a metal plate, then the X-rays. How long? Different times, sometimes very bad burns. Another group, physical castration, one testicle, both, which is more effective? As if this is a real question. And after the X-rays? Semen samples to test for fertility. Otto did it with a piece of wood, like a club, up the rectum to rub the prostate until the semen was discharged. So the boys were—humiliated? No, whatever's worse. Of course, later they were killed, with the others, so— He didn't make me do this. But I was part of it. Part of the experiments. He made me—complicit. Think what that means. To be part of it. He liked watching me struggle with this. And give in. We always gave in. Or it was the gas. So we were like him. What he did, we did. Complicit. Daniel? They were going to kill him anyway. The children were the first to go. Nothing would have saved him. It was the way things were there. But this other? A special torture. Making me part of it, the same kind of murderer, using science to cover what we were doing. No better than him. He took my soul. So let me ask you, if you were me, in my place, would you forget how such a man walked? Would you know him?"

Aaron looked at him, his mind swimming. X-ray plates and inflamed scrotums, whimpering. Mothers taking off their clothes, eyes wide with terror. The choking, gasping for air. All the stories, all of them familiar and yet each time new, looking into the dark pit of what was possible.

"Yes," he said, the expected answer.

"Yes," Max said, lying back on his pillow, closing his eyes. "It was him."

Aaron waited.

"And now I can't do it," Max said. "Not by myself. With this." He opened his eyes. "You have to help me. This one thing. Not a guard this time. A monster. It's worth everything to get him."

"How? Tell the police he's still alive? Because you had a feeling."

"It was him. You don't believe me?"

"I believe you think you saw him. Maybe you did. Let's say you did. How do you prove it? Otto Schramm back in Germany? Walking down the busiest street in Hamburg, where anybody could see him. It makes sense to do that?"

"Somebody did see him. Me." He raised his finger. "But he doesn't know it. That's our piece of luck. Our advantage. He thinks he's safe. Why not show yourself? Take a walk? He's arrogant. And he's supposed to be dead. Nobody expects to see him. So he's invisible. Except to me. And now I've lost him. He's there and then—" He made a poofing sound.

"You haven't lost him." Trying to sound as if he meant it.

"You think he takes a walk every day?" Max shook his head. "Maybe a good-bye walk."

"You don't know that."

"He's arrogant, but he's not crazy—not that way. He can never live in Germany again. Even as a dead man. Too many people know that face. The risk— So, a visit only. A visit you can manage. If you're careful. Of course, a new passport. Helmut Braun is dead."

"Who?"

"The name he was using. How many years I tried to find that name. What good were records without a name to check? Once there was a letter from a Jew in Buenos Aires. He thinks he recognizes Schramm. Now Braun. But I'm already looking at so many. It's a common name. Where do you start? And anyway, what about all the other letters? The leads. Why this one and not them? Then, when he dies, the name comes out and I realize I had it all along. And I put it with the others." He looked up, catching the drift in his voice. "But now it'll be something else. So no point in checking the flight manifests—who would we be looking for? And this is Hamburg, planes from everywhere. By the time you check all of them he really could be dead."

Aaron looked over at him, drawn in, a crossword puzzle start.

"Why Hamburg?"

"Yes," Max said, nodding. "I've been thinking about that. Why here? Why does anybody come? To get a ship. But I think he would fly. The longer it takes, the more he's exposed. You know the first time, it took three weeks. From Genoa."

"To Argentina."

Another nod. "It's in the file. How the Ratline got him out. Elena can show you. You should know it. And maybe it gives you an idea." Already on the job.

"Max—"

"So why Hamburg? Why does a man make such a visit?"

"To see family."

"Yes. I thought that too." Nodding, partners now. "He was close to his family. Of course, according to them, he disappeared in '45. No idea where he is, if he's alive. But I think they were giving him money all along. The Schramms were rich. Probably through Switzerland, private. When the father dies, Otto's not in the will. I checked. Why? Because they can't forgive his crimes? No. I think they already had some arrangement. He got his inheritance that way."

"And when he died? What then?"

Max shook his head. "An Argentinian will. I requested it, but from here it's difficult. They ignore you. And, you know, after he's dead, I lost interest." He thought for a minute. "There was a child, but the wife divorced him after he disappeared. A case of abandonment. So more likely it's back with his family."

"You think it's a business trip? To see whoever's looking after the money now."

"But the family's in Munich. So why here? And to come all this way. It would be safer to go the other way, for them to visit him. Uncle Otto in South America. Uncle Helmut. Or whoever he is now. Unless—"

"Somebody here died."

Max smiled. "Exactly. So a dead man flies to see a dead man. How often can that happen? Quite a situation."

"If he did."

"Yes. So now we dig."

Aaron looked across at him. "And you're going to do this from a hospital bed."

"No, I'm going to get better. But right now it's you. And my friend Fritz. You liked him? A messy person, but a good mind. And an office with a staff. To look for things. A gentile and he does this work. Proving something, maybe. Not all of us were like that. It's a powerful thing, guilt. You should have some."

Aaron ignored this. "And what are we looking for?"

"Funerals. Hamburg, the suburbs. All the newspapers keep files. It's not a needle in a haystack. Say the last week. Two. No more than that. I don't think he'd risk that, such a long visit. Two weeks. Then we see."

"Unless the funeral hasn't happened yet. Maybe he just got here."

"Then he's still here." He sighed. "Two pieces of luck, it's a lot. But check the death notices too. Every paper. The *Abendblatt*, the *Morgenpost*, all of them."

"And if nothing turns up?"

"We think of something else. I've been doing this for a long time. Start with the papers."

"You know, even if you find something, it won't prove that it was him."

"No. But I think it would prove something to you. I need to do that. So first we put him here. The possibility of him."

"But if you're right, he won't be here for long. He'll be back in Argentina. As someone else."

Max nodded. "Your contacts will be useful. This place you work for, they have an office in Buenos Aires? Some people on the ground?"

Aaron said nothing.

Max closed his eyes again, moving away from it. "All right. Now maybe I should sleep. You'll call Fritz?"

"Max—"

"Even with my eyes closed I can see your face. Aaron, this is a monster. I have the money. I'll pay you."

"You don't have the money."

"I'll get it. You won't be out of pocket." He opened his eyes. "Do this for me, this one thing, and I'll do what you want. I'll give it up. But not him. After, you don't want the documents, you don't want them. Your decision. Go back to America. But this—" He slowed. "All right, enough. Read the file. Now let me sleep."

"You're going to sleep. Like this, all excited."

Max closed his eyes again, an answer.

Aaron leaned over and kissed him on the forehead. "Then sleep." He started for the door.

"One more thing," Max said. "The family was Schramm, but the mother I think was a Brenner. Look in the file. It might be on her side. Tell Fritz to check both."

Max's flat was a short walk from the hospital at the Steindamm end of Danzigerstrasse, a nondescript new building that had probably replaced a more graceful one lost in the Allied bombings. His office wasn't in the living room, a point of pride over Wiesenthal, but it wasn't far: a second bedroom down the hall had been fitted out with filing cabinets and two desks and a seating area of mismatched chairs where Max conducted his interviews, survivors pouring out their terrible memories while Elena's pen ran across her pad, her face impassive, the unimaginable now part of her everyday. "We could move a daybed in, make it a guest room," Max had said, but Aaron had insisted on the hotel across from the station, just a few streets away, grateful for the distance.

The Schramm file turned out to fill most of a drawer, old folders stuffed with clippings and yellowing reports and notes to the file, rumors of sightings and letters from strangers, all the paperwork of an obsession. There seemed to be no organizing method to any of it, but after a while Aaron saw that there were time groupings: the postwar years, when most of the testimonies had been collected; Otto's disappearance to somewhere in South America; and finally his death. Aaron looked at this first.

Clippings from both German and Argentinian papers, where the death, coming soon after Eichmann's kidnapping, was tabloid news—car crash or assassination? Had another Israeli team violated Argentine sovereignty? Except the other driver had been killed too, which would have made it a suicide mission, and would the Israelis go that far? Without a show trial at the end? There were pictures of the accident scene but none of Schramm, careful even in death to avoid the camera. *Stern* had run a slightly blurred picture of a party at the Buenos Aires Jockey Club a few years back, a group of men in tuxedos on a staircase, one of them Schramm. Aaron stared at it, then turned his head back and forth, trying to duplicate the angle of his sight line at the Alsterpavillon, but the face was too grainy to be recognizable.

He took out the first folder, which he guessed would have an SS picture, Otto in uniform. A high forehead, fixed military jaw, and Prussian cheekbones, but otherwise unremarkable, even pleasant, his voice probably gentle when he told Daniel to join the other children. But what would he look like now? Aaron tried the head trick again with the SS picture, moving it to refocus, but the thin face in the photo refused to become the one he'd glimpsed on the terrace. How could Max possibly have recognized him? Seeing him without seeing him. Could you really tell a man from his walk, as distinct as a fingerprint?

The best photograph, surprisingly, was in the Auschwitz folder, where Aaron had imagined there'd be no pictures at all. A snapshot, not formally posed, of Schramm with Mengele and two coworkers, outside a brick building on a cigarette break, Schramm smiling, as if someone had just made a joke. Who'd taken the picture? Presumably another member of the staff, just then behind the camera. Aaron looked at them carefully, trying to take in details, the gap between Mengele's front teeth, the nurse's mouth, open in laughter, white coats, Schramm's cigarette, but the picture itself, the fact of it, still seemed unreal. Enjoying a laugh just steps away from the crematoriums, the sun on their untroubled faces. What kind of people could they have been? What had made it all right for them?

Some of the personal testimonies, Max's evidence-in-waiting, were cross-referenced to Mengele's file and those of the other doctors, overlapping stories remembered in DP camps after the war and now fading on the page. Sara Sadowski, a Polish Jew forced to serve as a nurse in Mengele's hospital, the mad experiments to change eye coloring, dyes that made children go blind. Included here in Schramm's file because she had witnessed him giving Mengele assistance with his twins. For an exact comparative dissection, two girls had to die at the same time, so Schramm had killed one while Mengele killed the other, injections straight to the heart, instantaneous. Aaron glanced at the filing information at the top of the sheet. Recorded and signed January 1946. Sadowski deceased 1947. No cause of death given. Typhus. Tuberculosis, maybe. Camp diseases. No, a blank space, discreet, the other camp disease. Why then, having survived everything? But as he read through more of the file, one grisly brittle page after another, he saw that no one survived Auschwitz. One year, twenty—the distance was immaterial. It was always there. When Max finally died, the cause of death would be Auschwitz too.

More folders, a rat's nest of paper—leads that went nowhere, requests for documents that went unanswered, details on the other missing Nazis that might, someday, overlap and be relevant, the vanished footprints of people no one wanted to find. In the chaos after the war there had at least been an effort to track down the Mengeles, the Schramms, the worst offenders. But then they stayed missing and the world moved on. Aaron hadn't realized how easy it was to vanish. Take a new name, a new identity, and Max was helpless. Who was he looking for? After a while he had taken to drawing up hypotheticals, routes that had worked for some of the others and might have been used by Schramm. Bishop Hudal at the Vatican would use his contacts to get an Argentine landing permit. With that as identification, the applicant could obtain a Red Cross passport. Then, with both documents, go to the Argentine Consulate and apply for an entry visa, which in turn was used to get an identity card when he arrived in Buenos Aires, after which he disappeared into his new life.

Max had drawn the process out in a chart, diagramming the steps. But had Schramm actually taken them? There were other ratlines mentioned—a Croatian priest, a CIC line for Soviet defectors—and then, after Eichmann's capture two years ago, a flurry of notes into the file, details that might have been similar to Schramm's escape, more leads to check. With no one to check them. Aaron thought of the paperwork all the documents must have generated: visa applications, landing records, file after file, sitting in some office in Buenos Aires, undisturbed by Max's requests. What had happened to them all? Schramm's paper trail. Helmut Braun's. And then he had died and it didn't matter anymore. Even Max had given up, just a few things added to the file after the newspaper clippings, tying up loose ends now that he had Schramm's alias. The Red Cross passport, checked against Max's list, verified. The boat from Genoa, now also verified. His address in Buenos Aires, just for the record. Filling in the pieces of the puzzle just as Otto slipped between his fingers.

Aaron looked again at the *Stern* photo. Black tie at the Jockey Club. What had his life been like there? Aaron had somehow always imagined the fugitive Nazis literally hiding, cowering in a shack in the jungle. But Eichmann had been working a factory job, a man with children. Mengele was said to have invested in a pharmaceutical company, at least according to one rumor in Max's file. They went to restaurants. They read *Der Weg* every month. Otto went to parties at the Jockey Club. They had got away with it. Aaron looked at the Auschwitz picture again. Smiling Otto, the laughing nurse, Mengele with a cigarette. Maybe relaxing after a selection, or one of the experiments. No anesthesia. People who were going to die anyway. Children. You'll see him later. Had he smiled when he said it? Strolling down the selection line, waving Aaron's mother to the left. He had got away with it. Aaron closed his eyes a little, imagining the man on the Alsterpavillon terrace again, walking toward the sun. Strolling.

3

FRITZ FOUND NOTHING UNDER Schramm or Brenner—no deaths, no services. His staff had checked papers as far north as Bremerhaven, a wide arc, and added two more weeks, just in case, and had still come up dry. Now what? The brick wall of a dead end.

Aaron expected to find Max quiet and disappointed, licking his wounds. Instead he was sitting up in bed, talking on the phone, hands gesticulating as he spoke. When he saw Aaron, he leaned more closely into the receiver, not wanting to be overheard, up to something.

"How did you get the phone?" Aaron said when Max was finished.

"I asked them to put one in. I had a few calls to make."

"It's the last thing you should be doing. What happened to getting better?"

"I am better." And in fact his color was good, eyes brighter, engaged. Schramm was keeping him alive, real or not.

"What calls?"

"I made an appointment for you to meet with a friend of mine. He can't come here, so you be my legs for a few days."

"Why can't he come here?"

Max ignored this. "Did you look at the file?"

Aaron nodded. "Max, Fritz didn't find—"

"I know. It would have been easier, a funeral. But when is it easy? So you look at it another way. A man stages his own death. I didn't know before, but now that I do, the question is, why?"

"He's in hiding. That's what he does, disappear. Who knows how many—"

"Yes, but why then? I've been thinking. First, always look at the obvious. Why then? What's happened?" He paused, a theatrical second. "Eichmann."

"Months before."

"And he's worried ever since. If they can get Eichmann, why not him? So maybe Mossad is waiting to strike again."

"Were they?"

Max shook his head.

"How do you know?"

"I know. Anyway, you can ask them yourself."

Aaron looked up. "That's who the meeting is?"

"We need to bring them in."

"Bring them in."

"In case I need—" He stopped. "They were never looking for him in Buenos Aires. Of course, how can he be sure? But what does he know for sure? Who's requesting documents? Still after him?"

"You are," Aaron said. Now about Max. How many years since the *Time* cover?

"All these years he's protected. We can assume somebody would let him know there's such a request, no? Maybe this is how they got Eichmann."

"Max, you had nothing to do with Eichmann. You were never mentioned."

Max looked up, a shadow across his face. "No, Wiesenthal. But how does Otto know? Better to die and get everyone off your back. Once and for all."

"You didn't even know his new name until after he died."

Max waved this away. "So the old name. But there were still requests and somebody would notice." His voice grasping at straws now.

"I meant to ask you about that," Aaron said, taking them somewhere else. "The requests in the file. Did they just refuse? Some were from you, but some were official. The state prosecutor in Hesse, I saw. How could they just refuse?"

"Well, you delay. Things get lost, especially at the Information Bureau. You keep records and then they become compromising, they show how Perón was helping. Imagine, the president of the country being part of that. A Fascist sympathizer, but still— These are wanted men. Of course, he's working with the Church. That makes it all right."

"Bishop Hudal."

Max raised his eyebrows. "So you read the file." He nodded.

"Alois Hudal. The Nazis' best friend. He writes to Perón personally. Asking for visas. For 'anti-Communist fighters.' In other words, Nazis. A friend in the CIC told me."

"What did the CIC do?"

"Well, by the time they know this, they're fighting the Communists too. So, nothing. But the point is, he writes to Perón. So how much is already going on if he thinks he can do this? A direct approach. People think it was just Eichmann or a few big fish who got out, but it was hundreds, maybe thousands. Aliases, new papers, hiding places while they wait. Perón can't do all that. Only the Church had those resources. Plus they've been anti-Semitic forever. But Perón can let them into Argentina. And he does. And as long as he's running the show, nobody looks in the files. But later—it could be a political embarrassment. Not just to him. His people. So in '55, just before he gets kicked out, a lot of the records get destroyed. Sometimes you make a request now, the clerks are telling the truth, they don't have the files. Not anymore. Gone. The rats are safe." He held up a finger, telling a story. "Unless there are other files." He waited for Aaron's reaction. "It's a wonderful place, Argentina. So much paper. And everybody wants to be a big shot. Look at those uniforms. Not even Napoleon— Anyway, they're always fighting about something. Even this. The Foreign Ministry fights with Immigration. That's why you needed two documents, the landing permit from Immigration, the visa from the Ministry. And Immigration keeps its own files—character witnesses, recommendations. And these they don't put with the others, so Perón's people don't destroy them. Maybe they didn't even know they're there. But they are. You just have to go and find them. And now I have the name."

Aaron looked over at him. Years of work, making a trail map through the bureaucracy, maybe the only one who cared enough to know.

"Nobody's going to let you do that."

"I have people with access. People there. We need documents to make the case."

"At his trial."

Max nodded.

"Max, we're not going to Buenos Aires."

"So don't come."

Aaron said nothing, not biting. Take a breath.

"Anyway, he's here. You think. So why go—"

"But guess what's not here? There either." Enjoying himself. He nodded to the phone. "They just called back from Munich. A nice young lady."

"Who?"

But Max wanted to stretch it out. "I should have checked before. Sometimes you don't think, you just assume. Buenos Aires, all right, but even the police there— But they don't have them. They never had them."

"What?"

"His dental records." Finally there, a modest flourish. "They couldn't. They were destroyed during the war. In the bombing. All the records. Schmidt, that's the dentist. He did the whole family. I didn't think to check. You make mistakes."

"But Max," Aaron said, hesitant, being reasonable with a

child, "he lived in Argentina fourteen, fifteen years. He'd have a dentist there. With records. Why would they need Schmidt's?"

"It's not conclusive, recent ones. You want the whole history."

Did you? Or was Max just selling again?

"Dental records—it's hard to argue with that. I didn't. I thought, well, that's it. But they weren't complete. It's not proof."

"Somebody identified the body."

"Anybody can identify a body."

"That would be illegal."

"Down there, who knows what's legal?"

"Now you're just making a case."

"So make a different one. Tell me I'm wrong."

"I'm not saying that." He slowed. "I'm just saying nobody in the file pictures looked like the man at the Alsterpavillon."

"It's twenty years, those pictures."

Aaron nodded. "The body was identified. The dental records matched—I don't care where they came from, they matched. If he wants to play dead, why come here? No funeral, either side of the family. Fritz checked everywhere. Maybe he had a cousin who walks just like him, I don't know. Maybe the light was playing tricks."

"No cousin," Max said quietly. "All right, it's a case." He looked up. "But what if I'm right?"

"And now you want me to meet with Mossad and say what? Set up an operation in Argentina? When we don't even know ourselves."

"We know," Max said, but almost to himself, not fighting back. He glanced at Aaron. "Mossad can't operate on German soil. So, an interested party only. He knows me. He'd be interested in this. That's all. Be my legs."

"All right," Aaron said, making peace. "Where's the meeting?"

"Chilehaus. The office building in Burchardplatz. Like a ship. You're by the prow. Five-thirty, everybody's leaving work, meeting for a drink. Busy. Nathan likes that, accidentally in public. God forbid you should just meet in a bar, stay warm." He looked up. "But he's good."

"OK," Aaron said, getting up to leave. "I'll be back. Now, why don't you give the phone a rest for a while? I can't believe they let you have one."

"I asked nicely," Max said, a glint back in his eye.

Aaron picked up his coat. "Max," he said quietly. "What if—?" He stopped, as Max looked up at him. Let it go.

But Max finished for him. "What if I'm an old man who doesn't see so good." He nodded. "What if. Then I'd have to go out of business. You make that kind of mistake—" He looked away. "You know what you worry about, you get old? What if you can't tell anymore? Like a painter doesn't know his painting's lousy. Too old to see what's there. Just what he wants to see. So maybe I want it to be Schramm and that's who I see. I know. Sometimes it works like that. What if." He looked back. "What if I saw him and he wasn't there? Then I'm—"

Aaron said nothing, then put his hand on Max's arm. "Not yet." The hand tighter now, a conversation. "Stay off the phone."

"Send Elena over."

"You're supposed to rest."

Max nodded. "Send her."

In the corridor, Aaron stopped for a minute, not sure where he wanted to go. Back to Max's office and the Schramm file of blind alleys? Back home to his office and the piles of field reports with their own blind alleys? How long had he been away? Days, a week, long enough to have left it behind. Without wanting to be here either. He'd come for Max and now couldn't wait to leave his room. It wasn't hospital claustrophobia, the smell of disinfectant, the nurses in and out, the overheated air. Max's room was filled with something else, triggered at the Alsterpavillon, crammed into files, the inescapable memory of Poland, the miles of chimneys, somewhere Aaron had never had to go before, where Max still lived.

"Herr Wiley!" The W pronounced as V, German.

Aaron looked down toward the nurses' station, Fritz in a hurry, brushing past people, jacket rumpled, shirt coming untucked on one side. Aaron imagined flecks of ash on his tie.

"Good, you're here. I was afraid—" He stopped, catching his breath. "He's up?" Nodding to Max's room. "He'll want to hear."

"What?"

"Come. Both," he said, guiding Aaron back into Max's room. "So you're slipping," he called over to Max, a tease. "Now, who thinks of everything?"

Max waited, eyebrows up.

"Not Schramm. Not Brenner. Lessing. His wife."

"His wife," Max said. "Yes, Lessing, I remember. But she disappeared, as Lessing. I thought she remarried." He looked up. "She's dead?"

Fritz nodded. "I saw the notice and at first I didn't connect. No mention of Schramm, of course. No marriage. But something in the back of my head, so I checked. And there it was. Lessing. So he comes back for the wife. Quite a love story."

"*Quatsch*," Max said, waving his hand.

"Is there a funeral?" Aaron said.

"This morning. It's good I found you." He glanced at his watch. "Ohlsdorf, so we should hurry."

Max looked straight at Aaron for a minute, not gloating, the wordless look its own triumph. Then he turned to Fritz. "Don't be surprised if he's not there. To show himself to people— But find out where the grave is. Watch that. That's where." He shook his head, an almost involuntary smile, and lay back against the pillow. "The wife. And he comes back. So did she know all along where he was? See him? Maybe the divorce was like the car crash. Another trick." He turned, waving them off. "Go find out. Watch the grave, yes? That's where he'll go."

Ohlsdorf Cemetery was near the airport, so they went north toward Barmbek, then out of the city.

"One of the largest in the world," Fritz said, suddenly a tour guide. "Over two hundred thousand graves. But very beautiful, like a park. My father's there."

"What if he does show up? What do we do?" Aaron said, thinking out loud. "I mean, we can't just grab him. Like that. Where is it anyway? The funeral. Some kind of chapel?"

"They have ten. You have to ask at the gate. Don't worry, there's time. See the camera, the bag on the backseat? Check if there's film. If he does show, we'll want that. Otto Schramm. It's a front-page picture."

"We should tell the police."

"Get the picture. Prove it's him. Then you've got something. They'd need a reason."

"For Otto Schramm? He's a war criminal. He's been on the Most Wanted List since the war."

Fritz nodded. "*Genau.* The publicity would shame them into it. So we get the picture. Otherwise, it's the usual. The wanted list? Bonn sends it to the consulate in São Paulo. Maybe somebody looks. Maybe somebody's an old Nazi and lets it sit in the tray. The Brazilian police? They need a request. No one is looking for these men, not really. Stangl, from Treblinka? He lived in Brazil as Stangl. All these years. But since Eichmann, people take an interest. Even Bonn moves a little. For years it was forget, forget, but now it's news again. The Schramms, they're not so safe anymore."

"That's what Max said. That's why he faked—"

"And then Max sees him. Ha, a resurrection. It's a great story." He turned off the main road. "If he shows."

The elaborate gates of Friedhof Ohlsdorf opened onto a gravel courtyard and a formal Wilhelmine mansion.

"I'll find out where the service is," Fritz said, opening his door.

Aaron watched him scurry up the broad steps. Could they really have built this just for the cemetery, or had it been some prince's house, the park behind once filled with deer. No rows of crosses, but wide swatches of green, the graves discreetly clustered behind hills, landscaped, statues and monuments and old trees, a place for people to walk on Sundays. Fritz came back carrying a map.

"It's this one," he said, pointing to a chapel symbol on the map. "Keep it open. It's easy to get lost." He put the car in gear again. "You know, before, when you said, do we grab him? You have to keep in mind that he's not going to allow that. Are you—can you handle something like this?"

"We can't just let him go. They have security guards here?"

"I'll talk to the undertaker. Of course, if he doesn't come, then I'm a fool. And no story either."

"See who else comes. Maybe a story there too."

Fritz shook his head. "Doctors. From the nursing home. Well, the *Klapsmühle*—what's the English? Loony bin. That's where she's been."

Aaron looked at him. "The things you know."

"Gretchen, my secretary."

They followed the winding road to the northern edge of the grounds and parked near a few other cars down from the chapel.

"You go in," Fritz said. "Somewhere in the back, yes? Dressed like this." He smoothed his jacket. "I'll go see the undertaker. Find out where the grave is."

Inside, a string trio was playing Bach. The chapel was simple and nondenominational, rows of chairs facing a lectern and the customary German sprays of flowers, large wreaths with satin ribbons, even one of the tall horseshoe arrangements you saw in old movies, this one marked *Schwester.* Aaron took a program from the attendant and found a seat near the back, away from the small group of mourners but still part of the assembly. No one turned, curious. Behind him he could see Fritz huddling with the funeral director, both looking over the room, like headwaiters counting the house.

There weren't many. A half row of people Aaron took to be staff, nurses and aides, dressed for a formal occasion, admiring the flowers. A blonde woman down front, Dresden doll pale, shuffling notepaper, maybe the eulogy, a younger woman next to her, late twenties and also blonde, possibly her daughter. A few scattered others, so random they might have been people who wandered in off the street. No Schramm. No one standing in the back or in the side shadows. No one strolling outside. No one in tears either, except for an old woman in a heavy coat, sobbing quietly, a maid or maybe the old nanny.

The trio changed to Mendelssohn. And just then, for a second, the younger woman turned, not far enough to look back at him, but enough to make half her face visible so that Aaron suddenly took her in. A dark, tailored suit, expensive, hair pulled up off her neck in a bun, every strand perfectly in place, the brooch, the pearls, the makeup, everything put together, shoulders back as if she were being held in place by a coat of armor. Except her neck, catching the light in a white flash, thin, a girl's neck, the one part of her that seemed exposed. There was something of

Claire in the way she lifted her head. He leaned forward to see her better, then stopped, embarrassed. The old cliché, the second wife who looked like the first, men attracted to the same woman, over and over.

But why so tense? When she turned, the skin on her neck tightened, all her movements alert, the way a bird's head responds to every sound, aware. She turned to the front again as the older blonde patted her hand, but sat stiffly, uncomfortable, a woman who didn't really want to be here.

Fritz slid into the seat next to Aaron and followed his gaze. "American," he whispered. "A Mrs. Crane."

Aaron raised his eyebrows, miming, Who?

Fritz shrugged. "That's how she signed the book." He pointed to the map. "The grave," he whispered. "They buried her this morning. No graveside service, just this. By request." He tipped his head toward the funeral director. "He says nobody's been around. Either place."

The music stopped.

"He could be there right now," Aaron whispered. "While we're all here."

Fritz shook his head. "There's another funeral. Nearby. He wouldn't risk it. A crowd. So, later. Unless he comes here." He glanced around the room again.

"One of us should go," Aaron said. "Just in case."

Fritz looked at him, then gave up and nodded. "I'll take the camera. Max said he'd go to the grave." Talking himself into it.

Without the music, the room had gone silent, expectant.

Aaron looked down at the program. Beate Lessing. Finally the older blonde woman stood and went to the lectern. The younger woman was facing straight ahead, getting through it.

"Good morning. We are here to honor the life of Dorothee Maria Lessing. Most of you knew her only these last years. When you cared for her. Made her comfortable. Made her life possible. But I want to talk to you about Doro, the girl she was before—before she wasn't herself. Before all the bad things happened, before the war. What a happy person she was."

The old woman who had been sobbing nodded her head at this.

Aaron shifted in his seat. And why shouldn't she have been happy? He could see the life Beate was now describing. The big house in Munich, with its heavy Sunday dinners, a sideboard gleaming with silver. Maids to polish it. Parties. Trips to the mountains in the summer. The lake house. More parties, showing off her new dress.

Around the room, the others had begun to nod too, the prewar dream they'd agreed on, not the smashed shopwindows and roundups.

Meanwhile, in Munich, Doro was in love with life, always ready to laugh. And one night she must have met Otto. Still a medical student or now in his SS uniform? The straight military jaw, the easy manner. How had they actually met? Aaron wondered. One of her parties? But of course they didn't meet, not in Beate's memory. No Otto, no marriage, just her sister as she was before the bad things happened.

How much had she known? Enough to drive her mad? Had

he told her about the experiments? Or just anecdotes about colleagues in the East, war stories, like everybody else. And then climb into bed, a husband, not a monster. But she'd divorced him. Because she knew? Or some simpler, more ordinary unhappiness?

"Sometimes I think," Beate was saying, "that she was another victim of the war. Not in the air raids. Those she survived. But the rest—it changed her. Her spirit was too fragile, maybe too fine to survive all the bad things."

There they were again, the bad things. If Otto hadn't told her, she would have heard the stories after. Not just rumors, but in newspapers, on the radio, the reports of the trials, the testimony. Had she believed them? Or was Otto still the man she'd met at a Munich party, Poland some grim war duty no one talked about. But she'd divorced him.

"When she moved to Hamburg, to start a new life, it was already too late. The sickness was in her. War damage. Still, you remember, always a kind word for everybody. Even at the end. Still Doro."

She stopped, upset, then gripped the lectern more tightly and went on. Doro's gentle nature. Her love of animals. Aaron looked at the program again. No other speakers. Just a benediction from Pastor Muller. Behind him, a door opened. He swiveled, a reflex. Not Schramm, a white collar, glasses, probably the pastor, holding the door to close it quietly. Then, having managed the door without a sound, he tripped on a chair leg, dragging it, a loud scraping noise and a clatter that startled the room. Beate stopped, people turned to look. And Aaron saw her face. A sudden prickling sensation in his scalp. The same high cheekbones, softer, not as chiseled, but the same. The high forehead. The face in the SS photo. There had been a child. Aaron looked away, as if not meeting her eyes would make him invisible, another piece of furniture, and when he looked back, it seemed to have worked. She was already facing Beate again, the hapless pastor now working his way down the aisle. The same cheekbones. He felt short of breath, taken by surprise. Not Beate's daughter. Doro's. Otto's. A Mrs. Crane. Who didn't want to be here.

The benediction was general and impersonal—Muller clearly had never known her—and Aaron left before it was over, hunching down as he crept out, careful with the door. In a crowd this small you'd be expected to pay Beate your respects and explain your presence and what would he say? He turned right outside the chapel, heading to the spot Fritz had pointed out on the map. Did she know? Or was he dead to her too? Not even mentioned in the eulogy, erased. And not here.

Fritz was standing with a group of mourners at an open grave not far from Doro's. The coffin had already been lowered and the crowd was breaking up, drifting down the slope toward the road. Aaron stopped by a tall plinth with a limestone angel hovering over it, an elaborate monument in a field of simple markers. He looked around, a quick survey. Two of the mourners getting into cars. Cemetery workers busy at another grave. An old couple with a dog, out for a walk. The hill was banked with shrubbery but otherwise open. Impossible to visit her grave and not be seen. Fritz came over, fiddling with the camera case.

"So what do we do?" Aaron said. "Walk around? He won't show himself if he thinks we're—"

"Just sit for a while," he said, dropping down on a bench. "People use it as a park. Anything happen inside?"

Aaron shook his head. Why not tell him about the daughter? But not yet.

Fritz lit a cigarette, eyes fixed on the grave downslope. Some rhododendrons behind them, a tree to one side, a clear vantage point.

"You know, this could be a great thing for Max. A big one like Schramm." Fritz patted the camera case. "Then there's only Mengele."

And all the others, Aaron thought. Thousands. How many had it taken, all working together? Enjoying a smoke break.

Some new mourners had begun to arrive, leaving their cars and following a casket up to its grave. Another delay, the slope filling with people again. Why hadn't she spoken at the service? Her own mother. But she was here as Mrs. Crane. American. And maybe she was. Everyone in the family had become someone else. Otto and Doro, now her. They had become other people. Not like Herschel, becoming Henry Wiley to fit in. They'd become other people to escape.

"Not so many for this one," Fritz said, looking toward the new funeral.

A woman in a veil, leaning on someone's arm, men standing by the grave, holding hats, the scene from before, repeated, this time a minister in a surplice, heads bowed. Except at the back of the group, where two men were stepping away, hats still on. What was the etiquette here? The others had removed theirs. Aaron watched them back away and head slowly down the slope, not together, one following the other, the man in front making his way carefully, an old man's walk. And then, as the hill flattened out, he picked up the pace, arm beginning to swing, out for a stroll. Aaron sat up. The walk unmistakable, just as Max had said, as good as a photograph.

"It's him," he said quietly, as if Otto could overhear them.

Now Fritz sat up too. "You're sure?"

"Yes," Aaron said, suddenly Max. "It's him."

The two men had stopped at Doro's grave, one standing a few steps behind the other, both of them now taking off their hats. Otto. He lowered his head slightly, a formal paying of respects, and stared at the grave. Thinking what? How long since he'd seen her? Locked away for years. As Lessing, not Schramm, even his name no longer part of her life.

Fritz began to get up. "Slowly," he said. "We don't want to spook him." He eased the camera bag over his shoulder. "Head for the funeral."

Down the hill Otto was still standing at the grave, the other man looking to his side, keeping watch.

"Who's that, the bodyguard?"

They were walking toward the service, not too fast, moving figures in the landscape.

"Remember, we just want to get a picture. Something to go to the police with. No heroics."

They had reached the funeral service now, and Fritz took out his camera, snapping a picture. The minister looked up, annoyed. Down the slope, the guard turned his head at the click. Fritz took another picture.

"So they won't think anything of it," Fritz mumbled to Aaron. "A guy with a camera."

They began to move down, Fritz fiddling with the camera, absorbed, as if he hadn't noticed Otto and his friend.

"The light's good, but we'll have to get it fast. We need his face and he's not going to stick around and pose. They'll run for the cars. If we get a plate number— Here we go. Watch the other guy." Barely whispering, close enough now to be heard. They were almost at Doro's grave, heading toward the parked cars, the logical route down from the funeral.

The other man looked up as they were about to pass, but Otto stayed fixed, staring at the grave, his back to them. Impossible to stop and wait for him to turn. The element of surprise. Now.

"Otto," Fritz said, raising the camera.

Schramm whirled around in place, startled, then heard the click. Another. Eyes frozen in surprise, but only for a second, then he ducked, away from the camera, and started running. Another click, then a shout from the bodyguard, leaping on Fritz, fast as a snapshot, everything a blur, then a crunching sound, Fritz groaning as he went down, the bodyguard grabbing the camera and smashing it against the headstone, ripping out film.

"Hey!" An involuntary yelp, Aaron still trying to catch up, everything too fast.

The bodyguard reared back, as if he hadn't known Aaron was there, then shot a fist forward, catching him in the nose.

A stunned throbbing pain, blood spurting. Aaron looked up in disbelief. The surprise of it, the panic of not knowing what to do. He put his hand to his face. Was his nose broken? No time. The guard had turned back to Fritz, his real victim, and was kicking him, so hard that you could actually hear the crunch of bones breaking, Fritz screaming. Violence that had its own momentum, past the point now of protecting Otto or destroying the film, vicious, taking pleasure in it, the way SA thugs had kicked people in the street, not just to hurt them but to feel their own wild power. Aaron watched, stunned. People had started running down the hill from the funeral. Shouts. A few of them just standing, trying to take it in. Something they'd seen years ago, the old nightmare. Still here, not wished away at some trial.

"Stop it!" Aaron yelled, lunging for the guard and then suddenly flung to the ground, not even aware of being thrown, hitting face-first, his nose throbbing again.

The guard picked up the broken camera and threw it at Fritz, a flash of contempt, and then started running, ahead of the crowd coming down the hill. Fritz made a gasping sound.

"The plate. The license plate."

Aaron managed to get on one knee, then pushed the rest of his body up, swaying for a minute as he got his balance, pain shooting across his face. He staggered, another step, then found his footing, a colt, and started to run after the guard. Another pain on his side, where he'd fallen. He heard voices behind him, the startled funeral party. Ahead the bodyguard was moving fast, catching up to Otto, both of them too far now, getting into a car. Even part of a plate number would help. But they were gone.

Aaron saw the car pull out and then disappear down the winding road. He stopped, shaking, the sight of Fritz being kicked still in his head. And now Otto was still dead, out of reach, and Max had nothing, not even a piece of film. Except Aaron knew. Not just the walk, but the way his head had snapped around when Gruber said "Otto," the look on his face. Someone knew.

4

NATHAN WAS RIGHT ON time, coming up to Aaron just as clerks and secretaries were spilling out of Chilehaus. In the early dark the redbrick building looked like something out of an Expressionist film, all angles and shadows and a high ship prow corner. The only light in the street came from the office windows, so at first Aaron couldn't see his face, just the shine of his head, the hair cut so closely that he might as well have been bald. Not tall but broad-shouldered, fit. An able-bodied seaman look, even a dark peacoat.

"We can walk this way," he said, steering them away from the crowd and down toward the old warehouse docks, looking over his shoulder as they crossed the street, as if they were being followed, maybe the way he always walked. "What's wrong with Max? He didn't say."

"His heart."

"It's serious?"

Aaron nodded.

"And that's why you're here? Compassionate leave." A knowing inflection, making a point. "I didn't think you had such things at the Agency."

Aaron looked over at him.

"I like to know who I'm dealing with."

"And?"

"A desk man. Agency training but no field experience. Excellent performance reviews. Not a troublemaker."

"What else? Am I a dossier yet or just a phone call?"

"I like to know, that's all." They were at the Zollkanal, a brick warehouse looming opposite, dark. No ships in the canal, gone now to the deep water on the other side of the Elbe. "When you deal with the Agency—"

"You're not dealing with the Agency. I'm here for Max."

"All right," Nathan said, letting it go. "So what's so important he couldn't tell me on the phone?"

"Otto Schramm is alive."

Nathan stopped. "Otto Schramm."

"I know. He's supposed to be dead. But he isn't. He's here."

"Here. What, having coffee with Bormann? With Mengele maybe."

"Max saw him."

Nathan glanced behind, then started walking again, turning in to one of the dock's service streets, away from the water. "Max saw him," he said, still taking it in.

"So did I. I know what you're thinking. I thought so too. You get to that age—" He wagged his hand by his temple. "But I saw him too. This morning. I've got a friend in the hospital to prove it."

Nathan tilted his head slightly, an I-don't-follow look.

"He tried to get a picture and Schramm's—bodyguard, I guess, didn't like it, so—"

"He get the picture?"

"No. They smashed the camera. Then him. Real storm trooper stuff. Heavy on the kicking. So Fritz's got a few ribs taped and half his head bandaged up."

Nathan took a breath. "Fritz from the newspaper?"

Aaron nodded.

"And where was this?"

"Ohlsdorf. Schramm's wife died. So, her funeral. That's why he came. To pay his respects. Something like that anyway."

"He's so sentimental?"

"He's here, that's all I can tell you. I saw him with my own eyes. Fritz too. Not just Max. He's here."

"But not anymore, after this. And what am I supposed to do with this information?"

"Max thought you should know. Your people. He'll need your help."

"My help."

"He can't do this alone."

"My friend, I am one man here. I help people emigrate. Sometimes I get information for Bauer, the prosecutor in Frankfurt. From the archives, in Israel. Bauer wants to make a series of trials. Here. So we help him. We want trials here too. By Germans, not by us. That's what I do."

"Everybody knows Mossad—"

"Everybody knows what we tell them. Mossad is everywhere. No one is safe from us. The invincible Mossad. The truth? Not so invincible."

"All he's asking—"

"I know what he's asking. Another Eichmann. Do you think anybody would agree to that? Another operation like that? Put people on the ground? Halfway around the world. Safe houses. Exfiltrate a man. Where is all this money coming from? Some secret fund in the Knesset? We don't have resources for this. It's that simple."

"You did."

"And we made our point. Eichmann was worth it. A trial before all the world, so everyone could see. A stand-in for all the others. Now let the Germans put the rest on trial."

"The small fry."

"The small fry murdered people too. Max knows that. These trials that Bauer wants? Max was the one who—" He broke off. "Ach," he said, waving hand. "But now Schramm. So Israel blamed again. Acting like gangsters. Kidnapping. On foreign soil. More people yelling in the UN. Just like before. Right under their noses. Because we're so good." He shook his head. "No, because we were so lucky. And had money to plan. Every detail, so nothing would go wrong. It worked, once. Not twice. This isn't what we do."

"And what happens to Schramm?"

Nathan didn't answer for a minute, buying time by lighting a cigarette.

"I don't know. Maybe he stays dead. It was good, that death, whoever arranged it. We believed it." He looked up. "It's really him? So you, what do you want to do?"

Aaron hesitated, thrown by this. "Me? I want what Max wants. To put him on trial."

"Where? Israel? We're out of the trial business."

"For Schramm?"

"Yes, I know," Nathan said, weary for effect. "A monster. But you know how many monsters there are out there? And how few of us? You see this?" He lifted his hand to his throat. "There are millions of Arabs who want to cut it. Like this." He made a slicing motion. "And smile while they're doing it. Butcher us. Wipe us out. That's what Mossad does now. We fight for our lives. Not look for Nazis. Not Eichmann, over and over." He took a long pull on the cigarette, then tossed it to the ground. "My parents were killed at Auschwitz. Max isn't the only one. I know. To get someone like Schramm— But we have to survive first."

"Then how does he pay?"

"I'm not God. I don't know. Maybe he doesn't. Maybe he dies again. For real, this time. Another accident. If God arranges it."

"Or someone else."

Nathan looked over. "Not us. We are not assassins."

Aaron raised an eyebrow.

"We protect Israel. That's all. Not *nakam*. You know *nakam*? Hebrew for vengeance. If we began—where would it stop? Six million lives later? Jews can't afford *nakam*."

"So he gets away with it. What's Hebrew for justice?"

Nathan stared at him for a second, then looked away.

"Well, justice. Everybody has a word for that. But what is it? Something maybe doesn't exist."

"You don't mean that."

He waited out another silence.

"You're sure it's him?" Nathan said finally.

"Sure."

"They said you were careful. In your work. So, all right, maybe it is."

"That must be some source you have. Even my performance reviews."

Nathan gave a half smile. "Ears everywhere. So people think." He looked up. "You know what Max will do? What he always does. Go to Fritz, the newspapers. A press conference. The Nazi hunter gets his man. So we lose face if we don't act. Where was Mossad all this time, with their ears everywhere? And then what? Argentina won't arrest him. They've been protecting him. And how do they admit— Anyway, what law has been broken there?"

"There's an extradition order."

"To Germany? And what will they do with him? A show trial. You think there's such an appetite here for that? Poland, where the crimes were committed? Israel, another diplomatic crisis? Everyone against us again?"

Aaron looked at him, dismayed. Nobody, not even the Israelis. Max the only one who wouldn't let go.

"It's an impossible situation for us. It's better if he's dead," Nathan said. "Better for Max too. At his age."

"Except he isn't dead."

Nathan lifted his head to respond to this, then stopped. "Listen to me. Nobody else will tell you this. They'll say what you say. Who could argue? But nobody wants him. Except the newspapers. The newspapers want him. What does he look like now? How did he live all these years? The newspapers can do this for weeks. Longer. For them, gold. But for everyone else, a problem. These Bauer trials, the ones Max is helping with, they can make a difference. Maybe even some justice for a change, who knows? But this, this circus—let him stay dead. He'll be dead soon enough anyway, so it ends the same." He paused. "Nobody wants these men."

"So what do I tell Max?"

"Tell him—" He stopped, frustrated, then sighed. "Tell him we're grateful. I'll pass this along. Upstairs. See what they say. Meanwhile, if there's anything I can do here—"

"But you know what they're going to say."

"Sometimes they take a long time to say it. We're playing for time here, my friend. If he finds Schramm, he'll force our hand, yes. We can't just sit by. But what are the odds he can find him? Seventeen years he couldn't find him. Why now? What are the odds?"

Aaron looked at him. "Better. I'm going to help him." Something he didn't know until he said it.

Nathan took a minute, not saying anything, trying to read Aaron's face. "You think you know what you're doing. You haven't even started and you've got one in the hospital. Who do you think these people are? Max is a sick man. You do this, you're on your own. You're ready for that? A desk man." Nathan looked down. "Fritz's doing a story?"

"Not without a picture. Without that, it's just Max seeing ghosts. But he will. I find Schramm, it's a story. Then you've got the whole world watching. Mossad will have to do something then."

Another silence.

"I'll pass it along. That's all I can do."

"I'll find him. But I'll need help getting him out."

"Like Eichmann, a whole team?" He shook his head. "Those days are over."

"How many then?"

"You think this is a negotiation? How do I know? Find him and ask me again."

"But enough to get him out."

"To where? Germany?"

Aaron nodded.

"You need to see what this is. So let me ask you. If there's no trial at the end, there's no point wasting men getting him out. But there he is, walking around. No justice. So what then? He has an accident. That would only take one man. You prepared to do that? If that's how this ends? Would that be enough *nakam* for you?"

He thought of Fritz being kicked on the ground, Schramm walking down a line, nodding his mother to the gas.

"I'll tell you after I find him."

The nurse intercepted him as he got off the elevator.

"The doctor would like to see you."

"What's wrong?"

"He's this way," she said, leading him down the corridor, evidently not allowed to say. News only a doctor could deliver.

"Ah, Herr Wiley." The doctor stood up. A desk cluttered with paper.

"What's wrong?"

The doctor made a take-a-seat gesture. "He's had another episode."

"Episode."

"Attack. My English. *Ein Herzanfall.*"

"How bad?"

"Bad. One right after the other—it's difficult. Of course, he may—" He stopped, leaving it unfinished.

"But he may not. He could die."

A slight dip of his head. "I wanted to prepare you. Of course, a man of great spirit. He may—"

"Can I see him?"

"Yes. He's still lucid. That's a good sign."

Of what, Aaron wondered, when he saw him. Max's skin seemed pulled against his face, as thin and fragile as yellowing paper. A small plastic oxygen tube had been fed into his nose, the mouth gaping anyway, as if he couldn't get enough air. Aaron stared for a minute, eyes suddenly filling. I can't die now. After. God's final trick, taking him just when Schramm was in his sights.

"How did it go with Nathan?" he said, eyes still closed, his voice weak and scratchy.

"Good. He's talking to his people, set things up. He's excited."

Max smiled. "I knew."

"He's nervous about operating in Argentina again. But it's Schramm." Why not enfold them both in the story, what Max wanted to hear?

"Good," Max said. "If you have them, you can do it. Tell Elena to give you Goldfarb's number. He's a friend. Important in the Jewish community there. If it's for me, he'll help you."

"You can call him yourself. You should be out of here in a week. He can wait that long."

Another smile, this time fainter, an effort. "Don't kid a kidder."

Aaron took his hand. "You can do it."

Max opened his eyes. "No, it's the end," he said, his voice clear. "I saw him tonight. Otto. Not for real. The way I said before, when you see people. It's the brain talking to you. In his white coat, so I knew. Making a selection. This time left." He gripped Aaron's hand more tightly. "The way it was always going to end. To the left. I could see it in his face, that look he used to get. When he could decide. A god. Imagine, being able to decide death for people."

"Max—"

"Shh. It's all right. Now, then—what's the difference? He was always going to do it. He pulled me out of the line—for how long?—but he was always going to put me back. So it's now. But he doesn't know."

"What?"

"He thinks it's over. His face tonight. He thinks it's over. But he doesn't know about you. He thinks if I'm gone, he's safe." He clutched at Aaron's hand. "He doesn't know about you."

Aaron stared at him, at a loss.

Max loosened his grip. "And you'll have Mossad. With them you don't need luck. So you can finish it."

"Max—"

"Something else. I wish we could have spent more time together."

"We will."

"But I think I know you a little, how you react, so something else."

Aaron waited.

"When you go through the files, you'll find some things from your mother. I don't know why I kept them. Well, I keep everything. Elena says. And now it's too late. You'll find them. I want you to know how it was, what they mean. She wanted to get out, to be with you again. And Herschel. He never knew. I never said a word. But this man said he would help her. She was out of hope by then—they weren't letting anyone leave, not even for money—and the man said he would help. So she believed him. You look at those letters, you might think she stayed for him. But it was the opposite. It was because she wanted to be with you. You understand?"

"Yes."

"There's no blame. She thought she had time. We all thought that."

"How long did this go on?"

Max moved his hand. "I don't know. What does it matter? But then, when she knew he wasn't going to help, she had to stay with him anyway. Where else could she go? So it's another story from that time. Another story. You know, I used to think, they go down that line, the selection line, and to them we're like cattle—just something to slaughter. They couldn't see us. All the stories. Just cattle." His voice dipping at the end, but worked up, no longer peaceful.

"Maybe you should get some rest now."

"Later. I just wanted you to know. No blame, do you understand?"

"Yes."

"So, a few things. Keep Elena on—it'll be worth it to you. She knows where everything is."

"OK." Agreeing to anything.

"When you get Schramm, give Fritz an exclusive, all right? I owe him some favors and anyway he'll do a good job with it."

Aaron thought of the bandaged head in the other hospital, Schramm's latest victim. "OK."

Max nodded. "You're a good boy. Come, sit. You going to stand all night?" Keeping his hand, as Aaron pulled the chair over. "That's better. Now I don't have to look up at you." A weak smile. "Herschel's nose." He closed his eyes for a second. "So, no problems with Nathan?"

"No. He had me checked out. At the Agency."

"See."

Another silence.

"You know what you don't expect? You make a list—what you need to do. And what does it matter? You won't be here anyway. Everything goes through your head. What you did, what you didn't do, and none of it matters." Another pause. "But he doesn't know about you. So there's something."

A minute of silence, his breathing steady, in a light sleep. Aaron sat holding his hand, not knowing what to do. Max's body seemed to be shriveling, no bigger than a child's under the sheets.

"Do you know what I thought before?" he said suddenly.

"What?"

"Daniel. There won't be anybody to remember him now. After me. So he'll be free. I thought I let him go before, but I held on. Now he can go. All these years."

And then he did sleep, Aaron still by his side, cramped but not wanting to move, afraid of waking him. At some point he worked his hand out of Max's, so that the old man's rested palm up on the sheet. A nurse tiptoed in, but Aaron put a finger to his lips, and after checking the hydrating drip she went away. Now there was nothing but the swish of an occasional car outside, the faint hiss of the oxygen feed, and Aaron felt himself beginning to drift. The final to-do list that didn't matter. His mother yearning for him, not feckless. Seeing Otto in his white coat, the way it was always going to end. But he doesn't know about you. In the quiet, his head began to droop, following Max into his half sleep. How long could he sit here? All night? But once Max was gone, there'd be no one. Little enough to ask. And what was a white lie at such a moment, Nathan marshaling his commandos?

When Max stirred, a rustling in the silence, Aaron started, the movement like a hand on his shoulder. Faint noises now, maybe the beginnings of a death rattle, the gasping intake of air. Should he call the nurse? Max's eyes still closed, seeing whoever he was seeing. And then his hand closed on something tight, holding on, and Aaron watched, mesmerized, as it clutched and then, with a slight spasm, opened and let go, the hand flat and still, empty, as if nothing had been in it, not for years.

He walked back along the shore of the Aussenalster, shoulders hunched against the damp. He doesn't know about you. But he knew there was someone. A man with a camera, who had called out his name, unmistakable. He'd have to leave. But maybe not yet. He'd been safe here until he heard the camera click. Where? Aaron looked across at the apartment buildings lining the street. Any one of these lights, safe, bolted in. A house in the country, no neighbors. Some hotel down in Altona, transient. But not the Atlantic, just ahead, its bright lights pouring onto the sidewalk, shiny with wet leaves, the long lakefront veranda lined with columns two stories high, a porch built to catch the breeze. Where you stayed if you wanted to be seen, or were rich enough not to care.

Aaron stopped short, scanning the façade. The kind of hotel an American would choose, the only place to stay. He thought of her suit, the hair knotted perfectly in place, and saw her in the lobby bar, settled in a club chair, a drink at her side. With whom? Impossible to imagine Otto taking that kind of risk here. Too public. But she must have known he was at Ohlsdorf. Restless while the old nanny wept, keeping an eye out for him. Aaron's lead. Something Otto didn't know he knew. A back way to him.

He crossed the street and walked up to the Holzdamm entrance, behind a party of people getting out of a taxi, noisy as birds, the doorman in top coat and bright buttons, shooing them in. The lobby was busy, a Hamburg meeting place, and he headed toward the bar, not hesitating, as if imagining her there had actually placed her there. He looked around. Not in one of the chairs, not on a stool at the long bar, maybe not even in the hotel. But it was the obvious place, more than a hunch. He went over to the front desk and borrowed some stationery, writing out a note and sealing it. Crane, but what was the first name? Had Fritz said? No. Someone he could talk to just by lifting the house phone, if she was here. And then say what?

"I need to leave this message for Mrs. Crane. Would you see that she gets it?"

"Mrs. Crane?"

"Yes. American? I thought she said she was staying here. Would you check?"

The deskman consulted a book. "Hanna Crane," he said.

"Yes. I thought she said the Atlantic. Would the house phone put me through or do I need a room number?"

The deskman shook his head. "She's no longer here."

"She checked out? But we had an appointment—"

"Today. There was some family emergency, I believe."

"Oh," Aaron said, playing concerned. His only lead. He fingered the envelope. "Did she leave a forwarding address? I could send—"

"No, no forwarding address."

"But if it's family, she must be going home," Aaron said, working it out. "What address did she give when she checked in?"

The deskman looked up. "I'm afraid we can't—"

Aaron moved the envelope toward him. "You can write it then if you like. I just want to make sure she gets this. What will she think—me not showing up. Was her father with her?" Trying it.

"Her father." He looked at Aaron, a desk clerk's raised eyebrow, talking code. "I don't know. I didn't come on until this evening." He glanced down. "No one else is registered for the room."

"He probably went ahead. Would you send this, then? I'll pay for the postage, of course." While I read upside down as you write.

But again the desk clerk shook his head. "No mailing address. Just Buenos Aires."

"Ah," Aaron said, pulling back the envelope, giving in. "Well, then I missed her. Sorry to bother you."

He turned away, oddly elated. Gone, but not without leaving a scent. All Max would have needed.

II

BUENOS AIRES

5

IN THE UPSIDE-DOWN WORLD of the southern hemisphere, November was early summer, the jacarandas still blooming and the worst of the humidity a month or two off. After the coats and mufflers of Hamburg it was startling to see people in short sleeves. The flight had taken forever and would have taken even longer in the forties, Aaron thought, the time and distance disorienting, reminders that you were somewhere else. Downtown, on Corrientes, the lumbering buses and movie marquees were familiar, any city, but the faces on the magazine covers were unknown to him, famous in some other world. What must it have been like for Schramm, any of them, knowing they were here for good, through the looking glass.

Jamie Campbell, the station chief, had booked him a room in a residential hotel on Calle Posadas.

"It's on my hook, so nothing fancy," Aaron had said on the phone.

"So I hear. You're on leave. What is that anyway?"

"It means I pay. And nobody meets me at the airport."

"OK. I'll buy you a drink when you get in. Alvear Palace. Right around the corner from you. Put on a clean shirt. And maybe you'll tell me what you're doing down here. Or maybe not."

Given the irregular layout of the room, the hotel must have been an apartment building, chopped up now, with an elevator added in the middle, but the street was pleasant, lined with trees, and what did it matter where he stayed? He had the rest of the afternoon to walk, to see the city, and he strolled through Recoleta, then over to the Plaza San Martín with its European palaces and leather shops. Calle Florida was busy with shoppers, but the rest of the neighborhood had the sleepy emptiness of a rich district in summer, people away at country houses or traveling.

At the turn of the century, during the great boom, Buenos Aires had wanted to be Paris, and here and there it was, belle epoque mansions and iron grillwork and a subway station that could have been on one of the grand boulevards. But it was Paris and not Paris, the same dislocating feeling he'd had looking at the magazine covers—everything familiar and unknown at the same time. He felt oddly invisible walking the streets. No one would run into him, no one knew who he was. Even the trees were alien—forming classic allées, lining the broad avenues, but flowering with bursts of tropical red or twisting with exotic roots. It was an ideal city for walking, mostly flat and sprawling out toward the even flatter pampas, a kind of Latin Chicago, stretched between prairies and the gray metallic water at its edge. Except here no one faced the water, the riverfront a working port of docks and railway sidings. Paris but not Paris.

"You should have started without me," Jamie said, only a few minutes late. "This one's on expenses. I'm supposed to find out what you're doing here."

"Wonderful how they look after you, isn't it?"

"And you're not going to tell me. So let's enjoy the drink anyway. How do you like this?" he said, his hand taking in the red plush lobby.

"Quite a pile," Aaron said, following the hand.

The Alvear Palace was another dream of Paris, an art deco front with a Ritz-like bar to match, and an enfilade corridor in grand hotel style, chandeliers and deep-pile carpets and large swags of curtain.

"Just don't eat here. Unless you've got money we don't know about. Martini?" He signaled the waiter, who nodded, evidently familiar with the order.

"Did you get the address?" Aaron said.

"For Mrs. Crane?" He pulled out an envelope and handed it to Aaron. "Why do you want it? Can I ask?"

"I promised a friend I'd contact her. Fritz Gruber, a reporter. For a series he's doing. Sons of the Reich."

"Sons?"

"And daughters. She's Otto Schramm's daughter."

"Mm. You're a little late to the party, aren't you? That's old news now—at least here. The papers had a field day with it for about five minutes. Not much since. Rough on her. Socially. Invitations start drying up when they know you're a war criminal."

"She wasn't."

"But he was. It turns out. So it rubs off. Anyway, the ropes started going up for her right after it came out. Who Helmut Braun really was. Too bad. Nice woman. Ah," he said as the martinis arrived.

"You know her?"

"I've met her. It's a small town in a big city, the ex-pats. You keep bumping into the same people in the same places. Here, for instance. Fucking Rick's Café. Course, it's easy for her, she's just down the street, so this is her local. Maybe she'll show up tonight. Then you won't need that." He nodded to the envelope. "We're not supposed to do this, you know. Use the Agency for private business. Why the interest?"

"Me? None. The friend doing the book can't travel—he's in the hospital—so I said I'd help him out, that's all."

"While you just happened to be in Buenos Aires. Where everybody comes. On leave."

"What's wrong with Buenos Aires? It looked OK to me. I had a walk around."

"Oh, BA's fine. If you like steak. But it's a long way to come for a steak." He sipped his drink. "Sons of the Reich. You'll be heading out to Bariloche then. The mountains. They're still wearing lederhosen there. You squint and you're in Bavaria. Your buddy Schramm had a place there." Another nod toward the envelope. "But you knew that." Fishing.

"Who's Mr. Crane?"

"Tommy? His family was in business down here. His grandmother came from one of the cattle families. You know, Jockey Club people." Aaron looked up, seeing the grainy photograph. "But the real money was back in the States. Scrap, believe it or not. They made a killing during the war. Not that Tommy ever touched a rusty pipe. Just a swizzle stick at the Stork. Anyway, he was here—a family visit—and I guess it all looked good to Hanna, so she married him. She was just a kid, maybe she thought they'd be living at El Morocco. She stuck it out for a few years. Then after she figured out she'd heard everything he was ever going to say—back here. With a hell of a settlement, they say. On the town a lot. And then Braun turns out to be somebody else and it gets awkward. Easier to do your drinking alone."

"Does she?"

"It's an expression. I doubt it. She likes a drink, but not like that. She was upset, that's all."

"She didn't know? He was Schramm?"

"They say not. Not the kind of thing you confide in a child. So some surprise. Course, she can still see the Germans. They think he's a fucking hero. And Perón's buddies. Old Dr. Freude at the Intelligence Bureau. He protected him. They're all still here, more or less. If that's who you want to see." He took another drink. "What makes you think she'll talk to you about this? Five bucks says she throws a drink in your face."

"There she is," Aaron said, glancing over Jamie's shoulder.

She had stopped at the entrance, waiting for the maître d', giving the room a quick once-over, then turning back to her group. Another woman and two men, talking quietly and laughing, out for the evening. She had loosened the tight bun of hair, which now fell to her shoulders, and the funeral suit had become a cocktail dress, smart, drawing looks from some of the other women. But the posture was the same—shoulders straight, eyes fixed in front of her as she glided past the tables.

"Want to meet her?" Campbell said.

Aaron shook his head. "Too many people. I'll wait."

"Better with an intro."

"From you? Does she know who you are?"

Campbell shrugged. "They assume everybody at the embassy is Agency." He paused. "But that's not the same as knowing."

"I don't want to scare her."

He watched her for a minute. Easy with the others, everybody ordering drinks, the room dimly lit and elegant. Her life here, the same one she must have led in New York, only the seasons different. For a second he thought she had looked over at him, but then she turned to the man next to her, smiling, back in the small circle of their table. The same cheekbones. "How could she not know," he said, half to himself.

"What, about Braun? We didn't. Of course, we weren't looking for that."

"What were you looking for?"

Campbell shifted in his seat. "The Germans weren't happy when Perón had to leave in '55. As long as he was around, they had nothing to worry about. They were all on the same side. Now, you never know. So some of them would like him back."

"After all these years? Is that likely?"

"Here? A lot of people have fond memories. And every time

something goes wrong, there he is, sitting in Madrid, looking better and better."

"But not to Uncle Sam."

"Right. Illia may not be much, but he's still better than a fascist dictator with a bug up his ass about American influence. And a bad habit of nationalizing things. So every time his old friends in the army get together, we like to know about it. Same with the Germans. But the Germans are hard to turn. The reason they came here in the first place is we were trying to put them on trial back home. So not a lot of love lost there. And you know, over the years, you don't see yourself going crazy. How about a Nazi encore with the Church begging you to save the world from Communism? Sound good to you? It does to them. Some of them anyway. So we like to keep tabs on what they're up to."

"Including Braun?"

"For a while. But there wasn't much. The Germans all know each other. You see them at the ABC restaurant, having a beer, but that's as far as it went with him. Maybe he was too smart. Maybe he thought his money would protect him. But we never got anything on him. No Fourth Reich stuff."

"So she thought he was just a businessman?" Aaron said, looking over Campbell's shoulder again, her blonde hair like candlelight in the dim room. "She had to know."

Campbell shrugged. "Ask her. Let me guess the answer."

Now she was leaning forward with her cigarette, a lighter appearing like magic, her movements slow and practiced, almost languorous. When she sat back, the smoke seemed to form a curtain between her and the others, a retreat none of them noticed.

More talk, smiling, but not really following anymore, somewhere off by herself. Thinking what? Her face blank, veiled by the smoke. Maybe back in Hamburg, with memories of Doro. Maybe in New York with her boy husband. But not here. Smoking and smiling but not here. He looked for a second at the others. None of them knew her, had even seen her go. And suddenly, an impulse, like a jump of blood, he wanted to know, not just Otto and what she knew, but everything, what she thought behind the smoke.

"What else?" he said, still looking at her.

"It's all in there," Campbell said, indicating the envelope. "Field report."

"You had her under surveillance?"

"Part of the report on her father, that's all. We have a lot of time down here. What if he's using his daughter? As a courier, something like that. So why not check, just to be sure. We have the time."

"And?"

"Nothing. She shops. She goes out. She stays in. She likes the Alvear. She sees a shrink twice a week."

Aaron raised an eyebrow.

"Wouldn't you? Given the family. Anyway, that's nothing special in BA. Everybody sees a shrink. There's a whole neighborhood, all shrink offices. Villa Freud. Really. It's what people do here. Maybe the air."

"Who's the boyfriend?" he said, eyes back at her table.

"No idea. Not the first, though. She's not shy."

"Any of them serious?"

"You want to interview her or fuck her?"

Aaron shot him a look.

"Just asking. Two different things. You don't want to confuse them." He took a sip of his drink. "Unless you're doing one to get the other."

Aaron looked at him again. "I'll let you know how it goes. Since you're interested. You like peepholes too?"

Campbell put up his hand. "Just saying."

"Meanwhile, could you get a copy of the accident report?"

"Whose? Braun's? Why?"

"I'd like to know how she reacted. When she identified the body. I don't want to bring it up if—"

"She didn't identify the body. Rudel did."

"Who?"

"Hans-Ulrich Rudel. Luftwaffe ace. Everybody's best friend. If you're German. He put some money into *Der Weg*. Old pal of Braun's. Great minds think alike, or something like that. And since he was there—"

"He was there? At the accident?"

Campbell nodded. "Yes. They were together, but he was lucky. Why?" Alert now, afraid of missing something.

"Isn't it usual for the family—"

"Well, his daughter. There wasn't any question about it. Nobody knew him better than Rudel. And it's a hell of a thing, make her look at something like that. Then the family doctor backed him up. Markus Bildener. So they had two IDs. They didn't need her, put her through that."

Aaron sat back, glancing again over Jamie's shoulder. Had she refused to do it, be part of the plan? Or had she only been told later, the fake death something she had to accept? Uneasy with it, still nervous at Ohlsdorf, now hiding behind smoke.

"What?" Jamie said.

"Nothing. The martini just hit me. Right off the plane."

Jamie looked at him, his face cloudy with some interior debate.

"What are you doing here?" he said finally. "I'm really asking this time." What he had come to say.

"You mean Langley's asking," Aaron said. "They're worried about me? With all the problems of the world—"

"They don't want you to be another one."

"How?"

"Uncle chases Nazis. Dies. Next thing you know, the nephew shows up in Buenos Aires. Who comes to Buenos Aires? People looking for Nazis. So maybe some unfinished business. That could be a problem."

"The only Nazi I'm looking for is dead."

"Which is why I gave you that." He motioned to the envelope. "But not everybody's dead. You don't want to step on any toes."

Aaron stared at him for a minute. "Especially if they're our Nazis. Working for us."

Jamie took another sip of the martini. "However unlikely that would be."

"But it's a wicked world and you play the cards you're dealt. And so on."

"And so on."

"This is what you came to tell me?"

"Your uncle wanted to lock them all up. Maybe he was right—not very nice people. But sometimes a bad guy's useful."

Aaron picked up the envelope. "This one isn't. He's dead. Look, before you get yourself in a twist about this, I'm really just interested in their kids."

"Which ones?"

"You want a list?"

"The office insists."

"So somebody is working for us."

Jamie shrugged. "It's hard getting leverage. Sometimes promises are made."

"Like not putting him on trial? A big fish, then." Testing.

"We're not in the trial business." The sound of a door closing, Aaron standing outside.

He drained his glass. "So I don't talk to anybody without clearing it with you first, that right?"

Jamie nodded.

"But I'm cleared to talk to Mrs. Crane."

"If she wants to talk to you."

"How about the Eichmann kids? He wasn't on the payroll, was he?"

Jamie glanced up. "It's not a joke. We need to know what you're up to. You don't want to wander off the ranch."

"Wander off the ranch. Christ, Jamie, you're beginning to sound like them."

He looked over his glass. "I am them. So are you."

"I'm on leave. I'm not working for anyone right now."

"You're never on leave. Not in this job. You know that."

"So this is an order."

"A word to the wise."

"I'm just here to talk to their kids. You can quote that in your report."

Jamie looked at him for a moment, then let it go and signaled the waiter. "In that case, 'nuff said, and I'm buying." Then, a new thought. "You know, anything you write, you'd have to clear it with—"

"You'll be the first to know." He smiled, on the team again. "And thanks for this," he said, putting the envelope in his pocket.

"What do you think she'll say?"

"Probably what they all say. How nice he was. Devoted family man."

"Then what's the story?" Jamie said, taking the new glass from the waiter.

"You're a kid, you believe what you're told. Mostly. But then you grow up. Turns out Daddy was killing people. Lots of them. How do you feel about him now? You know some of the camp commandants had their families with them. Fritz talked to one son. He remembers playing in the backyard while the prisoners were marched past. Work detail. He never thought anything of it. The way they looked—starving, like skeletons—he thought that was the way they were supposed to look. How things were. Later he finds out what happened to them. Now how does he look at his father?"

"We don't get to pick our parents."

"Just our friends," Aaron said, raising his eyes. "The ones we make promises to."

Jamie shifted in his chair. "I didn't make them."

"That's what everybody in Germany says. My friend Fritz thinks, you talk to the children, you're talking to Germany too. How much did you know? Then, how do you live with it?"

"You see a shrink twice a week."

"That's one way. Or it never happened. Or it wasn't him." He took a breath. "Or it was. Then what? When do you become complicit," he said, thinking of Max, following Otto in his white coat.

"Christ, they were kids."

"But they didn't stay kids. Take Otto. He wasn't just killing, he was enjoying it. Medical experiments on kids. What do you do with someone like him? What if he's your father?"

"Well, that took care of itself. Luckily. For her, I mean."

"She still sees a shrink."

Jamie said nothing for a second, uncomfortable. "You know, all this business, who's a Nazi, it went away and now since Eichmann it's starting up again. All of the sudden everybody's a Wiesenthal, turning over rocks. You can't live in the past."

"It's not the past if they're still alive. If they haven't paid."

"But this one's dead."

Aaron nodded, checked.

"So now who pays?" Jamie said. "The daughter? Bringing it all up again."

But she knows, Aaron wanted to shout. They must have gone to the funeral together. Like a getaway driver waiting outside the bank. Aiding and abetting. And the only lead he had to Otto. Worth anything.

"She's already talking about it twice a week. Maybe she won't mind talking a little more. Fritz says the others couldn't stop, once they started. Some of them, it's a relief."

Jamie hesitated, then tipped his drink in a mock salute. "I still say she'll throw a glass in your face."

Aaron looked past him again. "Here's your chance to find out. She's coming."

Without thinking, Jamie swiveled to see, the movement catching her attention, so that she was forced to acknowledge him, a small smile. She detached herself from her group and came over.

"Jamie, isn't it? Hanna Crane. We met at the Carlsons'."

"I remember."

"I'll bet not," she said, pleasant. "Embassy people never do, but they have to pretend."

Her voice was clear, the English distinct, the trace of accent no longer German, just another tone, a verbal garnish.

"In this case, it would be hard to forget."

She laughed. "Aren't you ashamed? A line like that. Worse than the Argentines. They still act like Talleyrand—or whoever it was that all the diplomats got it from. Was it?"

"Metternich, I think. But still true."

She smiled again. "Well, all right. Then I'm flattered. Satisfied?"

She had turned toward Aaron, waiting to be introduced. At Ohlsdorf, her head at an angle, he had seen Otto in the sharp cheekbones, the high forehead, but now, facing him, the resemblance was fainter, the cheeks softened by full lips and bright, lively eyes that were taking him in, interested, someone new in town, maybe the way Doro's had been in the happy years.

"Ah, Aaron Wiley," Jamie said, still playing diplomat. "Hanna Crane."

"A colleague? You're at the embassy too?"

"No, just passing through."

"An old school friend," Jamie said.

"Passing through to where?" she said, skeptical, enjoying this.

"Bariloche," Aaron said. "I want to see the Andes."

She looked at him, surprised, then pleased. "Oh. It's very beautiful this time of year. Empty. Not like ski season. My father—my family used to have a house there."

"But not anymore?"

"No, we sold it. It was really my father who liked to go," she said, moving away from it. "Some wonderful trails out past Llao Llao. Funny to think of you hiking," she said to Jamie.

"I'm not. Just Aaron. But why funny?"

"I don't know. I just never imagined you being outdoors."

He had been facing Jamie, and now, turning back, he found her staring at him, and for a second he was back at Ohlsdorf, blending into the chairs, finally recognized. But it wasn't that. A more familiar kind of recognition, how men and women talked, a conversation in a look. What surprised him was the frankness of it, a direct stare, not coy, as clear as her voice. Who are you? Is something going to happen? Do I want something to happen? Jamie's friend. Which probably means the same work. Already lying. But you were looking before, across the room.

"But you must know the place so well," Aaron said, breaking

away from the look. "Anything you'd recommend? Restaurants? Anything I should avoid?"

"Mm. How long are you here? You're not going right away, I hope. Jamie, you should give a party. People love meeting new people down here. I suppose because there never are any." She smiled, easy with drink.

"A few days anyhow. If you think of any restaurants— Can I call you?"

She looked up at him, eyes laughing now, the line more forward than Aaron had intended.

"Or just let Jamie know," he finished.

"No, call. I'd like that." Looking straight at him, as if she wanted to see into him, who he was, and Aaron felt a prickling in his scalp, the flirting ritual now unexpectedly charged, not just erotic, duplicitous. I know something you don't know I know. "Jamie has the number, don't you, Jamie?"

"Somewhere."

She laughed again. "Jamie has everybody's number. So to speak." She turned to Aaron. "Really an old school friend? Of course you wouldn't say, would you? Never mind. Pablo's flagging me down," she said, glancing toward her party. "Nice meeting you. Cognac is good. Wonderful views of the lake." She smiled at his blank expression. "A restaurant. In Bariloche. You'll have to call for the others."

He watched her pass out of the bar area and into the main lobby, down the carpeted stair to the revolving door, shoulders straight, not looking back.

"Interesting to see you in action," Jamie said. "Two minutes and you're getting her number."

"She did most of the work."

"Mr. Irresistible. You could have fooled me."

"She thinks I'm with the Agency."

"You are."

"Then why not stay away?" Aaron said, thinking. "Most people get a little shy."

"Maybe she likes the idea. Playing with matches."

Aaron shook his head. "Not if you've got something to hide."

"What does she have to hide?" Alert again.

Aaron shrugged, deflecting this. "What does she talk about twice a week?"

He had dinner alone in one of the restaurants across the street from Recoleta Cemetery. The lamps had been turned on along the cemetery's high walls, wrought iron fixtures that once might have held candles, an eerie effect, but there was still enough natural light left to see the tops of the mausoleums inside, crosses and pyramids, angels and haloed madonnas, crammed together in a miniature city of the dead. Farther along he could make out the white façade of the colonial church—our lady of something. Pilar. The street was busy, a warm evening, the cafés full, his the only table for one. How many evenings had Max spent like this, sitting alone, only his document folders for company? You're on your own, Nathan had said, and now he felt the doors closing all around him. Mossad, with better things to do. The Agency, too compromised to help. But Max must have felt the same, filling his folders, year after year, the only one who still cared. You could get used to eating alone, maybe even prefer it. He thought of those final tense dinners with Claire, making conversation with nothing to say.

He refilled his glass, hearing Nathan again. On your own. You're ready for that? A desk man. Was he? He remembered the field reports he used to analyze, the solitude you could feel on the page. Men keeping secrets. Now him. No one in the noisy café next door knew what he was doing here, who he really was. His great advantage, a hunter whose scent hadn't yet reached his prey. But it would, and then what? He'd need help. Max had given him names, "well placed in the Jewish community," and Aaron imagined a line of old men, Maxes, adept at sifting through landing cards and visa files, more desk men. Who, then? Jamie, protecting his flank? Nathan? For the first time, it occurred to him that he might not be able to do it, that the hunt he owed Max might end in another escape. Otto still walking around.

He took out Jamie's envelope and opened it. The usual Agency top sheet with routing numbers and file destination, the usual Agency overkill, full bio, source redacted, when all he'd asked for was address and phone. Jamie had included a surveillance report. Aaron glanced at the dates. Just before the accident, her father still alive. He read through the first page, peeking into her life. A week as James had described. Shopping. Lunch at the yacht club. The opera. Dinner with Ricardo and Tina. A short weekend in Mar del Plata. Dr. Ortiz in Villa Freud (an asterisk here, his bona fides checked). Drinks at the Alvear. Dinner Sunday at the Kavanagh Building (cross-reference to Helmut Braun). He looked at the following week. Another Sunday dinner. Obligatory or had she looked forward to seeing him? Aaron imagined the Sunday roast and red cabbage, an evening in Munich. What had they talked about? What did they talk about now?

He flipped a page. More lunches and parties. Dr. Ortiz. The Brazilian Embassy, then the Chilean, stops on the endless rounds of embassy cocktail receptions, a chance to dress up. A day trip to Tigre. Hairdresser. Pablo. Aaron skimmed down, looking to the bottom. How far had the surveillance gone? Sleeping partners? But not here, a discreet blank at the end of the page. One day like the other, filling time, presumably the life she still lived.

Except she wasn't just filling time anymore. The secret must have changed everything, even idle moments now lived in sharp, wary focus. He thought of her at the ceremony at Ohlsdorf, the white of her neck, tense, a deer listening for any snapping sound, ready to dart away. He wondered what a surveillance report would show now. No more Sunday dinners at the Kavanagh. How did they communicate? Why not just call? Unless they didn't want to take any chances, kept an elaborate radio silence. But why would the police listen in? They wouldn't. The Agency hadn't; there was nothing to suggest it. Maybe suspicion became its own reason, a cautious new way of filling time.

He walked the few blocks home, night now, dark in patches away from the restaurant lights. He stopped at the corner of Avenida Alvear, looking across to the sloping pocket of park with giant ombu trees, the pale gray roots twisting under the black umbrella of leaves, as if they were moving toward him, alive, like the roots at Angkor Wat strangling the temple stones. On this side of the street, modern apartment buildings, some with terraces facing back to the cemetery, the preferred view. She lived in one of these, the address in his pocket, maybe even home now, looking down on him. But more likely drinking a Malbec with Pablo and her friends. Living her father's lie, telling no one, another field agent working alone.

He was scarcely through the door when the phone rang, noisy, jarring.

"I'm putting you through," the desk clerk said, a borrowed English phrase.

The radio crackle of a long-distance line.

"Aaron? Fritz." Talking quickly, almost gasping.

"My god, what time is it there?"

"The rates are cheaper after midnight. But three minutes only, please."

"You all right?"

"The ribs are still taped, but I'm living."

"In the hospital?"

"No. Home. And now a little time in the mountains, to rest."

"That's good."

"No, that's what the office will say. A convalescent. But I am coming to you. That's why I'm calling."

"They're sending you? I thought they wouldn't—"

"I decided I didn't like being kicked to death. I have some money. If we get him, I'll have more. Then the paper pays."

Aaron smiled to himself, hearing the rumpled swagger in his voice.

"I met her tonight, the daughter."

"Did she recognize you?"

"No. I don't think so."

"And now?"

"I get to know her better. She must know where he is. She's bound to make a slip."

A sound of agreement, a gentle grunt. "First, build the trust. That's how you get the picture. After an accident."

Aaron said nothing, uncomfortable, suddenly seeing faces caught by a flashbulb, grieving, stunned.

"And your—people there?"

"They think I'm working for you. Lining up interviews for the series."

"Well, now it will be true."

"You don't have to do this. You must still be—"

"He saw my face. So I'm careful. I don't leave from Germany. Austria. No trace. Nobody knows I'm there." Voice still rushed, caught up in some melodrama. "So. This telephone costs a fortune. I'll leave a message."

"You sure you can do this? Travel, I mean."

"You're like the doctor. Stay in bed. So now I'm Lazarus. Rising up. That's right, rising up?"

"That was a miracle."

"*Ja*, back from the dead. Just like Schramm." A small laugh. "I want to be there, when we get him. Let him see my face again. So he knows it's me."

"OK," Aaron said, not knowing what else to say.

"We help each other. And I get my story. This time, lots of pictures." Ambulance chasing. But isn't that what he wanted too? Flashbulbs. Press.

"OK," Aaron said again.

6

SHE WAS JUST LATE enough to make an entrance, forcing him to stand, waiting for her as she made her way past the deco barrel chairs to the bar. She was wearing a white pencil skirt with a row of pearls at the hem, a soft white cardigan draped over her blouse against the air-conditioning.

"This all right?" he said, indicating the table.

"Yes, fine."

"You really like the Alvear."

"It's close," she said, sitting down, smiling at him, someone with her finger on a checker, waiting for the opening move.

He looked toward the bar, signaling a waiter. "It reminds me of the St. Regis," he said. "Without the mural."

"You know New York. I thought it was Washington somehow."

"It is. But I travel."

"All the way here," she said wryly. "Ah, Carlos, *buenas tardes*."

They ordered martinis.

"Were you really at school with Jamie?"

"No."

She looked at him, surprised, the game skipping a turn.

"I'm afraid I've got you here under false pretenses." Moving a man out.

"Well, I'll give you this. You're the first who's ever admitted it."

She took out a cigarette, leaning forward to his light. "So you don't work together?"

"No. I'm here on my own. Not on business. Not his, anyway."

"Whose, then?"

He paused as the drinks arrived.

"Cheers," he said, raising his.

"Cheers. All right, so you get a merit badge for honesty. What are the false pretenses?" She looked at him, playing. "Or do I guess?"

"Not that either," he said, slightly disconcerted, not expecting this. "I mean, not *not* that. But that's not why I called." Fumbling, off balance.

She sat back, amused, and crossed her legs, a faint swish of nylon. "I'm all ears. And I've just sat down. Now, how did you manage that?"

"I'm doing a favor for a friend. A writer. He'd like to interview you—or have me do it—about your father."

"My father," she said flatly, sitting up, the smile gone. "Then you know who he was."

Aaron nodded. "He's doing a series about the sons—" He dipped his head. "And daughters of prominent officials of the Third Reich. What it was like growing up then, how people feel about their parents now. Nobody's talked to them before. He thinks it's a book."

She drew on the cigarette. "Prominent officials. You mean war criminals. So that's one false pretense. What are the others?"

"I'm sorry to be so—clumsy. There's no other way to ask, really."

"I don't talk about my father. Anyway, he's dead."

He took out a cigarette of his own, giving them a second.

"The piece isn't about him. It's about you. What you think."

"What I think. Another false pretense. Nobody cares what I think. You just want me to say terrible things about him."

"Were there terrible things?"

She looked at him. "Why don't you answer that yourself? Since you already know. Everybody knows. Otto Schramm. Dr. Evil. But now he's dead, so why talk about it anymore. It's over."

"I meant terrible things with you."

"With me?"

"Yes. What was he like as a father? How did you feel when you heard that he was dead?"

She was quiet for a minute. "How did I feel? Free. Does that surprise you? Not a very nice thing to say. His daughter." She looked up. "I felt free. All that weight—gone. You could breathe. I didn't have to think about him anymore. And I didn't have to talk about him anymore."

"You don't. But I think you should."

"Why?"

"It's important. A part of history."

"Being his daughter? It didn't feel like history, not at the time."

"What did it feel like?"

She looked up, alert. "It felt like being his daughter. Is this the interview? This is how you do it?"

He held up his hand, palm out. "I was just asking."

"But I'm talking. Isn't that the idea? History," she said, exhaling, dismissing this. "I think that's already been written. Do you think I'm going to say he didn't do those things? He did. What else? Apologize for him? To whom? The dead? Now that he's dead too? Maybe they're settling accounts somewhere. I hope so. But I don't have to." She put down the glass. "I don't want to be in a book. I don't want to talk about it. So there's your answer. Sorry if you've wasted your money. But it's only the price of a drink."

"That's not the only reason I called."

She sat back, eyes on him, assessing. "It's interesting how you do this. Good cop/bad cop. Except there is no bad cop."

"No cop."

"Now let me ask you a question. Someone works with Jamie but says he doesn't. Never mind." She waved away his protest before he could make it. "So maybe he's on his own. But still one of them. So what do you want from me? You. Not this made-up friend with his made-up book. You."

"I'm not sure yet."

Looking straight at each other, another swerve, the air charged.

"Not sure," she said.

"Is that why you came? You thought I set this up for the Agency? Why? Why would they want to talk to you?"

"I don't know," she said, still holding his gaze. "I came to see what you wanted—you know, someone in your—what? Line of work."

"So you're here under false pretenses too."

"Both of us. Imagine. So what's the truth? What do you want?" Her voice lower, slightly smoky, really asking.

"The truth? I didn't make up Fritz. Or the book. You can ask him yourself. When he gets here."

But she had moved somewhere else, interested in the game now, what was going to happen.

"And when's that?"

"A few days."

"So I won't know until then. If he's real. And meanwhile?"

He looked at her. "You'll have to trust me."

"I don't trust many people."

He moved his shoulder as the waiter put down a dish of nuts. "That's probably a good idea."

"Mm. It is. I've been married."

"So have I."

"What happened? Did you cheat on her?"

"No. We just—grew apart."

"Now it's your turn to ask."

"A gentleman wouldn't ask. Did he?"

She smiled. "Only when I wasn't looking. Except I always was—I knew every time. So maybe it wasn't cheating. Is it cheating if the other person knows?"

"If she cares."

She tilted her head slightly, considering some new idea.

"We both knew. And pretended we didn't know. After a while it was the only interesting thing in the marriage, wondering what the other one knew."

Aaron nodded. Her senses already trained to pick up anything off, what she was doing now.

"Well, that's out of the way," she said. "Sometimes it takes hours. Tiptoeing around."

"What does?"

"Wondering about the ring," she said, nodding to his left hand.

"I just haven't bothered to take it off yet, that's all."

"Yes? I thought it was another false pretense. Camouflage. You know." Almost flirting now, a couple peeking around hedges in some old drawing.

He twisted the ring, tighter than he remembered, then pulled it off and put it in his pocket.

"Better?"

She smiled. "Now at least I know what to expect." A second's pause. "Are you Jewish?"

"Does it matter?"

"Not to me. Not that you would believe that, I suppose."

"Then why ask?"

"I just like to know who I'm talking to. Especially about my father."

"I thought we weren't going to talk about him."

She ignored this. "What kind of axe you have to grind. Putting him in a book. Why? Everyone knows he's guilty."

"But what else? Who was he? That's the book." He waited a second, letting this hang in the air. "At least you don't think I'm making it up anymore."

She looked at him over her glass. "Maybe. I thought you were here for them—Jamie's people. They have their fingers in every pie down here. But why ask about my father? He's dead, they know he's dead. The police went through his papers. Why? Because they're police. And if they went through them, then your people know too. That's the way it works. What did you find?"

He opened his hands. "I just want you to see Fritz."

"No, something else." She put down her glass, finished. "Anyway, I don't want to be in a book. Why should I? And never mind about history. Whatever he did, it's finished. Was he a monster? You decide. You will anyway. But he was my father. You don't say such things in books."

"You were fond of him."

"Fond? Other things. It's complicated. Oh, here I am talking about him. It's a technique you have."

He shook his head. "I know it's complicated. That's why we're only talking to sons—daughters—of those who've died." Trying it, like a new fishing lure. "We don't expect people to talk about their fathers if they're still alive. It's too difficult."

"They're all dead? In the book?" she said, a nibble.

Aaron nodded. "We find it's easier. For the children. In a way, it's a chance to bury them. All the mixed feelings they've had over the years."

"It's so easy, you think," she said, looking down at her glass. "And what do they say? Are they ashamed? Proud? Well, how could they be proud? A Wehrmacht general maybe. Clean hands. Cleaner, anyway. But that wasn't my father."

"No."

She looked up.

"I don't know what the others said. You'll have to ask Fritz. Sometimes it's good to talk."

"I don't need another therapist," she said quickly. "You think that's the way it's done? Talk to some stranger on his way to Bariloche?" She stopped. "If you're going. Are you?"

"No."

She raised her eyebrows, intrigued. "Another pretense. So what else? Maybe everything. Who are you really? Israeli?" Looking at him, a question.

"No."

"If you are, it's too late. He's dead."

"American. Born in Germany."

"But not German. Jewish. So you don't have to answer for that."

"Neither do you. You were a child."

"That's right," she said, looking away. "I don't have to answer."

"When did you know?" he said quietly, a first step.

"Who he was? Always. I had to change my name too. What he did? Much later."

"How did you find out?"

"A magazine. There was an article." She made a wry face. "Maybe your friend wrote it. If he exists."

"But before that?"

"No one ever talked about it. Why would they? He was in the army—well, the SS, it turns out, but I thought it was just part of the army. So when the Americans won, they were arresting everyone, putting them in camps. Like criminals. We had to change our names so they wouldn't find him. That's all I knew. And then he left."

"Without you?"

"My mother was still well in those days."

Aaron felt the prickling again, knowing something she didn't know he knew, the simplest detail still a deceit.

"Then she got sick, so my aunt sent me to him."

"In Argentina?"

"Yes, Argentina. Who else would take people like him? The government even helped sometimes. Jobs, you know, places to live. Perón liked the Germans—he thought they should have won. So now he's Helmut Braun. An ethnic German from the Alto Adige—the first papers were Italian. And I was Hanna Braun. *Auf Wiedersehen*, Schramm. That was all right with me. Why not a new life? Germany was like a graveyard in those days. My mother—" She stopped, shifting back. "And Argentina—we were rich in Argentina. A big house. In Palermo Chico. On Calle Aguado. It's an embassy now, so imagine how big. The parties."

"So you weren't in hiding?"

"Not on Calle Aguado. Not Helmut Braun. The other Germans knew who we were, but we knew who they were. A protection racket. The Argentines didn't care. The war, that was a long time ago. Far away. And he could be charming, you know. Perfect manners. They love that here."

Aaron thought of Max, taken smoothly off the line. You'll see him later.

"And then Perón left and we had to be more careful. I was never told why, just that it wasn't good to stand out. He sold the house. No more parties. Of course, it was still safe, really. Perón wasn't the only one who'd helped. He still had friends here. But he was going through money living that way. So, a quiet life." She smiled. "And where does he go? The Kavanagh Building. On Plaza San Martín. You know, the tall one there."

"Yes," he said, back in the surveillance report.

"That's his idea of a quiet life. Moving to the Waldorf. So we lived there. With all the society people. And then I saw the magazine."

She took a second, suddenly at an end.

"What did he say?" Aaron said quietly.

"Say? Nothing. I didn't mention it. How do you talk about something like that? And then later, when I did—he said it was an exaggeration." She looked down, another wry smile. "That's what he said to me. It was all an exaggeration." The words uneasy, not practiced, what had really happened. "Maybe he even believes that."

Aaron held himself still, as if he hadn't heard the present tense.

She looked up. "But now it doesn't matter what he believed. A doctor. A scientist. That's how he saw himself. And all the rest of it—" She waved her hand. "An exaggeration. They're all like that, you know. Not just him. It was all someone else's fault. Look at Eichmann. He had nothing to do with it. I guess that's how they live with themselves." She met his eye. "Or how they did," she said. "Sometimes it's hard to believe—I think he's still here. With all his excuses. But that's in the past now too. And here we are. You wanted the story of my life? So now you know."

He sat back, taking her in, the soft white of the sweater picking up the dim light from the bar, surrounding her, shining on her skin, like the warm sheen of her pearl earrings. The voice tentative, not just being careful, haunted. He imagined her holding out the magazine, her life turned upside down. Not at all what he'd expected. But so what? Otto still walking.

"It's a start," he said.

"Oh, a start. What would be enough? Always another question with you, I think. No, the end." She put out her cigarette, a kind of punctuation mark.

"But I still don't know anything about you." Keep her in her seat.

"Then we're even, aren't we?" she said, looking at him.

"All right. You ask."

"Why are you here?" she said, the voice direct again.

"Right now, to see you. Persuade you to talk to Fritz."

"And the rest of the time?"

He waited a second. "I can't tell you."

She smiled. "The perfect answer. Now I can't ask anything more."

"About my work. There's still me."

"The one who's not doing whatever you do for Uncle Sam. Can you separate them like that?"

"Mostly." He looked up. "You're not part of the work. If that's what you're asking."

"That's good to know. If it's true." She tilted her head slightly, looking at him. "I would never know with you, would I?"

"That's true of everybody, don't you think? Who someone is—it's always a mystery in the end. Another drink?"

"No. One's the limit. Gentlemen take advantage."

"Not all of them."

"You'd be surprised."

"Then let's take our time finishing this one."

She sat back, settling in. "So you can ask me more questions?"

"Why don't you just talk, then I won't have to. I'll listen."

"Mm, like my psychiatrist. Not a word—it's like a vacuum, just empty space. So you talk to fill it up."

"How long have you been in—"

"Since I got back. After the divorce. I didn't want to do something like that again, so I thought I'd better sort myself out."

"And did it work?"

"Well, I'm still seeing him."

He took a sip of his drink. "How old were you when you—"

"Got married? Twenty. So what did I know?"

"No, found out about your father."

"Back to that. Fifteen, sixteen. Old enough to know it wasn't an exaggeration, that he was lying to me. I think I was more shocked about that than— You know, at that age everything is about what happens to you."

"Did you talk about it?"

"No, not the way you mean. But I started to listen. When he talked about this and that—never the war, just thoughts about things—I paid attention. Looking for clues, I suppose, to explain how he could do it. A doctor, that's what I couldn't understand, how a doctor could be part of that. But to him it made sense. Crazy sense, but—" She stopped. "Anyway, it happened. And he must have known what it was, really, or why would he lie to me about it?"

Aaron thought of Max's photograph, the laughing nurse. Who must have known too.

"He never practiced afterward?" Aaron said. An odd unexpected symmetry with Max.

"No. That would have made him easier to trace. He had to be Helmut Braun. Businessman. Nothing medical. So he gave it up—no medicine. Another thing to hold against the Amis."

"He blamed them?"

"Who would he blame, himself?" She shifted in her chair, suddenly restless. "This is a funny sort of drink."

"Why?"

"Talking about all this—" She glanced at her watch. "It's getting late."

"Have another."

"No, it's enough." She looked over. "I'll talk to your friend. The writer."

"Fritz."

"Yes, it would be," she said, rolling her eyes. "So it's a success for you. Mission accomplished. How did you do it?" she said, beginning a mock conversation. "I charmed her. We talked about the camps. She can never resist that. Just mention her father and off she goes. You won't have any trouble." She shook her head. "Who else does he have, in this famous book?"

"I don't know. Hans Frank's son, I think. Bormann's."

"So he thinks Bormann's dead."

"Presumed dead anyway. The son thinks so."

"Then let's hope he doesn't turn up someday after all. Think how the son would feel. Better to be dead and gone." She began putting her cigarettes into her purse. "Well," she said, moving the purse. "Such talk."

She lifted her head, about to force a smile, say something light, get up, but her face clouded, a flicker of unwanted recognition, and her neck tensed, the neck at Ohlsdorf. Aaron turned to see an older couple coming toward them, suit and tie, long dress, slicked-back hair and a gray perm, dressed for Baden-Baden, a trip to the casino after dinner.

"Hanna," the man said, then a flurry of German, quick and familiar, the sense clearly how nice to see you or what a surprise, but the words themselves indistinct, another language. She got up, Aaron following her lead. The man's manners, like his clothes, had a prewar formality, a hand kiss for Hanna and a half bow to Aaron.

"Trude," Hanna said to the wife in English. "I thought you were in Mar del Plata. Markus—oh, forgive me. Markus Bildener, Trude Bildener, Aaron Wiley. A friend from the States."

"Wiley," Markus said, nodding again, trying the name on as if it were a jacket.

Aaron said nothing, no response expected. Another appraisal.

"What luck to find you here. So elusive these days," Markus said, correct but accented, a stage German speaking English.

"Just busy. I didn't realize you were in town." Getting through it, but the neck still rigid.

"The States," Markus said, now turning to Aaron. "New York?"

"No. Washington."

"Ah, you're with the embassy here, then?"

"No, just traveling."

"We have friends in common," Hanna said quickly, explaining him.

"Yes," Aaron said, surprised but not showing it.

"Not Tommy, I hope," Markus said, and then, to Aaron's blank expression, "Hanna's first husband."

"Only," Hanna said. "Aaron's on his way to Bariloche."

"Very beautiful this time of year. And Buenos Aires is always a little dull in the summer, I'm afraid. Of course, there's Da Silva, bless him, he never stops. You're going to the party Thursday, I hope," he said to Hanna. "It's very important that you go. João's gone to such trouble. You know the Brazilians care about these things. And he was so fond of your father." The words deliberate, as if he were speaking in code and waiting for the decryption. He turned to Aaron. "But I hope you get to see a little of the city. You don't know the ambassador, then? A shame, because the residency is one of the finest houses in Barrio Norte. Wiley. There was a Bill Wiley a few years back, a commercial attaché, I think, but that was a changed name."

Aaron said nothing, letting him wait.

"Well, but you'll join us for dinner?" Markus said to Hanna.

"I can't. Aaron and I were just about to go, in fact."

"I meant both of you, of course. We're dining here, so you see how convenient."

"I know, but we can't tonight. We're meeting some people. So nice of you, though."

"A 'rain check,' then?" Markus said, the slang in quotation marks. "And of course we'll see you Thursday. You won't forget?"

But Hanna was saying good-bye to Trude, and then, after another series of half bows, they were on the long runner carpet, through the revolving doors, and out on the porte cochere.

"I couldn't face it," Hanna said, trying to make light of it, but Aaron had seen the wariness. "Sorry to use you that way."

"I enjoyed watching you in action."

"Lying, you mean," she said, a little flustered, but pleased.

"Who is he?"

"An old friend of my father's. Waiting for the Fourth Reich. You can imagine what the dinners are like. So thank you."

"Changed name," he said, half to himself. "I haven't heard that one in a while."

"They're like that. They still think— My father too. When I married Tommy—"

"He was Jewish?" Aaron said, surprised, another swerve.

"One grandfather. But that was enough for my father. A *Mischling*. Dr. Ortiz, my therapist, thinks that's why I did it. My father didn't talk to me for a year."

"But then he did."

"There was the money," she said, a faint edge to her voice now. "He never had a problem with that—taking money from the Jews."

Aaron looked at her. Not what he'd expected.

"I'm just down here." She nodded toward the end of the street, a good-bye. "Tell your friend to call."

"No, don't go," he said, meaning it. "Anyway, we have to have dinner now or your cover will be blown. You have to play it out."

"Is that how it works? In your business?"

"My business? My business is sitting at a desk all day reading reports to guess what someone will say at a conference and then try to explain it when he says something else. You're thinking of the guys in the field. They go to foreign cities—South America maybe—and women ask them out to dinner. Know anything nearby?"

She smiled. "Do you like steak?"

"Let's go."

"You're sure? I really didn't—"

"You just want me to ask you. The one and only time I've ever been asked to dinner. All right. Will you?"

They walked down the gentle slope to Posadas, past Aaron's hotel and across Avenida Callao to a restaurant already filling up and noisy, soccer jerseys and team photographs on the wall, people in open shirts and summer dresses, regulars, the tables crowded with carafes of red wine. The waiters knew her and made a fuss, steering them to a table against a wall, away from the worst of the noise, her Alvear clothes now giving her a kind of regal presence in the smoky room. The waiter handed them menus.

"Don't bother," she said. "It's all steak. The wine's the thing here. I don't know where they get it. Shall I order a carafe?"

She spoke to the waiter in Spanish, a fast exchange.

"What?" she said, catching him watch her.

"Your Spanish."

"I grew up here."

"No, I meant, did you ever notice how people become different in another language? Their tone, the way they move, everything. Different personalities."

"Then I have three. Wait till I tell Dr. Ortiz."

"All right. But there's something to it. What if we think differently in different languages? You know, if the structure of it changes the way we think."

"I'm not thinking much in any of them. This is good, though." She moved her finger back and forth to indicate the conversation. "I need to think in English. I'm an American now. My passport is, anyway. The one thing I got out of the marriage."

"But you moved back here."

She shrugged. "I like it here. New York is—well, over for me. I can't live in Germany. Given everything. It's easier here. You can disappear from the rest of the world."

"That's what I thought the first day here. The distance—you feel forgotten."

"Almost," she said, then let it go, not bothering to explain. "Here we are," she said as the wine arrived. They tasted it. "It's good for house wine, isn't it?"

He smiled. "You're a cheap date."

"Is that what this is? The interview's over?"

"It was your turn to ask."

She smiled a little, toying with her glass. "You said before 'guys in the field.' What do you call them?"

"Agents."

"Not spies?"

"They prefer agents."

She nodded. "OK. I've never had dinner with an agent before. Not that I knew of anyway."

"You're not having one now."

She ignored this. "I don't count Jamie. Everybody knows he's— Anyway, you're the dangerous one."

"How so?"

"It's easy to talk to you. So I keep talking. Isn't that what every agent wants?"

"Probably."

Another smile. "But you wouldn't know." She sipped the wine. "Anyway, you don't get everything. The German me. Or the Spanish me. You don't know how I think in Spanish."

"I don't know how you think in English yet. That's why we're here."

Another sip of wine, the noise of the restaurant a buzz behind them.

"I'm not going to win this," she said. "I'm enjoying it too much."

He looked up, the gulp of wine spreading through him, warm, enjoying it too, the talk, just being in the room, at this table, away from the flow of Spanish and bright overhead lights, their space.

"Win what?" he said quietly, the cat and mouse of the Alvear becoming something else, so that two things were happening at once, a different rhythm, aware now of her perfume, lost somehow at the Alvear, of glances coming from the neighboring tables, as if they were meant to act something out, aware of everything.

"Whatever we're doing," she said, inside the intimate circle too, just their table.

"Having dinner," he said, steadying himself.

"That too." She made a toasting movement with her glass. "And I'm enjoying it. You can put that in your report. Subject enjoyed herself."

"Then I'd have to say that I did too. They wouldn't like that."

"Better not then." She paused. "I wonder what you really want."

"Why couldn't it be just dinner?"

"Because it isn't. I'd know. It would feel different."

"Maybe I'm not doing it right. How does it usually go?"

"Usually? We sit down. You'd say something about how I look."

"How you look," he repeated, now looking.

"I didn't say it had to be true."

He raised his eyebrows, playing. "You look—wonderful. But you already know that. Do I do it piece by piece? Eyes—"

She smiled. "Then tell me something I don't know."

"How about something I don't know."

She waited.

"Why you came to dinner."

"A whim?"

"You?"

"Every now and then. Or maybe some reason of my own. Like you."

"Like me."

"Some reason you can't tell me. Remember? Now we'll both have one."

He looked over at her, momentarily checked. Two things happening at once.

"But let's pretend it's just dinner," she said. "And you think I look wonderful."

They ordered more wine when the steak arrived, perfectly charred, spilling over the side of the plate. Fried potatoes. He glanced around the room—did people eat like this every day? They talked about nothing, floating from one subject to another, the talk just an excuse to be there, across from each other. The neighborhoods of Buenos Aires, authentic San Telmo, leafy Palermo. A friend who knew Borges. Tango parlors, real ones. New York when the marriage was still fun. In the bright restaurant light her hair, deep gold at the Alvear, took on a white silver sheen, a film effect, her eyes dark, pooling. But brown, not Aryan blue, not her father's Nordic dream. His daughter. Not giving anything away. But also this other woman, sipping wine, talking about—what? A new museum in Belgrano. Neither of them really paying attention. Putting the sweater behind her in the suddenly warm room, turning to hang it over the chair, the movement pulling her blouse against her skin. Where was Belgrano anyway? Laughing at something. All of it just an excuse to look. Not what he expected.

And then later, with the last of the wine, a new intimacy, not drunk or sloppy, but easy with each other, knowing, as if something had already been discussed and decided. Taking their time, tables emptying around them. For a few minutes they were quiet, not having to say anything. She rested her cheek on her hand, elbow on the table, looking at him.

"So what do you think? If I talk to your friend, do I bury him? Otto?"

"I don't know."

"No. I don't know either. I thought I only had to do it once—but here he is again. And maybe again."

"You can only die once."

She looked at him for a second, then took her hand away, sitting up. "Yes. Once. You're right. And he did. But the problem is he doesn't go away. I'm Schramm, then Braun, then Crane and he's still inside me—you know, his blood. My mother, I never told you—"

"No," he said, the word almost a gulp.

"She died. But before she died—"

He waited.

"She was—not right," she said, making a motion toward her head.

"I'm sorry."

"So that's what's in me. Two sides. Damaged goods."

"You don't really believe that."

"Why not? Who knows what's in my blood?"

"It doesn't work that way. You're not them. Blood's just—blood."

"So genes, then. Whatever they call it. You don't think I should worry."

"No."

"But you didn't have such a father."

He stared at her. Tell me where he is.

"It doesn't bother you?" she said. "That he's my father?"

"No," he said, sliding now, unable to stop.

"Maybe you even like it. There are people like that."

"No."

"No," she said. "So you don't care." She looked down at her wine. "Everybody cares. One way or the other."

"I'm not having dinner with him. I'm having dinner with you." He looked over. "And your genes."

"And my genes. Whatever they are. So that's nice," she said, forcing a smile. She sat back, fingering her glass, looking at him. "Aaron Wiley. Mysterious Mr. Wiley. So is Markus right? It's a changed name?"

"Uh-huh."

"What was it?"

"Gelb," Aaron said, pulling it out of the air, a yellow jersey on the wall.

"Yes? But it's not so bad."

"Not so American either."

"Tommy's was something I couldn't pronounce. His grandfather's, I mean. Lithuanian. Polish, maybe. From the East. Anyway, now Crane."

"Did he think of himself as Jewish?"

"No. How could he—and be with me? Sleeping with the enemy." She looked straight at him. "Maybe how you'd feel."

He said nothing, the question lying on the table between them, but the image in it alive, something he could feel, as if she had reached across and touched him.

"How do you know he didn't? Feel that," he said finally.

"Because you know. No one lies in bed."

"No one," he repeated.

"Not the bodies. People lie, but not the bodies. You know." Still looking at him, their eyes still.

"I wonder."

"Because you did? But she knew. I'll bet she knew."

"But I didn't lie."

She tilted her head, a new angle. "It's funny. I believe you. An honest man. Well, sometimes honest. That's what makes it—"

"What?"

"Interesting. Someone you don't know."

"A stranger."

She smiled. "No. Picking up people in bars, you mean? Not yet. You can ask at the Alvear. Tommy thought so. You know he hired a detective? Or maybe his father arranged it. Everywhere I went."

"And what happened?"

"I slept with him," she said, her laugh almost a giggle, young. "He wanted it. So he wrote a good report and they paid him. It was true, the report. He never found me with anyone. Except him."

Both smiling now, the jokes not really jokes, just something in the air that no one else felt, a way of touching.

She moved in her seat, leaning forward. "Why am I telling you all this? I don't talk to anybody about such things. Well, Dr. Ortiz. But that's like the confessional. It doesn't go any further. So why you, do you think?" A question to herself.

"I'm easy to talk to."

She thought about this for a second, her own idea circling back.

"Because you listen. Nobody listens, but you do. Everything I say. Listening."

"I'm being polite."

"No. Listening. Anybody else, we would already be gone—your room, somewhere. But we're here talking. That's what you want."

"And you?"

She caught his eye and then looked away, embarrassed, something new.

"I'd better get you home," he said, signaling for the check. "Look, we've finished the wine."

She watched his face, another direct look, saying nothing, as he paid the bill.

"Shall we go?" he said.

"You can't come to the building. I don't bring people home."

He looked back, an uncontrollable shiver of anticipation, the second when you know it's going to happen.

"Caesar's wife?"

"Tommy's wife. I got into the habit. It's a small town."

"I'm in the next block," he said evenly. "My hotel."

"Ah. Except you haven't asked me yet."

Not what he was doing here, what was supposed to happen. And then he was moving and it was too late. He reached across and took her hand, just grazing her skin, aware of it, helping her to her feet and collecting the sweater in what felt like one motion, a piece of choreography, his hand moving to the small of her back as they left.

In the street, a few steps away from the restaurant lights, she turned to face him, putting her hand at the back of his neck, faces close. Too late to stop now.

"Just tell me one thing. It's not because I'm his daughter. Somebody did that once. I don't know why. Get even, something like that."

What had that been like, to remember it now?

"He's dead."

She looked away. "Yes. I keep forgetting."

And then she pulled him to her, and all he could feel was her breath, hot on his face, her mouth opening, the little shocks of contact, not thinking anymore. He moved to her cheek, her ear, smelling her skin, excited by the tiny gasps near his ear, standing in the street, wanting it now. When she pulled away, just a little, it was only to catch her breath, his lips still on her, following some map of her face.

"It's not a good idea," she said, the words coming out in bursts, between kisses.

"What?"

"To go to bed with someone you don't know."

"No," he said, still kissing her.

"But I'm the one who wanted to. All night. Maybe that's why. To see what you want." Her breath coming faster. "And now I don't care anymore. I don't care who you are."

At the hotel, the desk clerk looked away as he handed him the key, concierge discretion. They had to wait for the elevator, a rickety iron cage, not looking at each other, waiting again as the door closed and the contact points met, the jolt of winches, the slow climb. When they were halfway to the first floor, out of sight of the desk, he pushed her against the cab wall, too late to stop now, a kid in a hurry. She laughed a little, surprised, then pressed back, the length of her body against his. He put his hands behind her, pulling her closer, excited now by where they were, the furtiveness, like teenage sex, something you weren't supposed to do. Just being here against the rules. And not being able to stop.

In the room she put her hand on his arm, a slowing motion, then unzipped her skirt and pulled her blouse over her head, a show for him, almost mischievous, watching him watch. When she was naked, she stood still for a second, a provocation, then pulled his hand over to her so that he could feel her skin, her breast, then the rest of her, wanting all of it at once. A woman's skin, the softness of it. No, hers. The way it smelled, moved under his fingers. Then she was at his belt, undoing it while he kissed her, and there was nothing to grab onto anymore. He thought of the cage elevator falling floor by floor, no stops, and when they fell on the bed it seemed part of the same fall, a kind of swoon, and she wasn't trying to slow him anymore, falling with him, faster, grabbing at each other to finish before they hit bottom. When he entered her she was already wet, almost there, and they seemed to go even faster, urgent, both of them gasping but not crying out, as if they didn't want to be heard, afraid of being caught, and then not caring, the pleasure rushing in, overwhelming everything. For one second, who they really were. Not thinking anymore, floating.

Afterward they didn't talk, didn't smoke, just lay there coming back. On the ceiling, there were flickers of light from the building in the next street. Where people were getting ready for bed, speaking Spanish, in their own world. Not looking for anybody. Maybe making love, clothes thrown on the floor. Then lying like this, at peace.

She turned onto her side and put her arm across his chest, letting it lie there, so they could feel each other breathing, then raised herself up, propping her head with her free hand.

"I should go," she said, moving her hand over his chest.

"No, stay."

She shook her head. "I sleep at home. It's a rule."

"Whose?"

"Mine."

"That's what men do. Cut and run."

"But I'm not a man."

"No." He leaned up and kissed her. "So stay."

"I can't," she said, beginning to move.

"Why not?"

She put a finger to his lips, then got up and went to the bathroom. He lay there, listening to the running water, wondering what would happen next, then sat up and lit a cigarette just to do something. When she came back and started dressing, she turned her back to him, suddenly private.

"It's late," he said.

"Not for here. People stay up."

"Should I come?"

"Don't worry, I'll be all right."

"Stay. Why not? We're both free."

"Well, free," she said, a frown, taking the cigarette from his fingers for a puff, then handing it back. She reached down, putting her hand against his cheek. "But it was nice. I'm glad."

"I'll call you tomorrow."

"No. Go to Bariloche. Or wherever you're going. It's better like this."

"Like what?"

"Like this. Something nice. It's enough."

"But I want—" he started, getting up, the sheet dropping as he stood.

"Look at you," she said, amused.

"I want to see you," he finished, not bothering to cover.

"To ask me more questions? No, it's enough of that too."

"Why? You don't want me to—"

"Not you," she said, putting a hand on his chest. "It's me I don't trust."

"Trust."

"I don't want it to be more than—something nice. I can't trust myself with that. So." She reached up and kissed him, a good-bye. "Let's say it was the wine."

"I'll call you."

She shook her head. "Something nice. Let's leave it at that. My purse—did you see—?"

"Over there." He pointed to a clump on the floor.

She smiled. "How did it get there?"

"I don't remember," he said, a faint smile back. "You must have dropped it."

"You see? So careless. I can't trust myself."

She turned at the door, another direct look, as if she were holding the moment, then went out. Now that she was gone, too late, he picked up the sheet and covered himself, standing in the middle of the dark room, not sure where to move, which direction, too many things happening at once.

7

SHE DIDN'T COME OUT until eleven. He had been under the big ombu tree since nine, perfect cover, the park benches hidden from her windows by the canopy of leaves. He had brought a newspaper, but it seemed unnecessary—no one took any notice of him. People were expected to sit here, a haven of shade. Her building was at the top of the rise, front door visible from under the tree. He tried to imagine her morning. A shower, coffee and a newspaper in her robe, morning light pouring in through the window. Maybe thinking about last night, whether she'd done the right thing. Getting dressed. A telephone call—to whom? Or maybe none of it. He could only see the door, a window, the rest of it something to pass the time.

She was wearing white again, or off-white, a crisp summer suit, pearls, dressed to meet somebody. He got up to follow. Even Agency desk men were given basic training, a summer course of tradecraft they'd probably never use, and now that he was here, he wasn't sure he could do it, keep the right distance, fall back, disappear in a crowd, never let her feel his eyes on her back. What if she took a taxi? The hotel with its rank of waiting cabs was a block away. But she walked, down Alvear past the big mansions, then the rows of new apartment buildings studded with air-conditioning units, toward the Plaza San Martín, where he'd walked that first day. Not in a hurry, maybe slowed down by her heels, but not changing pace either, suspicious, turning around. It would have been easier to do this downtown, getting swallowed up in the crowds, invisible, but she seemed unaware of him, and after a while he felt he had receded into the half-empty streets, the way he had at the Ohlsdorf chapel.

She skirted San Martín and started down Calle Florida, finally stopping at the Harrods branch, another piece of Europe. A minute or two at the windows, just looking, Aaron too far away to be reflected. When she went into the store, he held back. Stores were difficult, no crowds to melt into. What would he be doing on the women's clothing floor? He'd have to chance her coming back out the same entrance. He crossed the street to a bookstore, pretending to browse as he kept watch at the window. An endless wait, afraid he'd lost her. And then there she was, a flash of white, putting on sunglasses against the glare, a Harrods bag now on her arm. And as she reached up with the glasses, he saw her last night, raising her blouse over her head, naked for him. She looked up, and for a minute he wondered if she could feel him watching, be inside his head, some postcoital telepathy, but then she turned and started walking back to San Martín, just someone on the street.

At the corner she went into a bank, a day for errands, then crossed over to the belle epoque hotel at the top of the square and got a taxi. He waited until they'd turned the corner before hopping into one behind. When he told the driver to follow, he heard the absurdity of it, saw the look in the driver's eyes. Something that happened in the movies on Calle Lavalle, not in a cab rank on San Martín. "*Mi esposa,*" he said, as if that explained anything, but it seemed to work, a suggestion of infidelity, a chase the driver could understand. A burst of Spanish, probably some knowing street philosophy, then a conspiratorial wink, and he started the meter, heading down toward Retiro Station.

They caught up to her cab at a corner red light, then swung left behind it onto Libertador, heading north, avoiding the railway tracks and, beyond, the working port of cranes and warehouses and the slums squeezed in between. Libertador was broad, what seemed to be at least six lanes in either direction, an American width, flowing past parks and museums and the old rich houses of Barrio Norte. The cabdriver, waving his hands as he spoke, was creating some drama of his own about Hanna that required nothing but an occasional nod from Aaron. Where was she going? One of the embassies? The racetrack? Some apartment in Belgrano where Otto was waiting? And then, just past the entrance to the Botanical Gardens, they headed right, through the park, the way to Aeroparque, the old city airport. But where would she go without a suitcase, just a shopping bag from Harrods? Unless she wasn't the one going.

They followed the signs for the airport, but once they reached Costanera, the road along the water, her cab slowed, as if they were looking for the right turnoff. Finally, a right signal into the driveway of what looked like a pier, an Argentinian flag flopping in the breeze off the river, some nautical flags below it. "Dos Pescadores," the cabdriver said. Two Fishermen, maybe some whimsical name for a restaurant, a boat club. But a hopeless dead end. No cabs cruised here. He'd have to call from inside, after she'd gone, losing her. The cabdriver had slowed, watching her get out, and he must have come to the same conclusion because he parked just beyond the pier entrance, in the shade of a scraggly jacaranda tree. He pointed up at the blossoms, as if they were some romantic touch, right for the melodrama. Aaron opened his hands—Now what?—and the driver winked and cut off the meter, sitting back in a slouch. Now we wait, the story evidently worth a lost fare.

Aaron got out and had a cigarette, leaning against the door. She wouldn't stash Otto here, marooned beyond the docks. Even the airport, seemingly so close, would be too far to walk. The whole city was like that, everything farther than you thought. But maybe Otto wasn't in the city at all. Why not Bariloche? The sea breezes of Mar del Plata. Mendoza, drinking red wine. Anywhere. But there he'd been on the Binnenalster, in the heart of it all, not run to ground. He'd be here. While she had lunch. Maybe used the phone. Just a quick message, with a time and place. And then what? He threw the end of the cigarette on the road. Cloak-and-dagger stuff, how you thought when you had too much time on your hands. Just lunch. Maybe a glass of rosé. An old friend. But not that kind. Nobody lies in bed. He could still hear her, that gasp in his ear, the most erotic sound there was. Something nice. It's enough. But it wasn't enough.

Lunch took hours. But then he saw her coming out, two other women with her, all talking on the steps while they waited for their rides. Two taxis arrived, one for the others, one for Hanna. Kisses good-bye. She looked at her watch. Aaron nudged his driver, sliding down out of sight, the driver smiling with excitement. Something to talk about later. They retraced their route down through the park on Sarmiento, all the way to the end and then east on Avenida Santa Fe. There was traffic now, a busy shopping street clogged with buses, and when she stopped at a corner and got out, he assumed she thought she'd make better time on foot. He stopped the cab before they got to the corner, pointing to her, walking now, and handed the driver a wad of pesos. A grateful smile, but the faint hint of disappointment, missing the final act.

Aaron thought she would go into one of the stores, but she turned down a street instead, familiar with it. Calle J. Salguero, whoever he was. No doubt an important victory. Two blocks down, the street opened into a plaza, irregular, streets leading off it in several directions. A church at one end, children's playground in the middle, cafés on three sides. He saw the white suit heading left, a door just steps off the square. He stopped, taking a seat outdoors at a café, sight line perfect. He checked his watch, 3:50, then noticed a waiter checking his watch too, waiting for something. At first a trickle, one or two people, then more, emptying out of the buildings, several stopping for coffee, a small rush of business. Aaron got up and crossed the square. Plaza Güemes. Another unknown. He made his way to Hanna's street. Calle Charcas, which meant nothing either. Then the door, brass plaques near the bells. Dr. Ortiz. Of course. What had Jamie called it? Villa

Freud. Time up at 3:50, new patients in at 4, a tidal schedule. He went back to the café to wait, watching her building, glancing at the other customers. Not furtive, but keeping to themselves, not talking to each other, maybe thinking about what had been said, not said, in their fifty minutes. What people did here.

And what would she talk about? The man she'd just slept with or the more familiar subject, the tainted genes, the fear that she'd become her mother. Worse, her father. But that was crazy. Except we don't use that word here. If you were afraid, the fear at least was real. Was she actually lying on a Freudian couch? But people sat in chairs now. Talking about what? Doro, who stopped laughing and went away. A trip halfway around the world, everything new. The big house on Calle Aguado. A magazine article, blowing it up. Looking at him, knowing. What happened to birds when they were wounded, the strange inertia, not being able to fly. Maybe what Dr. Ortiz was helping her to do. Or not. Maybe she wasn't talking about any of it. Maybe it was just Aaron who wanted to know. Because it wasn't enough.

When she came out, 4:50 on the dot, she walked down Charcas, a more difficult street for him, residential, so that he was farther behind when she turned back up to Santa Fe and hailed a cab. No choice but to hope she'd gone home and follow her there. In half an hour he was back under the ombu tree, peering up, waiting for a light to go on. For all he knew, she was at the Alvear, hitting her limit with Pablo. But then there was a light in the window, oddly fluorescent, and he realized she'd turned on the television. In for the night. A blameless day. And maybe the next, and the one after that. Which was getting him nowhere. What would Max have done? Use whatever resources he had. Your contacts, he'd called them. Don't forget who Otto was. Use anything. But Max hadn't slept with her.

The American Embassy was across from the Parque 3 de Febrero, so Aaron suggested they meet there.

"What now?" Jamie said. "And what's wrong with my office?"

"People listen around corners."

"Tell me you're kidding."

"I need a favor."

"And you have to meet me outside to ask it. So it never happened."

"So you can say it never happened."

"All right, I'll bite. What?"

"I want you to put a tap on her phone. I need to know who she calls."

For a minute Jamie said nothing, shuffling responses, trying to read Aaron's face.

"First of all, we don't do that."

"Yes, you do. I see the reports."

"And if we did, I'd need a req from Langley. Official. The Argentines find out, they'd kick my ass out of here."

"They won't find out. They're not looking for this. Just a few days."

"Do I get to ask why? Or do I just operate blind?"

Aaron hesitated.

"Do you know how crazy this sounds? First you turn up in Buenos Aires, where nobody just turns up, with some airy fairy story and now you're asking us for a tap? So what the fuck is going on? Is this official?"

"No."

Jamie looked at Aaron. "You know you could have said it was and it would probably take a few days before—"

"And I'd have the tap. But that would leave you exposed. This way you can cover your ass."

"Wonderful. I can deny everything. I can also not do it and save myself the trouble. If it's not official, what is it?"

"A favor. I'll owe you."

"No, I mean what do you want it for? You don't put a tap on somebody just because you have the hots for her. Not in the Agency anyway. Who's she supposed to be talking to?"

Aaron looked over. "Otto Schramm."

Jamie stared at him, not moving. "From the beyond."

"No. Buenos Aires. He's alive."

"And she knows where he is."

"I think so."

"Funny you didn't mention this before."

"I didn't need the tap before."

"Sons of the Reich."

"That part's true. What would you have done? Put it in

your daily? Better to have some proof before you get everybody excited." He opened his hand. "So the tap."

"You're serious about this."

"He's here. That's why I came."

Jamie looked away for a second, trying to digest this. "That's quite a situation. Now what?"

"They make contact. We trace the call. I go take his picture. We need to ID him before anything. No mistakes."

"The Argentines aren't going to like this. Ever since Eichmann—"

"Let them take the credit this time. Make up for past sins. The Germans have had a warrant out for years. Extradite him and let them handle it."

"This isn't what we're here for. You know that, right? We're here to keep everybody happy, keep the OAS going."

"And save the Americas from Communism. I know. We still do all that. This is something else." He looked at Jamie. "It's Otto Schramm."

Jamie met his eyes for a second, then looked down. "I'll give you a week. And this never happened. You don't use the trace in evidence. You don't use it at all."

Aaron nodded. "You won't be sorry."

"I'm sorry already. I don't even know why I'm doing it." He glanced up. "That it?"

"One more thing?"

"Only one?"

"There's a big party at the Brazilian Embassy."

"And?" Jamie said, surprised.

"Add me to the list."

"As what?"

"I don't know. Second secretary, cultural affairs. That could mean anything. New in town."

Jamie threw him a look.

"Don't worry. I'll put on a clean shirt."

He had left her having lunch in Recoleta and got back in time to see her come out of the restaurant and head down busy Pueyrredón. It was the same as the day before—some errands, lunch, window shopping. She stopped at a bookstore on Santa Fe and talked to the clerk for a while, evidently a regular occurrence, familiar. Now what? He kept her blonde hair in sight in the crowd, fixed on it, wondering where it would go next, and it occurred to him that he wasn't just following her to find Otto but to find her, to know her life.

She'd been headed in the direction of Villa Freud but now turned right, no Dr. Ortiz today, circling back to Recoleta up Anchorena toward the German hospital. She went into a small office building. Five minutes, no more, and she was back, glancing at her watch, heading north again. Aaron stopped at the office building, checking the directory in the hall. A typical collection of small businesses—a lawyer, a dentist, a travel agency, a jewelry repair. The watch. Any of the others would have taken longer. He stepped back into the street. She was gone. For a second he panicked, cursing, but how far could she have gone? Some shop. And when he passed the hairdresser's, he caught a glimpse of her through the window. Getting her hair done for the embassy party. It's very important that you go, Bildener had said. Why? Had she skipped the last one? An old friend of her father's.

He kept going—people noticed if you stopped—and found a café where he could wait. But he already knew what would happen. The hair appointment, home to dress, maybe the Alvear, a night out. Without Otto, safely put away somewhere. There had to be contact. Now at least he'd know the calls at home. But why not one from the hairdresser's? Any café? A phone he couldn't trace. Patience. Max sometimes took years. But he didn't have years. He felt he was drifting through the days, the way she drifted through hers, both of them waiting. But she wouldn't just drift. Not her. He was walking just behind her, missing something.

Fritz left a message to meet at the ABC restaurant downtown in Calle Lavalle, a kitsch re-creation of a Bavarian inn, timbered with a sloping roof, squished between two office buildings. After the sunny glare of the street, the inside seemed dark, the country sconce lighting swallowed up by the paneled walls, a high border of heraldic shields hard to see. Fritz had already started on a beer.

"Do you believe this place?" he said. "A friend on *Stern* told me about it. You can't get food like this in Germany anymore." He nodded to a passing platter of pigs' knuckles and ham hocks and schnitzels Holstein. "They all used to come here. Eichmann once, they say. Mengele. They might even have met here. Imagine such an introduction. Would one know what the other looked like?"

"How's the jet lag?"

Fritz waved his hand. "Eat lunch here, you either have a heart attack or sleep all afternoon. I'll be fine. I met already with Goldfarb."

Familiar name, but how? Aaron mimed, Who?

"A friend of Nathan's. Also Max."

"Nathan?"

"He came to see me in the hospital."

"I didn't know you knew him."

"I didn't. I think he was checking up on you. If it was true it was Schramm."

"And?"

"He believes you. He said I was the proof. If it had just been someone who looked like Schramm, he wouldn't have done this." He touched his ribs. "So, no mistake."

"I thought he wasn't interested. No more Eichmanns."

"Otto's different."

"How?"

"Because he's supposed to be dead." He caught Aaron's expression. "Look, there are two stories here. Otto. Getting him. But then the other—how he lived here. Could fake his death. Think how many people must have helped. And think where—the police? The Intelligence Bureau? It would have to be. Even without Perón, the secret service protects him. Very embarrassing for the Argentines if that came out."

"And Nathan wants it to?"

Fritz nodded. "They didn't hide Eichmann. He hid himself. He came with a new name, passport. Works in Tucumán, then here, nothing special. An ordinary man, poor even. The Argentines can say they never knew. And then the Israelis come and kidnap him, take him out of the country. Outrage. Violating our sovereignty. How would you like it if they did it to you? Never mind what he did. You don't snatch citizens off the streets. So, they're humiliated—but they take the high ground. Lots of fists shaking at the Israelis. But this—now we have them protecting Otto. High up. Maybe even Perón himself. Get Otto and you can expose the Argentines, what they've been doing for years. Helping Nazis. And now Israel doesn't look so bad. So, a good story for them. That's why he helped me come."

"He helped you?"

"A little. Part of the ticket."

The waiter arrived with sauerkraut and a selection of wursts.

"I ordered. It's big enough for two," Fritz said. "It's all right?"

Aaron nodded, looking away from the heaping plate.

"So who's Goldfarb?"

"A businessman. Nobody. But he knows a lot of other nobodies. All the ministries."

"And what's he going to do for us?"

"So much paper in the world. But sometimes a trail. Who is Otto now? Helmut Braun died, so he must have traveled as someone else. And he was recognized. So now maybe he becomes someone else again. Another name. And that would mean new papers."

"He was recognized in Germany. As far as he knows, we're still there. Not chasing him here. Why get new papers?"

"Maybe. And maybe he's very careful. So let Goldfarb see

what he can find. If it's since Hamburg, it's recent. How many passport applications can there be?"

"Plenty. And he's doing this without a current picture, anything to match."

Fritz shrugged. "He has the time. His family was at Auschwitz. For him it's worth a little trouble." He speared a piece of boiled potato. "So, the daughter. Anything?"

"Not yet. No contact. And that's not like him. To stay in hiding. Look at Hamburg. He couldn't resist. So he has to come up for air sometime."

"And you'll be there." He looked over. "You're not hungry? The bauernwurst is excellent."

"She said she'd talk to you, for the book."

"Yes? What does she say about him?"

"It's—complicated."

"But she protects him. So that's not complicated."

"No." Where he always ended, circling back.

"She says he's dead?"

Aaron nodded. "Right on script. No mistakes. She said she was relieved."

"Relieved?"

"I told you, it's complicated. Isn't it like that with the others?"

"Sometimes. The interesting ones. The others—you know in their hearts they don't believe it. They can't. They say people exaggerate. What happened."

Aaron looked up. "That's just what Schramm said—it was all an exaggeration."

"Did she believe him?"

"No."

"But she still protects him."

Aaron put down his fork, uneasy, and took out a cigarette.

"You like her," Fritz said, leading him, a reporter.

Aaron shrugged this off, saying nothing.

"Maybe you should do the interview. She talks to you."

"She lies to me."

"Everybody lies. You learn that in this business. The trick is to keep them talking. Something comes out."

"Maybe. She's careful about him."

"Any photographs? A photograph would be valuable."

"You mean is there a family album? I doubt it. Considering."

"No, in the apartment. Pictures from childhood, something like that. Maybe letters. Something in the desk."

Aaron looked at him. "We just met for a drink."

Fritz was staring back. "You haven't—?"

"What? Broken in?" Thrown by this.

"Aaron," Fritz said slowly. "We need to know. It's serious, this. What we're doing."

"That's illegal."

"And Auschwitz was legal. So much for legal." He paused. "Just don't get caught."

"We can't—"

"They don't teach you this? Your people?"

"You've done this before?"

"Sometimes, how else?" He slowed again. "We need to know."

He reached into his pocket and pulled out a key ring, beginning to flip through. "You know her movements? How long she's likely—? Ah." He stopped and slipped a key off the ring, then held it out to Aaron. "It doesn't work with every lock. Maybe they're different here. But usually, yes. Here."

Aaron stared at the key, as if it were alive and if he touched it something would happen to him. Just a key, dull, not shiny. Don't.

He reached over and took the key.

"So try it," Fritz was saying. "It saves time. I thought they taught you how to do this."

"No." His stomach still queasy, but the key now in his pocket, some step taken.

"I have a friend, he can pick anything. It's useful. Does she have a maid?"

"I suppose. I haven't seen one. I'm usually following her."

"And she doesn't see you?" Fritz said, finding this amusing. "At least they teach you that." He wiped his mouth, finally finished. "Watch before you go in, if there's a maid. It's hard to explain."

"What? Going through her desk? Yes."

"Through everything. But a light touch, yes? Everything as it was."

He was under the ombu tree early, with a newspaper, but she didn't appear until just before noon, dressed for a restaurant lunch, a suit with handbag and white gloves. Which gave him at least an hour or two. No maid today, unless she turned up later, unexpected, a door opening in a French farce. He waited until she was well past the Alvear.

There was a locked door in the vestibule, where visitors were buzzed in, and the passkey worked, which meant that it would probably work upstairs too. No excuse not to go through with it now. No one in the elevator, the building in a midday hush, people at work or out somewhere, the faint whine of a vacuum cleaner overhead. In the quiet hall, mentally on tiptoe, he forced himself to walk normally. The key worked, just a minor jiggle while it found its groove. He stepped inside. From this point on, he was vulnerable, no explanations possible. Breaking and entering.

It was a modern apartment, international style, nubby off-white couches accented with pillows, bookshelves, swivel chairs with brass reading lamps, abstract paintings and pieces of sculpture. At first it seemed as impersonal as a hotel suite, but then the eye began to take in the details—magazines open on the glass coffee table, photographs in the bookshelves. Hanna as a child with Beate and presumably Doro. A group of schoolgirls at somebody's birthday. A table at the Stork, filled with glasses, only Hanna and another woman full face, the men off camera. Nothing of Otto.

He crossed over to the desk, still listening for the sound of footsteps, the room quiet enough to hear himself breathe. An appointment diary to the right of the desk pad, the entries for the last few days exactly what he remembered—Dos Pescadores, Dr. Ortiz, the hairdresser where he thought he'd lost her, even him, a drink at the Alvear. No notes. For an odd second, looking at the book, he wanted to know how everything had seemed to her. How had she felt about him? Not what she'd expected. But there was nothing but a name and time, her feelings still her own. Lunch today downtown. The embassy party later, underlined. Markus waiting, his eye on the door.

He flipped through her address book, lists of names he didn't know, any one of which might be the new Otto, but somehow he doubted it. Not something you wrote down. There was Bildener. Under L, a list of lawyers, in New York and here. More names. What exactly was he looking for? So quiet he could hear the clock.

He went through the drawers. Folders of bills, some letters from Germany, Beate keeping in touch, her own passport, nothing of Otto's. Another drawer with documents, the apartment lease, her divorce papers, all carefully in order, as if she were making it easy for him. See? I have nothing to hide.

He got up and went over to the bedroom, each step feeling like a violation, something he'd been told not to do and was doing anyway. Closets and closets full of clothes, everything personal now, the hotel feeling left behind in the living room. Racks of shoes, shelves with handbags. Everything hers, smelling of her. Sweaters. Blouses. In the top drawer, silk underwear. The sort of place where a passport or visa might be slipped under the panties, the intimacy of them somehow protective, where people wouldn't go. But he was there, the panties in his hand, and suddenly he felt his face grow warm, embarrassed by the odd pleasure of it, what a fetishist must feel, touching her by touching her things. He took his hands away. Another drawer, bras and nylons. Another, lingerie. He felt a silk nightgown, peach with a border of lace, imagining it on, the shoulder straps falling, her stepping out of it, then stopped, the pleasure mixed with shame now. Something a boy would do, making a woman in his head just by feeling silk, smelling it.

He went over to the bathroom. More nightgowns behind the door, a terry wrap. A makeup table, lights around the mirror, drawers of nail polish and powders and creams. A full medicine chest, the usual Band-Aids and iodine and cuticle trimmers. Rows of pill bottles, prescription, some from Dr. Ortiz, how she slept. He looked at the dates. Something she'd been doing for a while, putting herself to sleep. To dream what? A diaphragm case. Tampax. He closed the mirrored door, feeling embarrassed again, prurient.

There was a dress hanging from one of the closet doors. A cocktail dress, maybe what she was planning to wear tonight. Next to it on the bureau, a bag and gloves and jewelry already laid out, as if she didn't want to decide at the last minute. A gold charm bracelet, not girlish, real jewelry, something to dangle and flash on a glove. He picked it up, curious if any of the charms were personal mementos, bits of her life. But they seemed standard pieces—a dog, a little house, a shoe, a key, the key smaller than the others. He looked more carefully. Too small to be real, a toy. He put down the bracelet. What was he doing? Otto wasn't hiding behind her dresses.

He went back into the living room, checking behind picture frames for wall safes. The desk again, with the folder of official papers. If there was anything it would be here. In Spanish. What looked like a will. Her name only, clearly the sole heir. A Buenos Aires bank statement with a healthy balance, but not suspiciously large. The real money, Tommy's settlement, presumably still in New York in dollars, what rich Latin Americans did, handled by some lawyer or broker in the address book. He stopped, uneasy again. Money was private, a different kind of lingerie. He looked at his fingers on the paper, clumsy, intrusive.

A muffled sound outside, a door closing. He froze. Maybe the elevator, Hanna coming back, the maid arriving late. And he was sitting at her desk with her bank statement in his hands. What are you doing? What could he possibly say? He listened for footsteps, waiting to hear a key in the lock. But nothing happened. He breathed out. He glanced up at the desk photos again. The little girl in Germany. The glamour girl at the Stork. Now being followed, someone secretly rummaging through her life.

He put the folder back, then felt it blocked by something in the back of the drawer. He reached in, his hand stopping as he felt the cold metal. A gun. A box next to it. He pulled it out slowly, as if a sudden movement would set it off. A gun. Lots of people had guns. A single woman, a big city. Something you had for protection, nothing unusual. Except it sat there in his hand turning everything upside down. There was never anything innocent about a gun. He felt he was touching another part of her. Had she ever used it? Did she even know how? But here it was, blunt and heavy and cool in his hand, something he hadn't known about her before.

He put it back carefully. Everything as it was. But what if

he had missed something, some little detail that would give him away? A silk slip visibly disturbed, the fold no longer smooth, something. Or just the scent of him, the way you could feel another presence, even after it was gone. He checked the top of the desk one more time, the way it had been, then went over to the door, listening for any sound in the hall. Nothing. The click of the door behind him. The quiet elevator sounded like a roar. No neighbors. And then he was under the ombu tree, feeling relieved and foolish at the same time. She'd never know. But a risk he should never have taken. People didn't hide secrets in lingerie drawers. They trusted to memory or forgot them in files. Max, maybe Goldfarb, knew how to look at files. But memory had to be volunteered. Memory needed to trust you.

8

THE BRAZILIAN EMBASSY HAD once been a grand house, another dream of Paris, but not grand enough to have had a ballroom, so the party was spread over several ground-floor reception rooms, people moving between them like schools of fish, darting around the passing trays of champagne glasses. Aaron had expected a name check at the door, but no one had asked. Instead they were steered to an informal reception line where a silver-haired man was playing exuberant host, his voice switching from Portuguese to Spanish with an easy warmth, as lilting and relaxed as the music in the background.

"João, how nice to see you," Jamie said. "May I introduce Aaron Wiley. New with us. Aaron, Ambassador da Silva."

"*Mucho gusto*," da Silva said, an automatic response, then in English, "Another new one. Every week it seems. How busy you must be. But you are very welcome. It's your first time in Buenos Aires?"

"Yes."

"Well, you have an excellent guide. Jamie knows everything that goes on in Buenos Aires."

"Not quite," Jamie said. "Just the best parties." This with a complimentary nod. "And you have guests waiting. I hope we'll have a minute later."

"Oh, a minute. That sounds like business. Me, I prefer gossip. You can't gossip in a minute. Ernesto. But where is Gloria? Not ill, I hope."

And somehow, a kind of social swallowing up, they were moved along into the crowd.

"That's it?" Aaron said.

"It's a party. What were you expecting?" He turned as he picked up a glass of champagne, facing the door again. "Oh, right. Of course."

Aaron followed his look past the receiving line. She had come with a good-looking man somewhere in his forties. Tanned face, trim, a suit that might have been made for him. She was wearing the dress that had been hanging on her closet door, looking the way he had imagined her in it, and he felt, oddly, that he had chosen it for her, laid it out with the gloves and charm bracelet, knowing she'd look like this.

"I hope someday you'll tell me exactly what's going on. Not now," Jamie said, raising his hand, a tease, "that would ruin the story. But at the end. The way detectives do in books, when they explain everything." He took a sip. "Well, I'll leave you to it. Don't get into any trouble. I don't want to have to explain you."

"Trouble?"

"Right here in River City," Jamie said, pleased with himself.

"Walk with me for a minute. I don't want her to see me yet."

"Hard to get? I wouldn't bother. It looks like she's already got." He nodded toward the door, her escort, then looked up at Aaron. "What *are* you up to?"

"I'll tell you at the end," Aaron said, moving them farther into the party.

In a minute Jamie was stopped by someone, an Argentine, and Aaron drifted away before he needed to be introduced. It was an easy party to get lost in, crowded, everyone talking, the several rooms making it hard to keep someone in sight. The late afternoon light was pouring through the open French windows, then reflecting off the tall mirrors, and as Aaron looked around, it seemed impossible to imagine any kind of trouble. The women were beautiful, or at least beautifully put together, made up and dressed for display like pampered mistresses. He stood by a pillar near a drinks table taking in the room. Genial da Silva, the polished diplomats, rich businessmen and their watchful wives. The kind of party she'd been to a hundred times, what she knew. But then someone near da Silva moved aside and she was suddenly in his line of vision and she didn't seem to be at the party at all but off somewhere by herself, the way she'd been that first night at the Alvear bar. Her dress was simpler than the others, everything about her simpler, as if none of that really mattered, just her youth, the bright shine of her. He stared past the others, unable to look away, seeing her as he'd seen her in the hotel room, clothes dropping around her feet. Then he was in her bedroom, touching her things, the silk becoming skin, the same feeling. He looked away.

She was moving past da Silva now, into the larger party, her head turned toward her escort, listening. A waiter offering champagne broke into the sight line, then another couple, so that she was close to him, a few feet, when she looked up and finally saw him, surprised, then flustered, caught off guard. Her escort had turned to greet some other people, so they had a second alone, the others busy.

"What are you doing here?" she said, the thought just coming out, unfiltered.

"Jamie brought me."

"Here?"

"I wanted to see you."

"Oh," she said, an involuntary sound, a skip on a record, not expecting this, her eyes suddenly bright, pleased.

He looked at her, not saying anything, eyes talking instead, a private second. Her reaction unmistakable before she had time to think, the way a woman looks when she's happy to see you.

And then the second was over, the others turning to them, and she was flustered again, as if his being here was not only unexpected but inconvenient, ill-timed. She put her hand up to brush her hair back, a gesture to buy a minute, the charm bracelet dangling, just the way he'd imagined.

"Ricardo, Aaron Wiley, a friend from New York." Explaining him again. "Ricardo Moreno."

Moreno dipped his head, an abbreviated bow. "You're here with the embassy?"

"Just visiting."

"Ah."

"I had no idea he was here," Hanna said. "We bumped into each other at the Alvear bar."

"You were close friends in New York?" Moreno said tentatively, not quite sure how to ask, and Aaron saw that he was going to be jealous, protective, unless Aaron defused it.

"It was really my wife you knew," he said smoothly. "I don't even remember how you two met." Over to you.

"A friend of Tommy's. We were office widows—Aaron always working. And Tommy— But we managed without you both."

"Perhaps you'll see more of each other here."

"I'm only here a few days, I'm afraid." He turned to her, social. "When are you coming back to New York? Don't you miss it?"

"But it's the best time of year here," Moreno said, still looking at Aaron.

"If you play polo," Hanna said pleasantly. "Ricardo loves it. I still don't see why you won't play in the Open. You're good enough."

"But not young enough. Do you play?" A testing question, measuring.

"I've never even seen a match. But I know it's popular here."

"Once the season starts, people don't do anything else," Hanna said. "It's a ghost town."

Moreno smiled. "With parties every night. After each match." He turned to Aaron. "You mustn't listen to her. You really should think about staying on." A question, still testing, but gentler now.

"Oh god, there's Emil. Be an angel, will you, and run interference for a few minutes? I want to catch up with Aaron. You won't know anybody we're talking about, so think how boring. I'll come rescue you, promise."

Moreno, apparently easy now, gave another of his nods.

"He's jealous about you," Aaron said, watching him head over to a tall gray-haired man with Wilhelmine posture.

"He has no reason to be." She looked up. "Neither do you. Men."

" 'Office widow' was a nice touch. Why the little charade?"

"It's easier. Anyway, what could I say? That I don't know what you're doing here? Is that what you want?"

"I want to see you again."

She looked away. "I don't think that's a good idea."

"Yes, it is. I'll buy you a steak. We could just—go. The ambassador would never know."

"I can't."

"It's just a party."

"Really, I can't. Don't." She looked back up at him. "That's why you came? To see me? How did you know I—?"

"Bildener reminded you. I figured you wouldn't miss it."

"Bildener," she said, her voice edgier, nervous. "Oh. At the Alvear. Yes. You could have called."

"This is more fun. Besides, you can't hang up."

"No, there are people. So we pretend we knew each other in New York."

"It worked," he said, glancing toward Moreno. "I guess that's our story now. How did my wife know Tommy?"

"How did anybody?"

"Oh. Not really very nice for me. Did I know or was I the last to know?"

"The last." A small smile. "Your innocent nature."

"Did I ever make a pass?" He nodded to the room. "He'll ask."

"No, you're not that kind of man."

"I must have been crazy."

She looked at him, her face pink, flushed.

"Come with me."

"I can't. I can't leave here. Not yet."

"Is there a checklist? Five people you have to see? I'll do two, you do three, and then you're done." He paused. "I can't stop thinking about you." Knowing it was true the moment he said it. Following her blonde head in a crowd.

"Don't say that. Careful. Here's Markus."

Aaron looked up to see Markus Bildener and his wife coming, glasses in hand.

"Why careful?"

"He thinks he's my father. Protecting me."

"From what?"

"You. Anyone. A fortune hunter." She looked up at him. "Are you?"

"No. Are you rich?"

She smiled a little. "I mean it, be careful. He thinks you're with Jamie. Up to something."

"I am," he said.

She turned. "Trude, how nice. Markus."

"*Gnädige Frau,*" Markus said, a hand-kissing deference. "Mr. Willis, isn't it? Forgive me."

"Wiley." A nod to Trude. "Frau Bildener."

"So. Our Hanna is showing you Buenos Aires?"

"No, no, we just ran into each other," Hanna said. "I'm here with Ricardo."

"And his horse?" His idea of a joke. "A coincidence then, to find each other here. You know Ambassador da Silva?" he said to Aaron.

"No, a friend brought me."

"Ah," Bildener said. "Well, da Silva's parties . . . But I thought you were going to the mountains."

"I am. But there's more to see in Buenos Aires than I thought."

"Well, for young people everywhere is interesting. Me, I find it melancholy."

"Markus," Hanna said.

"Yes, it's true. You don't find it so sometime?" He faced Aaron. "Look at the *centro*, the Haussmann streets. They built a capital for an empire, but there was no empire. There never will be. They say Vienna is like that now, a capital without an empire. Thank god I'm not there to see it."

"You're Viennese?" Aaron said.

Bildener dipped his head. "But now a *porteño*. Be careful you don't stay too long. Like me."

"How long have you been here?"

"Since the war. Another empire lost. But history is like that, no? Rise and fall. Mistakes are made. And then you have to survive. So, a *porteño*, why not?"

"Markus, such talk," Trude said. "We were grateful to find a home here."

"Yes, yes, very welcoming. Maybe not so much now, with the Americans running everything." He raised his eyebrow at Aaron, testing his reaction to this. "But then, certainly. Europe was in ruins and we were eating. So yes, we were grateful. How could we not be? All the same, it's not—Vienna. You miss that."

"That's all in the past," Trude said.

"Yes, and here we are drinking champagne. So. I'm glad you could come," he said to Hanna.

"I promised I would," she said, looking away.

"It's good for you to get out. And you know he's fond of you, da Silva." He turned to Aaron. "The Argentines, they always look a little down their noses at the Brazilians. A mixed race. But of course with Hanna there's none of that."

"No?"

"She doesn't believe in race theory. A source of argument with—the older generation. So we wait a few years and then we see who was right."

"What would be the proof?"

Bildener looked at him, but didn't answer. "And meanwhile she charms the Brazilians. Da Silva said there was someone he wanted you to meet."

"Yes, all right."

"We shouldn't monopolize you then," Aaron said. "Maybe we'll run into each other at another party."

"Yes, that would be nice. Shall we have Markus introduce you to some people or will you be OK on your own?"

"Oh, I'll be fine." He looked at his watch. "I have to go soon anyway."

"You came with—Mr. Campbell?" Bildener said, wanting to know.

"Yes, that's right. Jamie. Do you know him?"

Bildener smiled. "We've met. A great interest in local politics. Not like the other Americans."

"Jamie?"

"Yes, you're surprised. It's like a hobby with him, keeping track, how the parties come and go, one minister after another. But not a Perónist, I think."

"Is anyone now?"

"Millions. You would be surprised how many long for his return."

"Is that likely? He's in exile."

"But not dead, Mr. Wiley."

"Perón was very kind to us," Trude said.

Bildener shot her a glance.

"And here we are talking politics and you have all of Buenos Aires to meet. Well, at least all of Barrio Norte. Hanna, you won't forget da Silva—?"

"No, of course not." She turned to Aaron. "I've got to go sing for my supper. I hope you enjoy the party. If you see Ricardo— Oh, there he is, I'll tell him myself. Trude, Markus—"

But as she said it, the name was repeated behind them, a booming echo. "Markus, my good Herr Bildener," the voice said, followed by a stream of Spanish.

Aaron looked up. A priest in a black cassock and pectoral cross, plump, a genial, florid face. On his head, incongruously, a zucchetto looking just like a Jewish skullcap, as if the religions had finally agreed on something.

"And Hanna, my dear child, what a pleasure." This in accented German.

"Excellency," Bildener said. A bishop then, the church hierarchy and its titles still vague to Aaron.

"English, please," Hanna said, taking his hand and nodding toward Aaron.

"Ah, an American? I should say North American. We're Americans here too."

"But still German," Bildener said, something important to him.

The bishop wagged a scolding finger. "Is that pride? A venal sin, you know. What difference could it possibly make? We are all children of God, surely." He grinned mischievously. "Even the Germans."

He laughed, the words bubbling out of him.

"Monsignor Rosas," Bildener said, introducing him.

"Luis Rosas?" Aaron said, blurting it out, not thinking. A name in Max's folders, a step on the ratline, lending Otto a helping hand.

Hanna glanced at him, surprised.

"I'm known to you then?" Rosas said, pleased, used to being recognized.

"Forgive me," Aaron said, backpedaling. "I heard the name but I can't remember where. Maybe it was someone else."

Rosas sighed. "Probably not. After the Catholic Alliance it was impossible to go anywhere. People would hear the name and think, aha, that one, the Catholic Alliance. Not the face, I didn't allow that to be used, but the name they knew."

"Ah," Aaron said, as if this answered it.

Rosas smiled. "Not a very popular group with your embassy. Why? I don't know. A mutual interest, stopping the Communists.

But the Americans, the North Americans, like to do things on their own. They never saw the special role Argentina could play, a Christian nation, untouched by the war. This loyal daughter of the Church. Who better to save Europe?"

By forging landing permits for Otto and the others, now Christian warriors, their sins absolved by the threat of the Church's true enemy. Aaron looked at him again. Not a pinched executioner's face, another Otto, but a jovial Friar Tuck figure, breezy, enjoying himself, a world away from the Auschwitz siding, the selection. But he must have seen it, that freeze frame of stopped time when everything had been morally clear, before it was an exaggeration.

"Monsignor, not another speech," Bildener said, a friendly tease. "Have some champagne."

"I must say, da Silva's parties. But look at you," Rosas said, taking Hanna's hands and holding them. "All grown up."

"I've been grown up for years now."

"And very lovely too, but to me— Still that little girl. Always wanting to confess. With nothing to confess. Good as gold."

Hanna flushed, embarrassed by this. "I didn't tell you everything."

"Then you can tell me now. When's the last time—?"

"I wouldn't dare," she said, smiling.

"I doubt it. You were such a good girl. People don't change."

She looked away, uncomfortable.

"Ah, still wearing your trinkets," he said, looking down at the bracelet. "I remember the little dog—no, it's different."

She moved her hands away, out of sight.

"It's a new one. Bigger." Uncomfortable again.

"Well, what isn't?" Rosas said, patting his stomach. "We're all getting—" He turned to Bildener. "You should see Jorge. So heavy, at his age. I had no idea he was here. In São Paulo, I thought. Nobody tells me anything. I said, how can you come to Buenos Aires and not let me know?"

Bildener had looked at him in a kind of alarm, then over at Hanna, who looked back, a moment between them, so that Aaron had the sense of missing something, distracted by Rosas's easy flow.

"Who?" Aaron said.

"Jorge Martínez," Rosas said simply, Bildener now looking at Aaron, reading his face. "An old friend. Some business here, he said," Rosas said to Bildener. "What business? Just in and out. When I think, in the old days, how we all—"

"Luis. Excellency," Bildener interrupted. "I'm sorry, I promised da Silva—" He reached for Hanna's arm.

"Ah, a higher authority."

Bildener stopped, realizing that if he took Hanna away he would leave Aaron with the priest. Aaron watched his body stall, then pivot, his thoughts being visibly acted out.

"I said I would introduce Mr. Wiley to some of our friends," Bildener finished, now taking Aaron's arm. "You'll be all right?" he said to Hanna.

She bowed to Rosas, a leave-taking. "It was lovely to see you."

"I never said. I was so sorry about—"

She patted his hand. "I know. Soon. It's been too long."

And then, before he could say anything else, she was gone,

melting into the crowd, Bildener's eyes following her, a kind of tracking.

"Such a pity," Rosas said. "To lose a parent so young."

Aaron looked at him. Did he know? Otto's old helper.

"Her father, you mean," he said. "You knew him."

"As Helmut Braun. A very pleasant man. Of course, it was a shock—I think to everybody," he said, including Bildener. "Well, but who are we to judge? Only God does that."

Aaron thought of several responses to this but was too taken aback to offer any of them. What would be the point? The lie as effortless as breathing. A man who'd helped murderers, happy to leave everything else to God.

"Ah, but here's my chance. Look at da Silva. Stuck with the dullest man in the room." Rosas giggled. "It would be a mercy to rescue him, no? Shall we do that, Trude? Enjoy your stay," he said to Aaron. "I hope we meet again." His nod like a benediction.

Aaron watched them go. "A man of the cloth," he said.

Bildener smiled a little. "His whole family was like that. Very social. The night before he entered the seminary, he threw a party for his friends. At a *milanga* in San Telmo. Cases of champagne. People still talk about it." He paused. "It's interesting that you knew him. His name."

"I still don't know how. Not the Catholic Alliance. I never heard of it. What is it, anyway?"

"A group against the Communists. Started after Poland fell. Now I think it's difficult for them. Perón supported them, so now they're Perónist. Out of favor. Luis was close to him. They say he arranged the papal visit. For Evita. But everyone takes credit for that, so who knows?" Another pause. "Maybe you take an interest in local politics too. Like your friend Campbell."

"No, I'm just passing through."

Bildener looked at him, skeptical, Aaron already part of a different story he'd made up. "But you knew Luis. Maybe it was that business with Eichmann. You were interested in that?"

"Eichmann?"

"The trial. Luis was mentioned. As someone who had helped him. Of course, not true. How would Luis know such a person? Another lie. Trial. If you can call it a trial. Everyone knew they would kill him. There was never any doubt about that."

"No," Aaron said.

"They just—take people. German people. Who knows what they did? Or didn't do? But do you think the Israelis care about that? Another German to put on trial, that's what they want. And the government here— Of course, this wouldn't happen before. Perón would never stand for that. On Argentine territory? Never. But now—you can't help but worry, if you're German."

"You don't think Eichmann was a special case?"

"We're all special cases to them. At least Otto's out of it now."

"But it must have been hard for her. Hanna." Looking up as he said it, her head visible across the room. She was talking to a small group, a clutch bag in one hand and a glass in the other, the Spanish Hanna now, not the one he knew. Bildener looked across with him.

"Yes, hard. So unexpected," he said, watching her. "They were very close, you know."

"I didn't. She never talked about him. In New York."

"Well, she had a different life there," Bildener said vaguely. He turned to Aaron. "I wonder if I can say something to you without giving offense."

Aaron waited.

"If I can speak for her father."

Aaron nodded, not sure where this was going.

"She married a Jew once and it did not go well for her."

"Tommy wasn't Jewish." Still not sure.

"A mix," Bildener said, waving this off. "Who knows how much blood it takes?"

"And?"

"You have a Jewish look. I know we're not supposed to say that now. A different time. Maybe it's a changed name, maybe not. That's your affair. But another Jew? No. I'm thinking of her, you see. That's why I say these things to you."

Aaron stared at him, the words like an icicle on his back, the cold dripping down his skin, Bildener's eyes hard blue.

"She thinks it doesn't matter, but it does. You can't mix blood."

Nothing changed. This one to the left.

"Go to hell," Aaron said quietly.

Bildener reared back, genuinely surprised. What had he expected? "I have offended you." Cocktail party politeness. "So maybe I shouldn't have said. Since you're just passing through." A slight nod, as if he were physically prodding him along.

"No. I mean it. Go to hell. Burn."

"So. I was right. A Jew."

"After they put you in a glass box. Like Eichmann. So everybody can see. I'll be in the front row."

"At my trial?" An exaggerated irony.

"No, at the freak show. With all the others like you."

"Stay away from her."

"Where everybody can see."

"You can change your name but you can't—" He stopped, eyes widening, a streak of fear flashing across them, seeing something in Aaron's face, the adrenaline rushing out of control. Stop. Leave.

Aaron turned and walked away, not toward anything, just away, his hands trembling now, feeling curiously exposed, as if everyone were watching him. What had just happened? An enemy he hadn't needed to make. A complication. Worse, not controlling it, a rage so close to the surface all Bildener had to do was pull a trigger. Where had that come from? Not from Max, plodding, methodically filling his folders. What good is mad? he'd said. You have to win the case.

He stopped at the bar near the open French doors. The last thing he needed, gas on a fire. He ordered a club soda and stood against the wall, calming down. Men in suits and shiny shoes, women in dresses and diamonds, talking louder now, the party swelling, Spanish and Portuguese and English. Monsignor Rosas had moved on from the ambassador, a ripple of laughter following him. Champagne the night before the seminary. Bildener had moved too, toward the edge of the room. Steady, not at all upset, the moment with Aaron forgotten, or maybe having served its purpose, driving him away. He was talking to a heavyset man whose jowls shook as he spoke, leaning in, intimate. Maybe the faithless Martínez, who'd put on weight, or another soldier in the Catholic Alliance, saving Poland for the Church.

"Sitting this one out?" Jamie, with a square glass and what looked like bourbon.

"It's more fun to watch."

"You're the one who wanted to come. Meet anybody?"

"Monsignor Rosas."

"The padre? He tell you how he's taking on the Commies?"

"More or less."

"Somebody should. We're not doing so hot."

"Are they? His group?"

"Marx or the Pope. They think it's a choice. They're surprised people don't make it."

"I gather he was friends with Perón."

"Everybody was. When he was Perón. But Madrid's far away."

"And we want to keep it that way."

"We don't want him back, that's for sure. What happened to your girlfriend?"

Aaron looked over his shoulder at the crowded room. "She's around somewhere."

But not nearby. The jowly man had moved away, heading down the hall toward the business end of the embassy, a row of office doors, closed for the party. Bildener was coming back toward the center of the room when he was intercepted by Ricardo, an awkward meeting neither of them wanted but had to get through. For a second Aaron imagined them talking about the

Argentine Open, the boredom cushioned by politeness, but then Hanna was there, handing Ricardo her glass while she moved her purse, the endless juggling of women at cocktail parties, purse, drink, cigarette.

"What about Jorge Martínez?" Aaron said.

Campbell looked up, surprised. "What about him?"

"What do we know?"

"You met him too? You really work a room."

"No, but he's here. So who is he?"

"Intelligence Bureau. Or was. A piece of work. Kind of guy makes lots of enemies. But the friends were the right ones. So when they were making—adjustments, after Perón left, they moved him over to the diplomatic corps. Out of the way. God knows what he had on them, but anyway, enough to save his ass. Some cushy job in Brazil. He's back?"

"Flying visit, in and out. He's a friend of Bildener's?"

"Back in the day. Now, I don't know. You don't hear much about the Fourth Reich these days."

Her words too, a sarcastic edge. Now she was handing Ricardo her glass again, apparently asking for a refill, then leaning forward to hear Bildener, close to her ear. Maybe something about the American friend's behavior. Or more paternal advice. Whatever it was, she barely heard it, distracted, looking around, then moving off down the hall, stopping a waiter to ask a question.

"Why the interest?" Jamie was saying.

Aaron shrugged. "Just curious. The monsignor seemed surprised he was here. So I wondered why."

"Like I said, he's a guy who made enemies. The way he made

them was torture, whatever nasty was going around. So it's not a good town for him anymore. People remember."

"Then why come?"

"He's Argentine. Maybe he came to see his mother."

"No," Aaron said, thinking. "Business. In and out. So what kind of business?"

"You have a suspicious mind."

She was looking at the doors as she passed down the hall, then evidently found the right brass plate and went in, a darting glance behind her. Where the man with the jowls had gone. Not the ladies' room.

"Jamie, you know what he looks like?"

"Big guy. I can dig up a picture if you want."

"You had him under—?"

"A person of interest."

"Oh?"

"They all were in the Intelligence Bureau. That's who ran things, so we needed to keep tabs. And one would lead to the other. They took care of each other."

Suddenly she was back in the hall, looking flustered, as if she had made a mistake and gone through the wrong door, a cover story, hurrying now, back to the party, stopping just for a second to adjust her glove, one of the charms snagged. She looked up, and for a minute Aaron thought she was looking at him, but Ricardo moved away from his group, handing her a glass. A quick smile, a gulp of the drink, back in the party, Aaron still looking over Jamie's shoulder, not sure what he'd seen, waiting for the man with the jowls to appear. But the hall stayed empty, as if he'd never been there or was busy behind some other door.

"So they ship him off to Brazil. But not to Rio, the embassy."

"Well, Brasilia now. They're not exactly lining up to go there."

"Still, he's a big guy. He'd want the embassy. But he's in São Paulo. So what's there, a consulate? He'd be happy with that?"

"It's São Paulo, for Christ's sake. We're not talking about some place up the Amazon."

Still no one in the hall. The party loud around them.

"Anyway, he'd fit right in there," Jamie said.

"Why?"

"It's where the Germans are. The tourists go to Rio, but the Germans go to São Paulo. All the big companies. So he'd have lots of friends. Old home week."

"Because that's what he did here."

Jamie nodded. "Recruit military advisors. Ex-Luftwaffe. To train the air force. All aboveboard, except for a new identity here and there. If they'd been more than pilots. And then the others, the ones the Intelligence Bureau took a special interest in."

"Like Otto Schramm?"

"Maybe. We don't know. And now— There may be records somewhere, but I wouldn't bet the ranch on it. Why don't you ask her?"

Aaron looked at him.

"Oh, that's right. She doesn't know you—" He stopped. "By the way, the tap? Nothing. I said I'd give it a week, but I don't think you're going to get anything there. Either she's careful or she's not in touch. Or you've made a mistake."

"Give it the week anyway."

"Nice woman. At least on the phone. Kind of girl you'd think about marrying, except for the family."

And then there he was, in the hall, closing the door behind him and heading deeper into the embassy, away from the party. Not the men's room either. The meeting no more than a minute or two, something you'd miss if you blinked. Just enough time to deliver a message. Which meant one of them would have to pass it on to Otto.

"Jamie? Could you put a tail on him? Martínez?"

"More official business? No. And no. You're out of favors, remember?"

"You have a file on him then?"

"Still no."

"A quick look. Back in a day."

"What do you think you're going to find?"

"I don't know. A needle in a haystack. If he helped Otto once, he might still be helping him."

Two people in the meeting. She was moving away, toward the other reception room.

"You know that's not what we're here for, right? Looking for Nazis."

"We should be."

Out of sight now, in the other room, maybe about to leave.

"I'll catch you later," Aaron said, patting his upper arm.

He walked through the crowd, turning sideways to slice between standing groups. She had gone into the opposite hall, the right way to the ladies' room this time, and he waited at the corner. He put his glass back on a passing tray. A single meeting, no more than a few minutes, maybe not even about Otto. But it must have been. An address, a number. He'd be so happy to see you. No longer strolling on the Jungfernstieg. At home. Somewhere near. Close now. Use anything.

She stopped when she came back into the hall, surprised to see him, a flash of apprehension. She had taken off her gloves and now held them with her purse, more juggling.

"Enjoying yourself?" she said, trying to be casual.

"Not much. I had a fight with Bildener. He tell you?"

She shook her head.

"He wants me to stay away from you. No Jews."

"Oh," she said, embarrassed. "That's about Tommy."

"I said I wouldn't."

She looked up. "Did you?"

"What about you? See everybody you had to see?"

"What do you mean?"

"I thought da Silva wanted—"

"Oh, that. Yes."

"So we're free to go. No one will notice."

"I can't leave Ricardo. We came together."

"That's before you got sick. You don't want to spend the rest of the evening in there," he said, nodding toward the ladies' room.

"Something I ate?" she said.

"Ask him to put you in a cab. That way he'll know you're going home alone."

"And where will you be?"

"Waiting for you. At the hotel."

She looked over at him, eyes alive now, as if he had touched her. "Just like that," she said.

"You're finished here," he said, curious to see her reaction, but she answered by looking around the room.

"I have to say good-bye to da Silva. He'll want to send a doctor. It's not so easy as you think."

"Ricardo will make your excuses. He'd be good at it. Just have him put you in a cab." He looked at her. "We'll play hooky."

A question mark, not familiar with the word.

"Never mind," he said. "I'll explain it later."

"You're so sure I'll come."

He took her hand, a good-bye, the skin warm to the touch, and felt her react to it, a reflex, pulling away.

"No. But I'll wait." He started to leave, then turned to her. "Come," he said, looking at her. "I want you to."

At Posadas he sat in the lobby, pretending to read a newspaper in a club chair near the revolving door, one eye on the street. Early evening, circles of dark under the trees. The desk clerk was busying himself with some papers, eyes down, an exaggerated pose of discretion. Aaron imagined her still at the party, trying to make her excuses, Ricardo hovering. You're so sure I'll come. But he wasn't. He turned the newspaper page, restless. Pictures of men in suits, the minister of this, the minister of that, a whole government he didn't know. Friends of Jorge, who'd helped Otto once. Maybe landing cards, maybe something more, the Intelligence Bureau impossible to refuse. Meeting with her, away from the party. Think it through. But he couldn't, Jorge as fuzzy as the men in the newspaper. What if she didn't come? If he'd overplayed it?

He got up and went over to the window, nervous, a teenager waiting for a date, not knowing what to do with himself. It had to mean something, meeting like that. She'd be careful now. But she'd come before. It's enough, she'd said, but it wasn't.

A black-and-yellow taxi pulled up in front, idling while the passenger paid. When the door opened, the long legs came out first, the skirt hiked up as she slid out. He felt an almost giddy sense of relief. Here. A bellboy rushed out to close the door behind her, bowing with deference. Not sneaking in, an arrival. Then she saw him through the window and smiled, some joke between them, knowing she'd come.

"Any problems?"

"No. He didn't believe me, but he had to save face. So now tell me. What's hooky?" Talking in a rush, her voice too low for the desk clerk to hear.

"Playing hooky. Not going to school. Doing something you want to do instead."

"And if you get caught?"

"More school. After hours. But the trick is not getting caught. To get away with it."

She looked up at him. "Playing hooky," she said, practicing the phrase.

"Are you hungry? Should we have dinner?"

"After," she said, her eyes meeting his, so that the word went through him, a shudder, as if a hand were touching his genitals.

They went back to the elevator, and when it left the ground

floor he kissed her, pushing her against the metal frame. "Wait," she said, but kissed him back, ready, her breath coming faster, the only other sound the whine of the iron cage as it rose past the next floor.

In the room, he thought it would be slower, making love to someone you already knew, but it was as before, clothes thrown to the floor, urgent, the hurry of stolen time. When she rolled him over and knelt on top, riding him, her breasts cupped in his hands, she began a gentle rocking motion, almost languid, that for a second seemed to promise a different rhythm, but then she was leaning down, kissing him, and the pleasure came rushing at them again and they went faster and faster to meet it, breathing ragged, making little involuntary sounds, until they were there, unaware of anything else.

Afterward they lay still, their bodies sweaty and warm, letting the breeze dry them. Now what? Ask her what Jorge had wanted? Tell her what he was doing? Feeling like this, his whole body flushed with well-being, and knowing it was wrong, some violation, not what Max had asked him to do. But how else to do it? He looked over at her, her face relaxed now, eyes closed, and he thought of how he'd felt seeing her get out of the taxi, a little rush of blood rising closer to the skin. I want you to come. And he had wanted it. But she'd met with Jorge, long enough to get a message, which she'd give to Otto. People don't lie in bed, she'd said. But they did.

She moved, leaning over him. "Is there a shower? I'm so sticky."

He nodded toward the bathroom, then watched her as she

got up and walked across the room, the way the back of her moved, something he knew now. When he heard the water start, he got up to get a cigarette. He looked at the desk, remembering emptying his pockets in the rush to get naked. Wallet, keys landing where they'd been flung. Her charm bracelet. He smiled to himself. Something she'd liked as a girl, according to Rosas. Even the same charms, the dog, the— He stopped, then reached over and picked it up. An empty ring. No key. But there had been one. He remembered seeing it in her apartment. Where he shouldn't have been. Noticed it because it was smaller than the other pieces. He stared down at the bracelet and saw her coming down the hall at the embassy, adjusting it on her glove, because something had got hooked. An empty ring. Missing the key. Not a charm, a real key. To what? Too small for a door. Thin, the kind you slid in and turned. He looked up. A safety deposit box. A number and a small key, all you needed. Now with Jorge. Not a message, a bribe, a payment. But what had she bought?

He reached over to her bag, listening to the water. The way he'd felt in the apartment, a small tingle of shame, no excuse possible if she walked in now. But she'd bought something. He opened the bag. The usual lipstick and handkerchief and small bills and cosmetics. And an envelope, stiff. He opened it and took out the paper. Folded over, like a book. In Portuguese, but Portuguese even he could understand. A resident visa. For Erich Kruger. He stared at the picture. The same cheekbones, sharp eyes. So this is what Otto looked like now. Like Erich Kruger, heading for Brazil. His future bought and paid for.

The shower stopped. He slid the visa back into the envelope

and put it in her bag. Why she had to go to the party. Something Bildener knew. Who else?

She opened the door a crack. "You really ought to try it," she said. "It feels wonderful." Happy, having made love.

And hearing her, he knew what he would do, saw the next few minutes unfold, like a preview. He'd go into the bathroom and they'd both get in the shower, their bodies soapy, rubbing up against each other, and they'd get excited again under the water, maybe even make love there or get back on the bed, not minding the damp, but maybe in the shower because they really shouldn't and that was exciting in itself. But they'd do it somewhere because now they needed to be closer than ever. Otto was going somewhere, about to show himself.

9

"HE'S MOVING TO BRAZIL."

"Brazil? When?" Fritz turned to face him. They were sitting on a bench under the ombu tree, an early meeting, waiting for her to come out.

"I don't know. But she got him a visa. As Erich Kruger. So anytime."

"What's in Brazil? I thought all his friends were here."

"But he's supposed to be dead. Which cuts into your social life. He'll make new friends. I think he spooked when you spotted him. And too many people here—" He let the thought finish itself.

"A visa," Fritz said, thinking. "So he's still traveling on an Argentine passport."

"Or a German one. Or—any. Maybe an extra he's had all along, in case he needed to run."

"Still, it's a name for Goldfarb. It's easier with a name. Erich

Kruger," he said, repeating it to remember it. "Now he knows who to look for."

"He'd better hurry up, then. Now that Otto's got the visa, there's nothing to stop him."

"He doesn't have it yet," Fritz said.

"No. So how does she get it to him?"

"She leaves it somewhere. He picks it up."

"It's an expensive thing to leave. Look how careful so far. She pays Martínez, but no money changes hands. Nobody knows what's in a deposit box." He paused. "She has to give it to Otto. And that's when we have him."

"If you see her do it."

He turned to Fritz. "We're going to get him."

Fritz nodded. "All right. I'll call Nathan."

"We don't have him yet."

"But he's ready to run. It's easier for Nathan to operate in Argentina."

"Why?"

Fritz shrugged. "More people on the ground here. Besides, who knows how the Brazilians will react? We need Nathan to get him out. So why wait until the last minute? I know. You want to do this yourself. Something for Max. But it's enough, to find him. You'd already be a hero."

"I don't care about—"

"No? I do. My page one. But what if he gets away? Then nobody's a hero. We should call Nathan. Now."

Aaron thought for a minute, then nodded. "I thought he wouldn't come until we found him. No wild-goose chase."

Fritz smiled and put his hand on Aaron's shoulder. "I'm going to tell him we did. So bring the cavalry," he said, a Western fan. He looked again at her building. "What time does she usually—?"

"Not until later, but I don't want to take any chances. Not now. She has to get it to him. You don't want to walk around with a thing like that in your purse. She's going to meet him."

But what if she didn't? After Fritz left, Aaron sat staring at the white building. She'd be making calls now, monitored by Jamie, her usual morning. A few women trickled in, maids. What would she do today? What she always did, just another day, if you weren't looking closely, seeing what else she was doing. Yesterday she'd gone to a party and now Otto had an escape hatch. He went over everything he'd seen in the last few days, each errand a possible cover for something else. Harrods, where she might have met someone. By accident. Dos Pescadores, arranging a boat. The office building on Anchorena. Not the watch repair. Why not the travel agent? Picking up a ticket, a matter of minutes. Nothing to see, if you weren't looking.

She came out a little after eleven and headed toward San Martín again, her route that first morning, when he hadn't known what to look for. Another stop at the bank on Calle Florida, standing in line at the teller's, so not a safety deposit box request, going down to the vault with the code and key. Just walking-around money.

She went back up Calle Florida to the belle epoque hotel at the top of Plaza San Martín and went in, asking for someone at the desk. Aaron waited outside, looking through the window. No messages written out, envelopes left. Instead she simply stood in the lobby, waiting, until another woman got off the elevator and hurried over, old friends. They left arm in arm, and for a second Aaron was afraid they'd get a taxi, but she turned left, heading home, pointing to the ornate buildings on the plaza, a guide. The other woman was talking excitedly, catching up. A friend from New York?

The day was pleasant, warm without the usual river humidity, and the walk through Recoleta seemed to have no plan, just a stroll through the neighborhood, the other woman barely noticing, still talking. When they reached the end of Alvear, Aaron thought they'd go up to the apartment, lunch at home, but they kept going across to the park, past the colonial church and finally to the big cemetery, passing through the Doric columns into the shady main avenue with the other tourists.

Aaron held back, waiting. He thought for a second of Ohlsdorf, when he'd first seen her. But that had been a cemetery of green hills, an Arcadia for the dead. This was a miniature city, all stone, a grid of narrow alleys sliced by diagonal paths, all lined with elaborate tombs, thousands of them, rising in some macabre competition, the owners building higher and higher, rich inlaid marble and bronze doors, so they wouldn't be forgotten, generals and Jockey Club presidents Aaron had never heard of.

Hanna and her friend had stopped to sit on one of the benches, looking at a plan of the cemetery, and Aaron slipped into an alley behind. It was an easy place to follow someone, even the long straight lanes broken by niches and cross streets, a maze. And if you were spotted, there was even the plausible excuse of playing visitor. Everyone came to Recoleta sooner or later.

They were moving now, following the map and stopping from time to time to look at the names, alone in some of the streets, an eerie quiet, the city noise out behind the high walls. What struck Aaron was how many of the tombs were neglected, forgotten even by their own, mausoleum doors with rusty padlocks, old flower vases now filled with fallen leaves, the occasional broken glass. Was there actually anything to steal? Then ladders and paving stones and piles of sand—the maintenance tools of any city.

They were there an hour, walking one end to the other, but they didn't meet anyone or leave an envelope on a quiet tomb for later pickup. She still had the visa.

They had lunch at the Café La Biela across the street, under a shady gum tree, waiters in vests sliding past the close tables. More chat, the lunch stretching on, another cup of coffee, and then finally they were done, the friend taking a taxi back, Hanna heading down Junin toward Santa Fe. Different streets but the same neighborhood as before, apartment buildings and shoe shops and fruit stalls, jogging west and south, no hurry, until they were back in Villa Freud, the polished brass nameplates on the doors, the quiet streets about to fill with people as the sessions neared their ends. Aaron smiled to himself and took an outdoor table at the café on the Plaza Güemes, looking toward Dr. Ortiz's building. He checked his watch: 3:50. The changing began, just as before, people seeping out of doorways, some headed to the café for a drink. Others began to appear, a few in taxis, everyone on time, wanting the full session, neither group looking at the other. Shall we pick up where we left off Tuesday?

He glanced through a newspaper. The other tables were

mostly singles, alone with their thoughts, maybe reviewing what they had said to their analysts. Fifty minutes was a long time. You could say things you hadn't meant to say. Aaron wondered if the conversation was protected, like a priest's or an attorney's. Would a psychiatrist report a crime? A wanted man? Or was the couch as sacred as a confessional? Where would she go afterward? A taxi. He looked across the square. A small rank to the left of the church if he needed to get one in a hurry.

But she didn't get a taxi. She came out on time, but instead of turning right, down Charcas, headed straight toward the café. For a second he couldn't move. The newspaper was a prop, not a screen. She'd see him, even sense him. Do something. She was almost at the corner when the light turned. A minute. Aaron stood up, chair scraping, and ducked into the café, a blur of motion, out of the sunlight. Still just steps away from the sidewalk tables, but now part of the dark interior, not there unless she was looking for him. He stood at the bar, watching as her head appeared through the window, still moving steadily toward Salguero, passing his table now. Had he left anything there, some telltale—? But there was only the English-language paper, and she seemed not to notice it, preoccupied. He waited another minute, then went to the door to see her turning the corner. She was going up to Santa Fe. A block between them should be safe. Another minute.

A flicker of movement in the corner of his eye. He turned his head toward Charcas and saw the man coming out of Dr. Ortiz's doorway. Maybe Ortiz himself, in a light summer suit and Panama hat, finished for the day. He looked up and down the street, then started for the café. Aaron glanced at his watch—give her another minute—then looked up again and froze. The unmistakable walk, the one Max would know anywhere, coming toward him. Not his back, what he'd seen at the Alsterpavillon, but him, full face under the brim of the hat, the picture in the visa. The walk. Aaron went still, as if any quick motion would scare him away. Still coming toward him, and for a panicked second Aaron wondered if he knew, had come to see him. But how could he know? The hat was disconcerting, tropical, and then in his mind's eye Aaron saw the SS hat, the way he must have looked walking down the selection line, separating the fit from the doomed. Nonchalant, like this, as if he were heading for a café table.

He took one near the street, facing across the plaza to the church, and ordered coffee and a brandy, at ease with himself, not looking into the café, uninterested in the other customers, someone else's patients. Except he didn't have patients. Was there really a Dr. Ortiz? Jamie had said there was. They checked. Some arrangement then. The waiter appeared with the tray. Early for a brandy, maybe a private celebration, the papers he'd been waiting for. Aaron put his hand on the bar, fingers trembling, just being this close. He was here. Now what? Fritz. Photographs. Nathan. He was here, the same café.

"*Un otro café, señor?*"

The waiter, wondering why he was standing there. Aaron nodded, not speaking, then started back to his table, deliberate, the trembling suddenly gone, his whole body alert. When he picked up the newspaper again, he was raising a rifle, looking through the sights, that moment of perfect calm before the trigger was squeezed, the end of the hunt. Afterward things might go wrong, a mistake, some unexpected mess. But not now. Now there was only the feeling of elation. Here he is, Max. In my sights.

Otto shifted in his chair, a glance around, as if he had sensed the invisible rifle. Aaron turned a page of the newspaper. Don't avert your eyes. It's perfectly natural to look up from the paper, see who had entered the café. Otto met his eyes for a second, then went back to his brandy. A man with a newspaper. Not Max Weill and all the other ghosts behind him. Here, in the café. Just when he thought it was safe.

Otto took his time with the brandy, sipping it, keeping his hat on. When he got up to leave, Aaron went still again. Too obvious to follow immediately, but what if he went up Salguero and found a cab? But he didn't. He went back to Ortiz's building and went in. It was only later, still at the café, that Aaron saw the lights go on and knew he was in for the night. Not just an office then, an apartment with a receiving room for patients, just like Freud's. In a street where nobody noticed who came and went, where Otto had gone to ground.

Goldfarb owned a sewing factory in Once, just a few blocks from the station. He was a short man, stooped, as if he'd been bent over one of his machines for too many years.

"All the Jews are leaving," he said to Aaron, waving a hand to include the whole neighborhood. "Belgrano. What's in Belgrano?

My business is here. You don't just turn your back. It's an honor to meet you. Max Weill's boy."

"Nephew," Aaron said, only half-audible under the noise of the machines outside the office door.

Another wave. "You should have seen him in the camps. After the war, the DPs. I don't think he slept. Always working."

"Did he ever send you a picture of Schramm?" he said, trying to steer the conversation. "To help you look."

Goldfarb shook his head. "We were working in the dark with that one. He had one in his files—laughing, I think, if you could imagine such a thing. But no copies. I saw it before I left Germany. So it was here," he said, putting a finger to his head. "Anyway, he may not look like that now. We change over the years."

"But nothing under Kruger? No passport?" Fritz said.

"Not yet. But if it's Argentine, we'll find it. If," he said, a cautionary finger. "Anyway, if you know where he is, just photograph him now."

"We will. But it's useful to have a link to the other identities, compare the pictures."

"So we'll keep looking. Meanwhile, I have something else for you."

Fritz raised his eyebrows.

"I was thinking. So it's not Helmut Braun in that car accident. But it's somebody. There's a body. So who is it?"

"And?"

"I thought, a man, somebody must miss him. So I checked the Mar del Plata police records. Who didn't come home? And I found a match, the right weight, the right height. Anyway, close enough. Here, take a look."

He showed them a photograph.

"That doesn't look anything like him," Aaron said, impatient, not interested.

"Forget the face. It was unrecognizable. But the body—"

"So who recognized it?" Fritz said. "Who identified the body?"

Goldfarb shot him a look. "Rudel. That fascist."

"And Bildener," Aaron said. "Anyway, we know it wasn't Otto."

"So who's this?" Fritz said.

"Giorgio Rinaldi. Still missing. Officially. Of course, we can't say for certain it's him, not now."

"But Bildener says it's Braun."

"You notice, not the daughter. She can never be accused. Nothing to do with it."

"Maybe it's true," Aaron said. "Maybe she didn't know."

Fritz looked at him. "Maybe. She does now."

Aaron glanced at his watch. "I thought you said Nathan was coming."

"He'll be here. He's setting up a team. To watch the house."

"You understand, there had to be somebody in the police," Goldfarb said, still back in Mar del Plata. "To tell Bildener. There's an accident. What you're looking for. So something changes hands and Rinaldi becomes— How else?"

There was a roar of machinery as Nathan came through the door, his bullet head shiny with sweat. The Hamburg sailor's pea-coat had been traded in for a warm-weather short-sleeved shirt that made him look uncannily like a young Ben-Gurion, stocky, with a wrestler's chest and arms.

"How do you hear yourself think in here?" he asked Goldfarb, clutching his arm, old colleagues.

"I don't think."

"Good sound cover, though," Nathan said, leaving the door open. "Fritz." Another shake. "And the hunter." He took Aaron's hand. "Nice work, for a desk man."

Aaron nodded, pleased. "I was lucky. He showed himself."

"So stay lucky. We have a team on him now, so you don't go to Villa Freud. He sees you twice, something clicks," he said, his voice gruff, in charge.

"Assuming he comes out."

"He has to buy food. She never brings anything, right? She's seeing her shrink. So." He turned to Fritz. "And we got lucky for you. There's a room for rent across the street. Not right across, too far for a regular camera, but a telephoto would get to the door. And if he walks down Charcas, he'd be coming to you. Just keep snapping. We still need a positive ID. I can't get more men without it. Christ, it's loud out there." He faced the factory floor.

"They wear earplugs," Goldfarb said.

"You get the papers? For the boys. They need something to show."

"You'll get them, don't worry."

Nathan touched Goldfarb's arm. "I know."

"And me?" Aaron said.

Nathan looked at him. "You? You do what you've been doing—stay close to her. She have any idea?"

"No."

"That must be interesting."

Aaron said nothing.

"Maybe you have a talent for it."

A sharp look now.

"All right, all right," Nathan said, an apology. "Just don't get confused. Remember who they are."

"She's not like that."

Nathan looked at him, about to say something, then dropped it.

"She did what we wanted. She led us to him. But she doesn't know that." He paused. "She never has to know."

"We just found him by ourselves."

Aaron shrugged. "You're Mossad. There's a reputation now. He's playing dead to get away from you. You don't need help."

"But we still need her. We don't know his plans. She does. When does he go to Brazil? How?" He looked over at Aaron. "Luckily we have an inside source. Close to her. There's no problem about that, is there?"

Aaron looked away. "What does it matter how he's planning to go? Aren't you going to—"

"What? Snatch him in the street? Another Eichmann?" He shook his head. "You staked out Villa Freud. What did you see? People in the street. Traffic. Cafés. Kids, for chrissake, in the playground. You can't just grab somebody there. Eichmann, it was different. He lived out of town. Nobody around. So, easy. And then what? Safe houses until we could fly him out. That's not going to work this time. We don't have an El Al plane warming up on the runway."

"So how do you get him to Germany?" Fritz said. "If you can't fly?"

"We get him out of Argentina first. Then we fly. And it so happens he's planning to get out of Argentina. So we follow him out." He turned to Aaron. "If we know how he's going. When. So we stay on her. Close."

"Why don't you just tail him? He goes to Brazil, you'll know."

Nathan nodded. "We have a team on him now. In shifts. One man at a time. But that only works if he stays put. Once he's loose, one man can't cover it. You need a whole operation. Otherwise, one slip and he's gone. And I don't have a whole operation. Yet. So, he comes out, we need to know where he's going. Let's hope he's not in a hurry. We need a little time."

"Why not just break the story?" Fritz said. "Once we have the pictures, we have him. Lazarus. Back from the dead. Everybody'll pick it up."

"But they'll never extradite him. They can't. Too many protected him. He'll disappear again. A phantom. Like Mengele. Then all you have are rumors. He's in Paraguay. He's in Bolivia. And he never testifies. But in Brazil, we have a chance. Don't worry," he said to Fritz. "Get him to Germany and you've got headlines. For days. They can't ignore him—he's on German soil. They have to do something." He turned to Aaron. "And Max gets his trial."

"If the Brazilians—"

Nathan shook his head. "The Brazilians won't know. You tell them, it could take forever. Even if they end up doing the right thing. Remember Eichmann? We need to do something like that.

Right under their noses. A quick transfer. But it takes people. So let's hope he gives us a few more days."

"They're not going to be happy about this. The Brazilians."

"And that's my job? To make them happy? I told you, back in Hamburg, it's not nice, this work. You have to have the stomach for it. To cut a few corners."

"A few corners."

"And you're not? With her?" He turned to Goldfarb. "Did you get the coroner's report? For Helmut Braun?"

Goldfarb nodded.

"Any mention of the tattoo? The SS ID?"

"Bildener mentioned it," Fritz said. "It's one way they identified him as Schramm. That, and the dental records."

"And tattoos don't lie. If they're there." Again, to Goldfarb. "But the coroner doesn't mention it?"

"No."

"Odd, yes? A tattoo he doesn't see."

"Mengele doesn't have one," Goldfarb said. "It made it easier for him, after the war."

"But Schramm did. And Bildener sees it, but not the coroner." He looked at Fritz. "So it's another story. Something else for Bildener to answer."

He looked at his watch, as if he were setting an operation into action, all business.

"What else? We don't want to be too long. Goldfarb has a business to run." A sly smile to him. "But you'll keep checking on Kruger, yes? Fritz, you get the pictures. See what else we can pick up in Mar del Plata. That's going to embarrass the hell out of the Argentines. I'll get more men. Meanwhile, we track his movements, get his routine. Maybe he's like Eichmann, home every day the same time, like clockwork." He looked over at Aaron. "What?"

"Nothing. It's just—to wait like this, when we have him. What if—?"

"We don't have him. You're like Max. He could find them—there was nobody like him for that. But you know, when you hunt, that's the first part. You find him. Then you have to bring him down."

She put on a slip afterward, covering herself.

"Why bother?"

"It's not decent."

He grinned. "But that is," he said, nodding toward the slip.

"It makes me feel better. Anyway, it's harder for you, to look," she said, playful, handing him her lighted cigarette.

"So Rosas was right. A good girl. Nothing to confess."

"Not to him."

"You never had impure thoughts?"

She smiled. "Imagine if I had said that to him?" She took the cigarette back. "How many Hail Marys. No, not then. The thoughts came later."

"I'm glad."

"Yes, and now what?" she said, stubbing out the cigarette. "Are you really going to Bariloche or is that one of your stories?"

"I got sidetracked," he said, stroking her arm. "Why don't you come?"

"To Bariloche? It's too German for me. Those funny hats. Strudel."

"It's supposed to be beautiful."

"It is. I told you, my father—" She stopped, then turned to him. "What happened to your friend with the book? Or did you make him up?"

"No, he'd still like to talk to you. I just thought you'd—rather not."

"Oh, rather not. Well. And when does that change anything?"

"All right. Just tell me when and I'll set it up."

She looked down. "Markus says I shouldn't do it. It's some plan you and Jamie have."

"To do what?"

"I don't know. It's Markus." A smile. "He said you were rude to him."

"I was."

"He's not used to that. He thinks you want to make trouble for me." She took a breath. "Do you?"

"No." He put his hand up to her head. "Is that what you think?"

She looked at him for a moment. "I don't know. What happens now?"

"We go to Bariloche. We go hiking. Or we don't go hiking."

She smiled. "And what do I tell Markus?"

"Why tell him anything? What business is it of his?"

"He acts like my father now. They were close. In Gemany. They worked together. So he thinks that gives him the right—"

"Worked together. During the war?"

"You mean at Auschwitz. No, Markus was too high up for that. He was back in Berlin. In Dahlem. The Institut fur Rassenbiologische und Anthropologische Forschungen," she said, the words flowing out in a perfectly accented stream, the German Hanna. He glanced over, in bed with someone else, but then she was back, her real voice. "He kept measurements. That's what he says anyway. My father sent him reports. From his experiments. So they knew each other."

"Measurements."

"From Mengele, on the twins. From my father, I don't know what. I never asked. What could they be? Something terrible. Listen to us. We talk about this as if it was some ordinary crime, a robbery. And Markus says 'measurements,' something innocent. My father says 'exaggerations.' Both of them pretending it was something else. Doctors. How can doctors do things like that?"

"Bildener was a doctor?"

"All of them. It had to have a scientific basis, what they were doing there. Someone in a white coat, how could it be wrong? And after, do they change how they think? They come here, a new name, but nothing else changes."

"Who was he before? Bildener."

"I don't know. You didn't ask. We were Braun. He was Bildener."

"Is he—wanted?"

"In Germany, you mean? No, he was never at Auschwitz. Only at the Institute. So he was never accused. The bosses always get away, no? Anyway, it's too late. Who could testify against him? The victims are dead. There was only my father and he would never—" She stopped. "And now he's dead too." The body identified, a stamped death certificate. "So Markus is safe." She looked out from the bed. "You think it's over and now here's Markus, another crazy man to be my father."

"But he's not."

"No. You know the difference? He never loved me. My father did. So who cares what Markus says?" She glanced at him, trying to smile. "What do you think? Should I talk to your friend? Will that make him go away? Bury him?"

"Who, Markus?"

"No, my father."

Aaron looked at her. "I don't know. I'm not a professional. Ask Dr. Ortiz." Waiting.

"Ouf. In del Plata. They all go to the beach in the summer. When you need them. Everybody leaves Buenos Aires." She put her hand up to his cheek. "Do you really want to go away? Not Bariloche. We could keep going, all the way down to Ushuaia. I've always wanted to go there—where the boats leave for Antarctica. The end of the world. Nobody would ever find us there."

"Nobody's looking for us."

"No, that's right." She laughed a little. "So maybe Bariloche's far enough. Warmer. To hell with Markus." She looked at him, straight into his eyes, trying to see inside. "Maybe I should listen to him."

He leaned forward, kissing her. "But he's crazy."

"Anyway, by that time—"

"What?"

"By the time we leave. Next week."

"Why next week?" he said, kissing her again.

"I have something to do. But then I'll be free."

"Why not tomorrow?" he said, trying it.

"No, next week. I can't leave yet. You can wait a few days. Then we can go anywhere. I'll be free."

"You're sure it's this week?" Nathan said.

Aaron nodded.

"Then we have to move. We can't wait."

They were sitting in Goldfarb's office again, the sewing machines humming outside, the desk covered with photographs Fritz had taken—Otto in his Panama hat, drinking in the café, getting into a taxi. A new man, Ari, had been introduced but had said nothing, studying their faces, a professional. Nathan turned to Goldfarb.

"We're going to need a safe house. Can you do it? Fast?"

Goldfarb opened his hands.

"I thought we were going to follow him out," Aaron said. "To Brazil."

"Maybe sit next to him on the plane?" Nathan said. "We don't have enough men. Here or there. We'll lose him."

"But you have enough for a grab? Then to guard him?"

"We don't have a choice. Let's say he's flying to São Paulo. Let's say we even find out the plane. Your girlfriend slips something. Or we track him to the gate. We still need a team to pick him up when he lands and I don't have it yet. So we have to move here."

"We do that and everyone who's helping him will know," Aaron said. "Then he doesn't fly at all. And we still have to get him out."

"I know that. I didn't say it was ideal. You work with what you have. And right now we have someone ready to fly this week. If you're right."

Aaron nodded again. "It's this week."

"I still say, let's just run the pictures," Fritz said. "Then everybody's in on it. Schramm's alive. They can't walk away from that. It would be a scandal."

"So the Germans request him. And the Argentines lose him. Checkmate. But we already have him. The Germans aren't going to put him on trial unless they can't do anything else. Unless he's there. So, Ari, what do we have? There's a routine?"

"Yes and no. What you saw," he said, turning to Aaron, "was unusual. Following her out. He waits an hour, another session, different people in the street. Then he comes out. Sometimes the café where you saw him. An early dinner. Or he takes a taxi. Another café, up by the cemetery. Tourists. Where it doesn't matter you eat early. Nobody notices."

"The same one?"

"So far. Alone. He reads a newspaper. A cigar with coffee."

"And a taxi home?"

"To the square, not the door."

"He never walks?"

"Not to dinner. Once a little walk after in Palermo Viejo. Half an hour maybe, no more."

"So?"

"The taxi's our best bet. There's a rank on the square, but if he sees one on the way, he hails it. So we make sure he sees one. Down Charcas, like always. We stop for the light at Bulnes, somebody else hops in. Off we go."

Aaron frowned, trying to picture it. "There's a café at Bulnes."

"So what does anybody see? A man getting into a taxi."

"And a man inside fighting him. What's Schramm going to do? Nothing?"

"Not after he sees the gun in my hand," Ari said. "It usually quiets them down."

"A gun? Then it's kidnapping," Aaron said.

"And what's your plan?" Nathan said.

Aaron ran the film clip in his head, the taxi pulling up, the man leaping in, the screech of tires as it drove off. He shook his head. "It's too public."

"You think we haven't done this before?" Ari said, annoyed

now. He turned to Nathan. "The taxi's our best bet. Two men, me and the driver. Nobody sees. And then we're at the safe house, wherever that is. Goldfarb?"

"Montevideo. Near Córdoba. From tomorrow."

But Nathan was looking at Aaron. "So?"

Aaron said nothing for a minute, thinking, then looked up.

"He's already in a safe house. We just need to make it our safe house."

Nathan peered at him. "Go on."

"He's already in hiding. So let's keep him hidden. With a guard. We don't have to snatch him. In public. We have him and nobody knows where."

"Except the daughter."

Aaron nodded. "Except her. And she doesn't want anything to happen to him, or why would she be doing this? So she does what you say. If anybody else knows he's there, comes looking for him, then they're part of Fritz's story. Pictures and all. Ortiz? If he comes back early? Not the best publicity, hiding a war criminal. But I don't think anyone knows."

"Except her."

"And you've got a gun on him."

"After we break down the door. Which the neighbors will love."

"There aren't any neighbors. We haven't seen anyone else come out."

"You ever break down a door?" Ari said, a slight sneer.

Aaron shook his head. "We just knock. Right after she leaves. So he thinks it's her. She forgot something. We have somebody in the street. Not me, somebody she won't recognize. You, maybe," he said to Ari. "The minute she hits the corner, you're at the door. He doesn't open, try this." He took the passkey out of his pocket. "Fritz here likes to sneak around. It works—you'd be surprised. No noise."

For a minute no one said anything.

"We might have to keep her there too," Nathan said finally.

Aaron nodded. "Let's see how she takes it. I don't think she wants any trouble. And she's probably the only one who can talk sense to him at this point."

"And when he doesn't show? For the plane. And his friends start wondering what happened?"

"But he does show," Aaron said. "As soon as you have your people in place at the other end. Then it's up to you. Maybe you get the Brazilians to fly him out for you. Maybe not. But he's there, not here."

"And he goes. Just like that."

"With somebody sitting next to him. To keep him company."

"When?"

"She sees him tomorrow—sees Ortiz—but I think that's too soon. She said she'd be ready next week, so I think it's the end of this week. Thursday. Her other day."

"Although it could be any time."

"It could."

"But you think Thursday."

"Does that give you enough time?"

Nathan looked at him. "Just a knock on the door. I like that."

"There's less risk."

"You sit at a desk, there's never any risk."

He reached into his pocket and handed Aaron a gun.

"What's this for?"

"We'll babysit in shifts. Make him think you'd use it."

She was late coming out. The 3:50 change had already begun, patients heading toward the plaza, the taxi rank, and she was still inside. Aaron watched the door through binoculars, the air still, just waiting. Fritz was fiddling with the telephoto lens, focusing on Ortiz's building. In the street, Goldfarb was circling in an off-duty cab, Nathan's backup plan, just in case.

"So where is she?" Fritz said.

"She'll be there."

"I want to get her coming out of the building."

"No, get Ari going in. Leave her out of it."

Fritz glanced over at him. "She's part of it. The story."

"She doesn't have to be."

Ari and Nathan were crossing the street from the square, entering stage right, the scene beginning. In a second everyone would be in motion, the extras melting into the café behind, the principals passing each other at the streetlight, but right now everything felt suspended, stopped in time, waiting for the music. Where was she? Aaron glanced up and down Charcas, the street emptying, the four o'clock patients already inside. A sleepy afternoon. A handful of people in the cafés. Witnesses. It had been easier with Eichmann. The walk from the bus stop down a dimly lit street, deserted. A stalled car on the side of the road, hood up, someone working on the engine. "*Un momentito, señor.*" And caught. Thrown into the car, a fast drive in the dark, blindfolded. Someone who didn't come home. Days before his family reported him missing.

The camera clicked as she started coming through the door.

"No. Wait for Ari."

Fritz lowered the camera an inch.

She was in a light summer dress and sandals, a full skirt that moved with her as she walked. No hesitation, no looking up and down, just heading toward Plaza Güemes as if she had heard the downbeat and had begun her steps. The rest came to life, Ari and Nathan passing her without looking at her, Goldfarb's cab turning the corner, starting to circle the block to be back on Charcas if he was needed. She walked across to the café, and for a second Aaron thought she would sit down, ruin everything just by being there, but she kept going, heading up to Santa Fe, no longer part of it.

Another click. Ari and Nathan at the door. A glance back to make sure Hanna had gone, then in. Now Aaron would have to imagine the rest. Second-floor front, an elevator, but better to take the stairs. Standing on either side of the peephole, out of range, a light knock. Then what? Who's there? Or a bemused, What did you forget? Or nothing, suspicious, playing dead, waiting for some explanation with the knock.

"They should be there now," Fritz said, his voice nervous.

Knocking again. Or trying the passkey, the sound rattling

Otto inside. Ortiz back early? Who else had a key? Maybe opening the door a crack with a chain lock. He hadn't planned for that, Otto checking before he opened the door. What else had he missed? It would only take Otto a second, seeing Nathan's head, Ari's hawk-like eyes, to know who they were. What it meant. Still, then what?

"Who's that?" Fritz said, raising the camera again. A click.

"Jesus, it's him," Aaron said. Not strolling, shooting out the door in a panic, turning down Charcas.

"That's it, come to Papa. Good one." Click.

No one behind him. A back door? Of course he'd have an escape hatch. Fire stairs, something. Which Aaron should have planned for. Walking fast, not running, head down, not wanting to draw attention. How long before Nathan and Ari knew he was gone? Getting away.

"Come on," Aaron said, almost a yell. Already at the door, then starting down the stairs, Fritz clunking behind him.

Otto kept coming down Charcas, not seeing them on the other side through the little park that divided the street. Fritz raised the camera again and snapped, the sound faint but distinct, stopping him in a second of panic. Behind him, Nathan and Ari had come racing out of the building. Now Otto started to run, no longer caring if anyone saw. Aaron dodged a car to cross the street mid-block. Intercept him. Otto, running, looked up, startled, then looked behind, Ari running now too, fast, a leopard about to bring down a gazelle, all of them panting. Another click.

Otto swerved out into the street, barely missing a car. He was grunting now, breath coming in gasps. The driver who'd just missed him shouted something in Spanish. He looked around, Ari and Nathan still closing in, and started again for Bulnes, the café on the corner, anywhere public, no longer thinking, an adrenaline spurt. Aaron jumped, coming down on his shoulders, as if they really were animals, the kill moment. Otto fell, a sharp squeal, bringing Aaron down with him, two brawlers, what they had wanted to avoid, a scene. Otto wriggled, slipping out of Aaron's grasp, and got up again, running back into the street, another car braking, Goldfarb's taxi. Ari, there now, slammed him against it and opened the back door. Plan B. "Get in." Barely words, just sounds.

Otto pushed away, fumbling in his pocket and pulling out a gun, pointing it at Nathan, who stopped, frozen. Otto took a step away from the car, testing the waters, ready to bolt. Another click. He whirled around to the sound, an instinct, one second of distraction, enough for Aaron to chop at his wrist. Otto half-turned, trying to hold on to the gun, loose now in his hand, and fired at them, an explosion in the quiet street. Heads turned in the café. Otto swung the gun, pointing it back at Nathan. A second, nobody moving. Then Aaron chopped again, grabbing the gun as it fell out of Otto's hand.

"Fuck," Ari said, clutching his leg, the blood already starting to spread. "The car," he said, gasping.

Otto started to spring away, one last escape, and fell into Aaron, who smashed the gun against his head. A yelp, still trying to run but blocked now. Aaron hit him again, opening the skin, a streak of blood, and shoved him into the backseat, Ari climbing in after. Another click, Fritz still snapping.

"You go," Nathan said to Aaron, nodding toward the front

seat. He touched Fritz's arm. "Come with me." Pulling him away from the car.

"What about—?"

"Now. Here," he said to Ari, handing him some handcuffs. "Cuff him. He'll do anything." He looked in the back. "What the hell?" he said, taking in Otto's bleeding head. "He going to be all right? What about you?" he said to Ari. "You need a doctor?"

"What, because I have a bullet in my leg?"

"I know somebody," Goldfarb said from the front.

Nathan turned from Otto to Aaron. "You weren't supposed to hurt him."

"He had a gun on you."

Nathan stared at him for a second, then nodded, a thank-you. "Tough guy."

A moan from Otto. "Who are you? Jews?"

"Here they come," Nathan said, spotting someone at the café door. "Give me the gun." He took it from Aaron and shot it into the air. The man ducked back inside the café. "That should give you a minute. Now get the fuck going." He handed back the gun. "Don't shoot him unless you have to." He closed Aaron's door. "So. Keep it simple. Now look."

"We got him, didn't we?" Aaron said, swiveling around to face the backseat, Otto slumped against it, groaning, his nose running with blood, his pale old man's hands lying still in the cuffs.

Nathan followed his look. "Otto Schramm," he said, shaking his head. "The fucking master race." He glanced back at Aaron. "Maybe he knows where Mengele is. Then we get them all."

10

GOLDFARB'S SAFE HOUSE WAS in a scruffy neighborhood on the western fringe of downtown. Second floor over a storefront, good sight lines both ways, dead bolt in the back. But who was planning to attack? Otto had become a ghost again, no trace left in Villa Freud but a broken chain lock where thieves must have tried to get in. After Goldfarb's doctor had put a few stitches in his forehead, he had fallen asleep, exhausted, a patient with a bandage. Aaron stared at the face, everything familiar, just like the pictures, except now the skin was thin and dry, the cheekbones close to the surface. Receding hair gray, some white. The face old and childlike at the same time, the way people look when they sleep. He had wet himself earlier and no one had bothered to change his pants, the wet blotch drying but visible.

"Still out?" Nathan said.

Aaron nodded.

"I brought his clothes."

"You went back?"

"We had to see if he left anything. That could ID him. But just this." He lifted a small case. "The good doctor travels light."

"Plane ticket?"

Nathan shook his head. "Just a wad of cash."

Aaron thought of her at the teller's window in Calle Florida. Regular withdrawals, nothing to call attention.

"You took a chance going there."

"Not to Ortiz's. Nothing happened there. That anyone saw."

"And down the street?"

"I had a coffee. On Bulnes. Crime is getting worse. In broad daylight now. Probably drugs. Two got away, one with a camera. That would be Fritz." He looked over. "We're OK. Nobody's looking for Otto."

"Yet."

"Funny how the body shuts down, isn't it? You'd think he'd be jumping around, all excited, but he's out. You OK for another shift? I want to check on Ari. We can't take him to a hospital with a bullet—"

"Fine." He looked up. "What about the visa? She didn't give it to him?"

Nathan patted his jacket pocket. "Here," he said. "No passport, though. I figure that comes last minute with the ticket. Whoever's helping gets it for him so he doesn't have to show, until the plane."

"Careful."

"Seventeen, eighteen years he's careful. And he's still here.

Even when he's not, officially. But now—" He looked at the couch. "Now his luck's run out." He turned back to Aaron. "There's coffee over there if you need some. Don't take any chances—you want to be wide awake with him. I'll bring some food when I come back. You're sure you're OK? You're not used to this."

"I'm learning on the job."

"Huh."

A sound came from the couch. Nathan turned. "Good morning. Evening." He dipped his head in a mock bow.

"Who are you?" The voice full, not vague and scratchy, trying to regain some authority.

"Your worst nightmare," Nathan said.

"Israeli?"

Nathan said nothing.

"What do you want with me?"

"I'll let you wonder about that. It'll help while away the time."

"You think I'm Eichmann. I'm not Eichmann."

"No, you're Otto Schramm."

Otto reached up to feel the bandage on his forehead, an awkward move in handcuffs.

"You're all right," Nathan answered before Otto could ask. "Stitches come out, you'll be like new."

"Do I have to wear these?" Otto said, holding out his hands. "Is this necessary?"

"You're a desperate character."

"Desperate," he said. "And how do I go to the bathroom?"

"You'll figure something out. Otherwise, one of us will have to hold your dick for you."

Otto gave him a look of scorn, something not worth answering.

"Want some clean pants?"

"You're going to kill me."

"Not us. So you might as well have the clean pants while you're waiting. Aaron, give me a hand, will you?"

Otto held up his arms, a reflex, then dropped them, resigned, as they unbuckled the belt and pulled off his pants.

"Why not just do it? Not go through this—charade. One Eichmann isn't enough for you? You're going to kill us anyway."

"That's not up to me. But just so we're clear about this? I wouldn't *mind* killing you, and if you try anything, we will. Like that." He snapped his fingers. "And you're not holding any cards. We have men in the street out front, covering. More in the back." His voice steady, not looking at Aaron. "You leave this room without us, they have orders to shoot. No questions. In the room you've got a trained officer." He nodded to Aaron. "Unfortunately a little trigger happy. He's been reprimanded. So don't make him nervous. Any quick moves, you'll be dead—you understand?"

"*Fantastisch*," Otto said, his mouth twisted in contempt. "The great Mossad."

"You just keep working on how to take a piss."

The new pants were on now.

"Where is the bathroom?"

"Over there. Aaron, show him."

Otto got up slowly, a little stiff, then looked at Aaron. "I can do it."

"Not alone," Nathan said.

Otto shuffled across the room, Aaron following, looking down at the thinning hair. He had always imagined Otto tall, towering over his selection line in polished black boots, but he was shorter than Aaron, surprisingly slight, about Max's height.

Nathan waited until Otto finished.

"I knew you could do it," he said, a tight smile. "Get some rest. Don't make Aaron nervous. I'll send Fritz with some food," he said to Aaron, then turned back to Otto. "You'll recognize him. He's the guy your buddy tried to kick to death in Hamburg."

"In Hamburg," Otto said, thrown by this, the net wider than he'd imagined. How long had they been stalking him?

"So don't make him nervous either."

"Go to hell," Otto said, but his voice had lost its force, deflated, and he sank into the couch. "How long am I here?"

"Not long. So try to make the best of it. You want to start by telling us the flight number?"

Otto looked up. "Flight number." Marking time, waiting.

"To São Paulo."

His eyes widened slightly, thrown again, not expecting this. Hamburg. São Paulo.

"Go to hell."

"Well, maybe it'll come back to you." Nathan checked his watch, then nodded to the telephone on the side table. "It works. Call if you need anything. Fritz should be here in an hour. Herr Schramm," he said, tipping his head. He glanced around. "Not much of a place, is it? If you hadn't run, we could still be at Ortiz's. Much nicer."

Otto watched him go, not saying anything, then sat looking at his hands, shoulders slumped, his whole body sagging.

"I heard you before," he said finally. "You're not Israeli. So who are you representing?"

"Representing," Aaron said, turning over the word, formal and snide at the same time.

"An American voice. So who sent you?"

"Max Weill."

Otto's head snapped up, all attention.

"Max Weill," he said, disconcerted. "He's alive?"

"No, he died."

"So," he said, as if this had settled something. "When?"

"After he saw you in Hamburg."

His head went up again. "He saw me?" Confused, thinking of Ohlsdorf.

"When you took your walk by the Binnenalster. A dead man. But he knew it was you. You should have stayed home. If he hadn't seen you, none of this would be happening."

Otto made a short waving motion with his hand, weighted down by the cuffs. "Who knows why things happen. So," he said, brooding, "he's dead." He looked up. "And who are you?"

"His nephew."

"Herschel's boy?"

Aaron nodded, surprised, forgetting he had known the family.

"His blood. And now you've come for your pound of flesh." A faint, wry smile. "Jews."

"Not your flesh. I don't want any part of you."

"What do you want, then?"

"What Max wanted. Put you on trial."

"Then you're wasting your time. Do you think I would ever let that happen? Eichmann was a fool. Talk, talk, and they were going to kill him anyway. Trial. A farce. From me—you get nothing. I'll never testify."

"But other people will."

"And what? I sit there while they point their fingers at me. What do they know about it? Any of them. Max. I saved his life. I pulled him out of the line. And what thanks? Hunting me down, like some vermin. After I saved him."

Aaron looked over, unable to speak, the mad rationale flowing out of Otto's mouth like spittle.

"He was a good doctor. You know we were at university together? So I knew. The others? To them, just another one for the ovens. But I knew. So I saved him. He survived the war. What were the chances of that? Unless someone saved him. But he never understood that, how it was."

"You murdered his son."

"Murdered. It's not correct, that word." He gestured with his hand again, a dismissal. "He was going to die anyway. I made it easier for him. A matter of minutes only, with the gas. Not like some of the others. For them, a difficult time."

"In the medical experiments."

"We were asked to do that," he said, explaining the obvious. "There was never such an opportunity before. For tests."

"On children."

"They were sent there to die," Otto said, not hearing. "And now useful. You can still read them, the reports, the test results.

At Dahlem, the Institute. They didn't die for nothing. They made a contribution."

Aaron looked at him. Radiation tests. Endless crackpot measurements. All sitting in file drawers somewhere in Berlin. A contribution.

"You made him help. Max. You made him do what you did."

"I didn't send those people there. It was not my decision. And so many. Train after train. We had to do the best we could under the circumstances. Medical decisions. Who was fit for work? Who had typhus? You had to watch like a hawk before it spread. And the requests would come. From the Institute, from the Wehrmacht. How long could a pilot survive in freezing water? Useful information for the war." He paused. "Mengele and the twins—I never took that seriously. He was obsessed, I think. And the guards, I don't answer for them. Some of them were—sadists." Searching for the word.

"Sadists," Aaron said, as if he hadn't heard correctly.

"Not all. Some. There were terrible things. People thrown into the ovens before they were dead. Terrible. But in our section, only the right procedures. What doctors had to do." He looked up. "That's the way it was there. You think it was my idea, to make such a camp? And now who answers for it? The people responsible? No—" He stopped, not bothering to finish, talking too much.

"You haven't answered yet."

Otto ignored this, looking down again, brooding.

"Do you want some water?" Aaron said.

Otto shook his head. Another silence.

"How did he die? Max."

"His heart."

"So, a long life. I saw him on a magazine once. With Wiesenthal. And that's how he spent his life? Looking for camp guards? To accuse them—of what? Doing what they had to do?"

"No, bringing them to justice."

"*Quatsch*. There was no such thing. Not at Auschwitz. What would justice be there? He was a sentimentalist, Max, always. That made it difficult for him—to do the work. A doctor, you can't be a sentimentalist. Death is part of the job. It's all around you. Those people were corpses. But useful. That's what mattered."

"Living corpses."

Otto shrugged, a point not worth arguing.

"Corpses. Like bodies in anatomy class. So you learn from them. You did your work."

"What did you learn?"

Otto looked away, ignoring this, scanning the room, then came back to Aaron.

"Such a waste, looking for guards. All these years. A good doctor. He gave it up?"

Aaron nodded. "He didn't feel he was a doctor anymore. After that."

Otto shrugged. "Foolishness."

"You stopped too."

"I had a new identity. A German doctor? How long would that have taken them?"

"Who's them?"

"At first the Allies. The Amis," he said, nodding to Aaron. "So eager for justice. But those days? In Europe? Everything a mess. It was easy to get away—get a new name."

"And Red Cross papers. And a priest to help."

"So you know all that."

"The ratline to Argentina."

Otto looked up, amused. "They call it that? I didn't know. We're the rats?" A kind of warmth in his voice, suddenly like hers, what he must have sounded like at parties, an easy charm. "So, Argentina. A new name. And it was good here, for years. Nobody was looking. The Amis went home, Adenauer was busy. No one cared about some businessman in Buenos Aires. But then the Israelis came and things changed."

"They came for Eichmann."

"Then why not me?"

"So you killed off Helmut Braun."

"Nobody looks for a dead man. Not even the Israelis."

"Max thought you were dead too. Until he saw you. Your one mistake."

"Not the only," he said, his voice weary, then smiled at Aaron, the smile a kind of lure. "But imagine, it's Max who finds me at the end, not the Israelis. Not that it matters. Now they have me anyway. So now what? Jerusalem? Another glass box? Maybe the same one, it would save expense. Did they keep it? Waiting for Mengele, if they find him. Are you going after him next?"

"No. Only you."

"Ah. Something for Max. You're the faithful dog? Here's the scent. Bring him back? So you can take me to Jerusalem?" he said, his voice rising, lifting his hands to show the handcuffs. "That's his revenge?"

"Not Jerusalem. Germany."

Otto stared. "Germany," he said, disturbed, taken by surprise. "A trial in Germany? No, I won't do that."

"It's not an invitation. There's a warrant out for you."

"A trial in Germany? To be a spectacle there? No," he said, visibly upset. He looked up. "What makes you think they want a trial? It was enough, after the war. Now it's—it's another time. People want to forget."

"They used to," Aaron said, nodding. "But now there's a prosecutor in Frankfurt who doesn't. He thinks it's time to take a look. New trials. What Max knew would happen. Why he kept collecting evidence, even when no one wanted to see it. Not just guards, the bosses too. Doctors. You'll be a star attraction."

Otto made a growling noise, not a word, just a sound. "To Germany," he said to himself, and when Aaron nodded, "Then why do they want to know the flight number to São Paulo?" A question he'd been waiting to ask, eyes on Aaron, watching his face. Think.

"To see how long it'll be before anyone misses you," Aaron said easily, the answer just coming out, as if he'd been cued. "Whether that would affect the plans."

"The plans. And what are the plans? Another plane? They're going to drug me?"

Aaron said nothing.

"How did they know about São Paulo?" he said, not letting go.

"That would be telling."

"In other words, you don't know," he said, his voice sly now.

Aaron shrugged, not biting. "I'm just the babysitter."

"No," Otto said. "Max's hound. You said. How did you find me?"

"I tracked you from Hamburg. After Max saw you." He paused. "Why did you go? Take that risk?"

Otto looked away. "Personal reasons. A family matter."

"Your wife's funeral."

"You're so well informed, why do you ask?"

"But why? You hadn't seen her in years. She'd never know if you were there."

"It's an obligation. Family. That's something you should understand. Why do you do this? For Max."

"No, for me. I don't think you should get away with it."

"Oh, the hand of justice again. And who appointed you?" He looked down. "She was my wife. I thought I owed her that much respect. To be there."

"After all this time. Did she know? About the camps? What you were doing?"

Otto looked away, quiet for a minute. "She was—sensitive. The bombs terrified her. That was it, I think, what made her sick." He took a breath, moving on. "So, yes, there was some feeling there and I had to go. And then, at Ohlsdorf, some idiot with a camera—the other one, that was you?"

Aaron nodded.

"So you followed. But here, how did you find me here? A dead man."

Aaron looked over. Think of something plausible, away from

her. "It wasn't hard. Once I saw that Bildener had identified the body. I recognized him from Max's files. At the Institute. So I knew he'd lead me to you. And he did."

"Markus," Otto said, frowning. "He should be more careful. More like Trude. A sphinx, that one. It's his temper. He just says things. He was always like that." He stopped, looking up. "And from him to my daughter?"

Aaron, caught, made a half nod. They looked at each other, not sure where to take this.

"She's not—" Otto said. "She knows nothing."

"She knows you're alive."

"She had no part in that. Any of it."

"She helps you."

"She's my daughter. My family."

"Another obligation?"

Otto shook his head. "She didn't want me to go. To Germany. She disapproves of me."

"But she got you the visa for Brazil."

Otto glanced at him, uncertain how much Aaron knew. "So I can go there. Disappear from her life. Really be dead this time. That's what she wants, for me to die." His voice growing faint. "And now a trial," he said, thinking out loud. "What this will do to her."

"I can't help that," Aaron said, answering something else.

Otto looked up. "You? No, you're the hound. You find the game. With your good nose. Then the others shoot." Another silence, the air in the room suddenly thick. "So why do you do it?" Otto said. "You never said before. What purpose does it serve? To make an example? For whom? The other Nazis? When you sniff them out? To see me hang? There's some satisfaction for you in that?"

Aaron shook his head. "You're just the excuse. To talk about it. So people remember."

"But they won't. You can't bring them back, you know. Max's son, any of them. Not even with a trial. That scale that's supposed to go like this?" He motioned with his hands, balancing. "When justice is served? It doesn't work." He raised one side higher than the other. "The victims are gone. In the air. No weight."

Aaron stared at him, not saying anything. What Max knew too. But kept going anyway. As if it matters, he said. We have to act as if it matters. Otherwise—

But Otto was talking again. "So, I'm just an excuse. At least the Israelis really hate me—there's some dignity in that. Not just be an excuse for this circus. And what do you think the verdict will be? That's what they'll remember. The circus, not what happened. Nobody wants to remember that."

Aaron took a breath. "But they should."

A wry half smile. "Another Max. A sentimentalist."

This time it was Jamie who wanted to meet in a park, the southeast corner of Las Heras, near the Diaz entrance. Dog walkers, mothers with strollers, kids in shorts heading for the soccer pitches, everyday Buenos Aires, except for the two men on the bench in the shade, Jamie with his hat still on.

"Now what?" Aaron said.

"Consider yourself back at work."

"What happened to my leave?"

"It's usually a week. If you're still in mourning, do it on your own time."

"And we had to come here to tell me this?"

"I said back at work, not back at the office."

"Meaning?"

"They want you to keep doing what you're doing. In fact, they're sending help."

"What I'm doing."

Jamie looked away, uneasy. "They heard about the tap. They asked me, I told them. I had to. I said I authorized it because I believed you." He turned to face Aaron. "That Schramm was alive."

"And?"

"No good deed goes unpunished. Now they believe it too. And they're all excited."

"I thought you said they weren't in the war crimes business," Aaron said, apprehensive, off balance.

"They're not."

Aaron waited. "I'll bite."

"They think it's a unique opportunity."

"To do what?"

"Recruit him." Jamie moved his hand, short-stopping him. "I know, not what you had in mind. All the Nuremberg stuff. But they're not interested in that. What they're interested in is him."

"As a unique opportunity."

"At first they just wanted me to close it down—the tap, you playing detective—and then they saw the beauty of the thing."

"Tell me."

"You've got a guy officially dead. Who wants to stay that way. That gives terrific leverage to someone who knows he's not. Expose him and he's nailed as a war criminal. Work with him and you've got someone with a perfect cover—he's who he says he is because he can't be someone who's dead."

"Jamie, he's Otto Schramm. We going to recruit Bormann next? You don't get better cover than that—he's been dead for years. We think. Mengele? Why not all of them?"

"Because they weren't close to Perón. Schramm was. Is," he said calmly, laying down a fan of winning cards.

"OK," Aaron said, "let's start over. Tell me how this works again." Trying to slow things down, his mind racing. Otto under Agency protection, invulnerable.

"Most of the big guys down here, when they get thrown out, they either get a bullet in the head or go live on a beach somewhere. Drink rum and fuck the local talent. What they don't do is come back. But Perón wants to."

"Does anybody want him back?"

"Plenty. The fan club never gave up, and the others—well, look who they've had since. So Perón looks better and better. Forget the economy almost tanked before they threw him out. Now he's the good old days."

"It's a long time to be away."

"But he keeps in touch. You have to hand it to him, he knows how to play the game. He's even got the Church thinking he looks good again. I thought when he left in '55 he'd be stuck in exile with Stroessner in Paraguay. End of story. But no, he goes to Panama next, then to Trujillo in the Dominican Republic."

"To the beach."

"But not drinking. Receiving delegations. Of Argentines. Even Trujillo thought he was a troublemaker. And then, the jackpot, Franco takes him in last year. Spain's still the mother country to a lot of people down here. It gives him credibility. So now he's like a fucking government in exile, plotting with this one, that one."

"And?"

"And we don't have anybody close to him, who can tell us who's coming to visit, who he's talking to. We're operating in the dark."

"Assuming he's worth bothering about in the first place."

"We have to assume that. Argentina's important and he's always hated us. He still thinks Germany should have won. Not to mention, he has a nasty habit of nationalizing companies when things get tough. We don't want that. We want him to stay in Madrid and enjoy the bullfights. We want to know what he's up to."

"Which is where Otto comes in."

Jamie nodded. "Perón knows him. As Schramm. Then as Braun. And now that Braun's dead, he'll know him as somebody else. Pick a name. A loyalist, someone Perón can trust. With messages. With—you name it. Really trust. Because he'll have this special leverage over him—he knows who he is."

"The same leverage we have."

Jamie nodded.

"So Otto's blackmailed twice."

"That's the beauty of it."

"If you think gossip about a tin-pot dictator is more important than trying a war criminal."

"That's one way of looking at it. But it's not the way we're looking at it, so do yourself a favor and make your peace with it. It saves time in the end."

"It's wrong, Jamie. We can't do this."

Jamie looked straight at him, the silence speaking for him.

"So we let him get away with it."

"He did get away with it. They're dead."

For a minute neither said anything.

"Twenty years now they're dead," Jamie said finally.

"But he's not."

"And what good is that to us? Or maybe they send him to Spandau. He can see Hess at breakfast. What good does that do? Five, ten years and he's sorry and he won't do it again? We know what he did. We knew in '45. This is about now. Nineteen sixty-two. What do we do with him now?"

"Make him one of us."

"We work with a lot of people. They're not all Eagle Scouts. You know that. This way we get something out of him. What do we get if he's sitting in Spandau?"

"I didn't come here to save his ass."

"But now you're here. And you're back at work. This is what we do, remember?"

Aaron looked at him, saying nothing.

"If it makes you feel any better, he's not exactly getting a free pass. You're on a leash like this, you're only as good as your last piece of information. It's always hanging over your head—what we know. Not a happy life if you're the worrying type. Kind of house arrest."

"Don't," Aaron said.

Jamie lowered his voice. "You need to get comfortable with this," he said slowly, serious. "You need to be on board."

"Because?"

"You'll be making the approach."

Aaron felt air rush out of him, as if he'd been punched.

"Me," he said, almost a whisper.

Jamie nodded. "You won't have to sell it very hard, but you don't want to take no for an answer either. So."

Several voices in his head, everything happening too fast. Throw a switch.

"That's assuming we find him," he said.

"I thought you said you were close."

"Close isn't there."

"No. That's why the reinforcements. They get here tomorrow, the day after. We don't want to take a chance on losing him, so you have a team now. Another tap if you want it. Martínez? You thought he might—"

Aaron shook his head. "There's no contact there."

"How do you know?"

Play it out. "Tap him, then. It can't hurt. You already have a file on him."

"As long as your arm." He paused. "You all right?"

"Just thinking. What if he says no? Won't do it?"

"What choice does he have?" He looked over. "But you'll make that clear to him. The options. That there aren't any." He leaned back on the bench. "It's the kind of thing that gets noticed at Langley. After that leave business. I mean, what the fuck was that? People don't take leave. But now you'll be flavor of the month. New asset in place, perfect leverage. Give Madrid something to do for a change. Nice." He looked over. "This could do a lot for you. Even put BA on the map for five minutes. So don't fuck it up."

"And if he gets away?"

"He won't. You'll make sure."

"I'm not a field guy."

"But you've got the direct lead. You've got her."

"What do I say to her?"

"You don't say anything. You just find him."

"And then he disappears?"

Jamie opened his hands.

"No. She has to know he's OK."

"All right. We'll arrange it. A little good-bye. Of course, we do this, she'll know. About you. She's not going to like that."

"No," Aaron said, a clench in his stomach. "Any of it."

"On the other hand, he'll be safer with us than he is here. Remind her of that. We don't want any trouble."

Aaron shook his head. "You don't know her."

"Not like you."

11

"WE'RE NOT HAVING THIS conversation."

"Some beginning," Nathan said, looking at him, eyes suddenly sharp.

They were walking down Córdoba, past the central synagogue, on their way to the safe house. It had rained earlier, a surprise storm, and wisps of steam were rising off the road as it dried out in the hot sun, mixing with the diesel fumes from the buses.

"I had a meeting yesterday."

Nathan waited.

"Someone from the Agency."

"I'm supposed to hear this?"

"What do you think?"

Nathan stopped for a second, turning to him. "I think you're crossing a line." He stared for another moment. "Are you sure you want to do that?"

"They want to use Otto as an asset. I make the approach. They're sending a team to find him. Once they get here, it's just a matter of time. We can't wait. We have to get him out."

"They don't know you found him?"

"Not yet. I'm close. But if he gets away—"

Nathan looked at him. "You're prepared to do this?"

"I came here to bring him to trial."

"Even if it means—"

"This is more important."

Nathan made a wry face. "They give you the heave, call me. I could always use someone—"

Aaron smiled. "I'm not that Jewish."

"It's not a question of how much." Nathan pointed his thumb back to the synagogue. "The Jews who built that thought they were German. But the Germans didn't think so."

"We can't wait for Thursday. If it is Thursday, the plane. And how do we get him to go now? We put him on the plane, he'd be kicking and screaming all the way to São Paulo."

"Unless we calm him down."

Aaron shook his head. "We need a private plane."

"Just like that. Who has that kind of money? Besides your people."

"They're not going to be my people much longer if we don't get him out of here. They find him and I'm—"

"On the wrong side," Nathan said, nodding. "Not where you want to be. We don't either. We can't get into a pissing match with the Agency. They're our friends. They want to protect a Nazi, we have to look the other way. Klaus Barbie, in Bolivia. We know he's there, but we can't touch him. Eichmann was different. He never worked for them. And guilty as hell, so who cares if the Israelis want a little payback? But not with our people." He turned to Aaron. "How do they want to use him?"

"Keep tabs on Perón. Be one of his buddies in exile."

Nathan thought for a moment. "He could do that. Not bad." Nodding, a professional.

"Not if he's in a courtroom in Frankfurt. So what do we do? Can you get the plane?"

"After I walk on water. Anyway, he'd have to have a passport if he flies. Even private. Which hasn't been delivered yet. We don't have enough time to make him a new one. When do your people get here?"

"Tomorrow, the next day. It won't take them long to pick up his trail. That's what they do. Plus, they'll be all over me, which cuts into guard duty."

"So we move him. If we can't fly him out, we'll have to drive him out," he said, working it through as they walked. "That means getting him up the river. First bridge to Uruguay isn't until Puerto Unzué. It's a hike, maybe a hundred and fifty miles, but they're not as fussy about passports on the bridge. Somebody sleeping it off in the back? Any papers. So the first step is move him to Tigre, up in the delta. We could get a boat there or go on, if we drive. Keep our options open."

"Uruguay," Aaron said, as if he were tracing his finger on a map.

"We can't operate here. Risk another run-in with Argentina. Tel Aviv orders."

"So fly him to Brazil from there? Or straight to Germany? Can you do that?"

Nathan kept walking for a minute, then took out a handkerchief and wiped his forehead. "Christ, it's hot." He turned to Aaron. "Not now. I'd like to, but sometimes things change in the field. There isn't time now to set up something like that. We're in a bind. In a few days, whoever's helping him here knows what's happened and starts pushing alarm buttons. And we have to guess they have some powerful people they can call, people you don't want after you. Then your people get here and start pushing their own buttons and my hands are tied because that's the way it is, we're not going to take on the Agency. And you need to deny knowing about any of this. Which is why we're not having this conversation, remember?" He stopped. "There's not enough time. It's complicated, getting someone out, getting him to Germany. And now who's going to help? I told you in Hamburg, sometimes you have to make other choices."

Aaron slowed as they turned in to their street, a vise clamping around him, squeezing.

"You're going to kill him. That's why you want him out of Argentina. They're sensitive, since Eichmann. So, Uruguay. You're going to kill him there."

"What would you do? You wanted to find him. You did. Now what do we do with him? What's the most useful thing?"

"That's what he said, about the children. Useful deaths."

"You tell me. What? He starts eavesdropping for the CIA, he doesn't pay at all. Not even prison time. A nice life. And

Otto Schramm stays dead. Instead, now his body's found. And identified—we make sure. The whole story comes out, everything Fritz has, how Otto did it, how he managed to hide. Everything you wanted him to say on the stand."

"Not everything," Aaron said quietly. "He won't answer for what he did."

"He'll answer to us." He met Aaron's eyes. "Look, we still get the story out. Who helped him, who helped the others. Expose them, finally. And this—what?—execution. Who did it? Nobody knows, but everybody can guess. A powerful message, an execution. It tells the others, no one's safe, we're still coming for you. So maybe Mengele gets nervous a little. The people who helped Otto. Even Barbie begins to worry. Who do they target next?" He stopped. "It's a powerful message."

"That's not what Max wanted."

"It's what we have. There's no glass box waiting this time. You take the best you can get."

"Just bump him off. Otto Schramm."

"What's the punishment for Auschwitz? What would fit? Hang someone six million times?" His voice almost a growl.

"Just once. In public."

Nathan waved his hand. "An auto-da-fé. Except we do the burning."

They started walking again.

"How are you going to—?" Aaron said.

"I don't know yet. And you don't want to know. You're as surprised as anyone when you hear. But there won't be any mistake what it is. Not an accident."

"And Fritz has his story."

"With a few cuts. People who aren't in it anymore. You, for instance."

"And you."

"You want to leave a little mystery. But Otto—it'll all be there. All his crimes. Corroborated by Max's files. Fritz can work around a few things and still have the story. Maybe he's getting Schramm to tell him some details right now." He cocked his head toward the next block. "He's good at that."

"He's there?"

"It's his shift."

More planning, working them in odd shifts, so Otto never knew whom to expect. Keep two steps ahead. Planning Fritz's story. Even planning to use Max's files. Aaron's files now. Had Nathan already spoken to Elena, busy back in Hamburg copying? He felt the air go out of him again. He stopped.

"You were always going to kill him. That was the plan."

Nathan looked away, uncomfortable.

"Nathan."

"You're like all of them. You want to hunt, but not to kill. What do you think happens at the end?"

"Were you ever going to fly him back? Tell me."

Nathan mopped his forehead again, waiting a minute.

"I told you in Hamburg. I don't have the resources."

"Just the resources for this."

"We don't look for these guys—we can't afford it. People come to us. With information. Most of the time, it's 'I saw Bormann,' some nonsense. But Max. Max you listen to. And then

Fritz. So now it's serious. We have a chance to catch him. Otto Schramm. And you were the way."

"So you lied to me. To get Otto."

"And what did you do? With her?" He looked up. "I'm not blaming you," he said quickly. "You do what you have to do. And it worked. We have him."

"There was never going to be a trial."

"Would it make Israel safer? Would it make the Arabs hate us less? It's a question of priorities."

"No. What's right."

"What's right. For the Jews? You want to help? Plant a tree in a kibbutz. Twenty dollars. You'll feel better and they'll get a little shade." He stopped. "I'm sorry." He wiped his forehead again. "This heat. I know you mean it for the best. I listen to you, I can hear Max. What else matters? Make things right. Hunt them down. And then after? Get someone like me to end it." He held up his hands. "Not so clean. But this is how it ends."

"With my help," Aaron said, suddenly back in the hospital room, the echo of Max's scratchy voice. He made me complicit.

Nathan just looked at him, not sure how to take this.

"I could go back to the Agency," Aaron said.

"And tell them the truth? That you've been holding out?" He paused. "What has changed for you? You don't think he deserves this? Why? Now you talk a little and he's a sad old man? There were sad old men on the selection line." A breath. "He's Otto Schramm. What other ending can there be?"

Aaron looked down, suddenly seeing the scene, as vivid as film, a building site somewhere outside a city, deserted, Otto being dragged, struggling, a punch thrown, his body flung against a wall, face bloody from before, now holding his hands out as the bullets are fired, the shocked expression, slumping down to the floor, the freshly poured concrete stained with blood, more bullets to make sure, a final kick, the body awkward, twisted, the way it would look in police photos when the half-built house became a crime scene, with flashbulbs and measuring tape and someone covering his face with a sheet.

"It's murder," he said.

"No, justice," Nathan said, then checked his watch. "We don't have time to split hairs. Can you relieve Fritz? I'll arrange for the car with Ari." He unlocked the downstairs door.

"Do you think he believes we've got the building surrounded?"

Nathan shook his head, starting up the stairs. "He's not stupid. You see the same people all the time, you think, so where are the others? But I don't think he cares. He's not going anywhere." He glanced back at Aaron. "He doesn't know he has a job offer in Madrid."

He stopped suddenly on the stairs, hand outstretched, a signal for quiet. Aaron looked over his shoulder to the landing. Nothing. Nathan reached into his pocket, still quiet, pulling out the gun, and took a step, his body tense, listening. Aaron followed, now seeing the door halfway open. Nathan crept along the side of the landing, then stood back to the wall next to the open door, a policeman's move. Then a creak as he pushed the door gently, opening it wider, moving his head to get a better view, then flinging himself into the doorway, gun held out, ready to fire.

"Fritz," he called out.

More silence. Nathan motioned with his hand for Aaron to cover the other side of the door.

"Gun," he whispered, nodding to Aaron's pocket.

Another push, the door fully open now, a sharp intake of breath as Nathan looked across the room. Fritz was splayed on the couch, head back, eyes still open, bulging, some grotesque stage effect. His clothes were twisted on him, not his usual untucked carelessness, but gone through, pockets turned inside out, his thick legs stretched out stiffly to the coffee table he had kicked over.

"Christ," Nathan said, almost a hiss, then followed training procedures, moving around the room with his gun still out, back to the wall, pushing the bathroom door open, then checking the kitchen area, the bedroom, before he was sure the apartment was empty.

Aaron stared down at Fritz, the gray skin of the dead. Not every death is the same. He could still see the surprise of it in Fritz's face, the panic as the air ran out, a big man not used to losing a fight, astonished at his own death, mouth open.

"His neck," Aaron said.

A series of round bruises, purple with blood that had welled up to the surface.

Nathan looked around the floor, then spotted the flung handcuffs, open now but still paired by the metal chain. He picked them up, then held the chain near Fritz's neck, matching the links to the bruises.

"He used these," Nathan said. "From behind. Bastard probably asked for the bathroom. Goes behind the couch. Then gets the key out of Fritz's pocket. After he was finished."

Reconstructing, something he'd seen in a police movie as assistants put evidence in bags. Aaron barely heard it, his mind numb.

"Fritz," he said, in the ambulance again with Max, the hospital, Ohlsdorf.

"He should have been more careful," Nathan said, his voice distant.

Aaron looked up. "He was careful."

"We needed two people."

Aaron felt the side of Fritz's neck, as if there might still be a pulse, the skin already cool.

"Close his eyes," Nathan said, squeamish.

Aaron ran his hand down Fritz's face, putting him to sleep. My fault, he thought, not even sure how. The story of a lifetime. Headlines. What drowning must feel like, gasping for life, Otto pulling the chain with the strength of the desperate, listening to him gargle, make noises, his feet kicking, held in place by the tight chain. Then finally the quiet. Otto killing again. Hadn't the others been strangled too, climbing over each other to get out of the locked chamber, away from the gas? Aaron reached down and patted Fritz's pockets, feeling for any bulk, then looked up at Nathan.

"Otto took his gun."

"How long, do you think, is he dead? Do you know about these things?"

Aaron shook his head. When did rigor mortis set in, the

blood pool downwards, drawn by gravity, all those signs he'd read about.

"An hour?" Nathan said. "Two? So whatever, a head start. To where, though? We should cover him."

Aaron looked at Fritz again, then took an afghan off the couch and draped it over the body.

"I'll get Goldfarb to move him somewhere. He knows how to do these things."

"He can't just disappear. What about his wife? In Germany." What was she called? Ilse.

"Maybe later. Depending on how we tell the story. For now, crime is a serious problem. A risk in coming here."

"So she may never know."

"What, that he was killed by a Nazi? Not a thief? What's the difference? He's dead." He avoided Aaron's look, moving over to the window. "So where is he?" he said, peering out, as if Otto might appear at the corner.

"Anywhere. If he's had an hour he could take a taxi to the airport. The next plane out."

"No passport."

"Then domestic. Go to Mendoza. Regroup. He could be anywhere."

"No, it's not useful to think like this. Anywhere. He doesn't think that way. Where would he be safe?" He looked over at Aaron. "Who would take him in?"

Aaron met his eye. "He wouldn't go to her. He keeps her out of it."

"But he might. At such a moment."

"It's the first place anyone would look."

"Including us. Where else? Not Dr. Ortiz's In his mind, now Israeli territory."

"A hotel somewhere. He could call for help. Anywhere."

Nathan made a face, annoyed. "Not anywhere. Somewhere. All right. I'll get Goldfarb and we'll clean up here." He glanced at the body, then back at Aaron. "We're down a man now. You'll have to check out her place."

"He's not there. She's not part of this. A messenger."

"You want to keep her out of the story, that's your business." Another look at Fritz. "You get to write it now. But you can't change who she is."

Aaron said nothing.

"If he's there, find a phone somewhere and call. If he's not, meet back at Goldfarb's." He moved to the door. "Leave separately, just in case. Five minutes. You all right?"

Aaron nodded.

A last look back at Fritz. "I'm sorry. These things happen," Nathan said, his voice flat.

"He should have been more careful," Aaron said, matching the tone, an echo from before, but Nathan missed it, already on his way out.

When he was gone, the room seemed utterly still, a mausoleum quiet. Aaron looked down at Fritz's draped body, then leaned over to pull back the afghan from his face. Not sleeping. Dead. These things happen. But they weren't supposed to, hadn't even been imagined when Aaron met him at the Alsterpavillon with a newspaper under his arm. How many more? And too late now to stop, with Otto loose, wondering when his luck would run out, when they'd tire him, panting in some hole, finally caught.

But running where? Who knew he was alive? Bildener? Who identified the body and now had to keep his distance, so careful he had Hanna get the visa. Corrupt Martínez? Probably back in São Paulo, arranging more visas. Monsignor Rosas, hiding him again in the folds of his cassock? Who else? He heard Nathan's blunt, gravelly voice. You can't change who she is. The faithful messenger, twice a week, wishing he were elsewhere, but showing up for her session. Who else would he turn to? Blood.

He caught a taxi on Montevideo and took it up the long hill to Recoleta, getting out at the Alvear, then walking the last block to the park. The day had turned cloudy again, an early dusk, so there were a few lights on in the building, but her windows were dark. He looked at his watch. She'd be home soon from wherever she was. A shower and a change for dinner, new jewelry, the usual. Ready to go to Bariloche next week, when she'd be free. One more meeting, then getting him on the plane. Or would she say good-bye at Ortiz's, handing him the ticket, all checked in?

Another light came on, not hers. Maybe Otto was already here, sitting in the dark, waiting. Except he wasn't. Trust your instinct. The first place anyone would look. A man who'd been hiding. He'd want to move fast. No long drives up to the delta. Get out. Which meant a plane. There were two airports. Ezeiza, where Ari would look, but old Newberry, the Aeroparque, was closer in, a quick taxi. But he'd still need a passport. And Hanna wouldn't come until Thursday, his lifeline. Aaron stopped. The only one? Hanna couldn't go to the airport, not with a dead man. They were too careful for that. She'd wait for word that he'd got off safely, but someone else would give him the passport, not Thursday, maybe even now, why he'd chanced an escape, killed for it. Maybe it was already too late. Where was she?

And then, as if thinking about her had conjured her into being, she was at the corner, the familiar walk, not hurrying, not meeting anybody, lost in thought. About Otto, almost gone? About him, a trip to the mountains? He sat up, the whole street alive with her, and moved down the bench, deeper into the shade. She was wearing a skirt and silk blouse, pearls, the way she had looked when they first met at the Alvear, and for a second he was there again, the swish of nylon as she crossed her legs, the ironic look, not sure what he wanted, the light behind her on her hair, before anything had happened between them. Even now, watching her, hiding, he felt an unexpected light-headedness, happy to see her, wishing they could talk. No, wishing they could start over, back at the Alvear, Jamie introducing them, this time without Otto, without anybody, just them. And then she was through the door.

He waited until the light snapped on, then waited a few minutes more. If Otto was really there, surprise or not, she'd draw the blinds, keep him out of sight. She'd ask about the cut on his head, what happened. Would he tell her about Fritz? Then feverish planning, what to do, still behind closed blinds. But they stayed open. She passed by the window, not looking out, unconcerned, alone.

Where would he go? He lived in Villa Freud under siege. His lifeline came to him, twice a week, regular as a clock. Then an early dinner in the café on Plaza Güemes, still invisible under his Panama hat. And so to bed. But what about the other days? Aaron tried to remember Ari's surveillance report. A rambling walk through Palermo, but that had been an exception. The café. Home. Except when he went to the other café, up in Recoleta. Always the same days, a routine? A tourist café near the cemetery, where no one would notice an early diner. Another lifeline? Why there and nowhere else? He tried to picture the report. An Italian restaurant, like half the restaurants in Buenos Aires. A predictable name. Café Roma? No, Napoli. Probably one of the restaurants past the Café La Biela, lining the narrow park across from the cemetery. Just around the corner, in fact, a few blocks away. If today was the regular day. He checked his watch again. The cemetery would be closing soon, visitors spilling across the strip of park to the cafés, where a man was having an early dinner. Alone, the surveillance report had said. The same café.

Aaron got up, passing under the low branches of the tree, and headed down the street, the white basilica gleaming on his right. Café Napoli. If this was the right day. His other lifeline. No Panama hat this time. That had been left behind in the rush out of Ortiz's office. Clothes rumpled after the safe house. A bandage on his forehead. Not a leisurely meal—impossible when you're this alert, watching everything. Maybe just a glass of wine, something to hold the table, until somebody turned up with an envelope.

By the time he reached La Biela, the image was so fixed in his mind, details filled in, that he hung back at the corner, trying to work out the best approach. The minute Otto saw him, he'd bolt, another back-door exit. Stay away from the restaurant door. Aaron walked toward the café, keeping to the edge of the park. A block of restaurants, some with tables on the sidewalk, awnings down against the late sun. The Napoli seemed a cut above the others, plates rather than pizza, a waiter in a long white apron. Aaron walked closer, still in shadow. He had imagined Otto, back to the wall, just in from the door, but that table was empty. A few people, none of them Otto, a family outside eating gelato, a man in an open-neck shirt reading a newspaper, sipping espresso. No Otto, the restaurant scene a trick of his imagination. Or maybe he'd already been here. No, too early. He'd still be on his way, if he was coming.

Aaron took a table at the next café, partly hidden by trees. He ordered a coffee and waited. Think how to do it. Otto was armed, had just killed someone. Nothing to lose. So why come here? Not for dinner. To meet someone. He looked again at the man with the newspaper, a plainer version of Moreno, Hanna's escort, too soft to be sinister, just another idle *porteño*. The family eating gelato left. Behind him, a bell rang in the church, marking the hour. His table took in the approach to the Napoli from both directions. But no one came.

He almost missed him because of the walk. He'd been looking for the stroll, that hint of swagger, the old Otto, so at first he didn't take in the man hurrying up the rise from Vicente López. Disheveled, slightly out of breath, as if he were running late for an appointment. No hat, hair combed back with his fingers and now loose on the sides. The man with the newspaper looked up, surprised, and then stood, intercepting him. A conversation

Aaron couldn't hear, presumably what happened, what's wrong? A hand on Otto's upper arm. Sit. But Otto was moving, on the run, touching the man's elbow to follow him. Aaron had expected a meeting, even a drink, something changing hands, time to call Nathan, and now he saw that he would lose him again, Otto in motion, not stopping.

He stood up, throwing some pesos on the table, and put his hand in his jacket pocket, clutching the gun, pointing it so Otto would feel it when it pushed up against him. In motion now too, not thinking, coming up behind. Let Otto feel the gun at his back, come quietly, no scene. But the man with the newspaper saw him coming, too fast, and made a noise, a grunt of alarm, and Otto whirled around, facing him before he got there, both of them startled for a second, eyes locked on each other, the kill. Aaron kept coming, expecting Otto to run. Instead, a deeper instinct, he raised his hands and pushed Aaron back, knocking him down, crashing against a table as he fell, winded. People around them looked. Aaron felt a throb of pain where his elbow had hit the ground, and tried to pick himself up, staggering, clumsy, people rushing over to help while Otto and the other man ran across the park. Getting away.

Aaron gave a final push up, waving his helpers aside, and ran after him. Keep him in sight. Otto had stopped, blocked by a wave of people coming out of the cemetery, closing time, and now had to wade through them, people giving way to his pushing, some urgent hurry. The man with the newspaper was following, and for a second it looked as if one were chasing the other, so that someone tried to hold him back. An argument in Spanish, Aaron still plowing through the crowd. Otto turned around to look and, spotting him, went faster, streaking through the Doric columns of the portico, then the tall wrought iron gates. A guard, annoyed, called after him, "*Los muertos todavía estarán aquí mañana*," then, when the other man followed, "*Cerrado! Cerrado!*"

Aaron reached the gates just as the guard turned to shepherd out the last straggling visitors. "*Cerrado!*" But he was inside now, racing down the avenue to the plaza, out of sight, swallowed up in the quiet necropolis.

12

AARON STOPPED FOR A second, listening for running, any footsteps, but the air was suddenly filled with the guard's warning buzzer and then a shout in Spanish, evidently beginning a last sweep to empty the grounds. Aaron stepped back behind a tomb, out of sight. Which way had they gone? Maybe just around the corner, in one of the plaza streets, or deeper in, the maze of narrow alleys. But there was only one exit, back through the wrought iron gates. Wait here.

The guard was now using a police megaphone to say the cemetery was closing. Aaron followed the sound, moving in a circle left to right, and then jumped when it seemed to be coming from behind him, the odd acoustics creating echoes. He darted to the next tomb, hidden now from behind, a white stone Virgin Mary looking down from the roof. One more announcement from the guard and then he was shuffling toward the gates, finished. Where was Otto? He heard the clanging sound of the gates closing. No doubt a large, ornamental key. Did the guard stay the night, cozy in some station near the gates, or were the dead left to sleep? As the hill sloped down to Vicente López, the walls got higher and higher, impossible to climb. Any valuables in the mausoleums must have long since been picked over, like Egyptian tombs. Nothing to steal, nothing to protect. They'd be on their own, locked in.

It was then he felt the prickling at the back of his neck. What Otto wanted. All along, from the beginning, Aaron had imagined only one end—a newspaper exposé, a trial. Now he saw that there were two. He might die. Here. Otto wouldn't shoot to wound. Before the gates opened again, one of them would be dead. He took a breath, looking around. And Otto wasn't alone. He saw himself cornered in one of the alleys at the other end, a cul-de-sac, lined with granite tombs, no side passage to dart into, a shooting gallery. Let them come to him, to the center avenues with space between the tombs, somewhere to duck if you were dodging bullets.

The faint scrape of a shoe. He froze, trying to place the sound. With two they could be methodical, taking each end of a street, making sure it was clear, one after the other, until finally there was only the hiding place left. He had to keep moving. He ducked and ran across the avenue to a diagonal street, cutting back down toward the Junin side, crouching behind a tomb, waiting. Silence. And then, like a fluttering bird, a shadow flickered in the street, somebody coming with the sun behind him. Not closing in, heading west. They didn't know where he was. He looked around. A tomb like a small bank vault, a statue inside, a vase for flowers, all of it dusty, unattended, and padlocked. He had noticed that before, the padlocks, which made the mausoleums impossible hiding places. The maintenance sheds were locked too. He had to stay outside, hugging the backs of the stone tombs, the stacked bags of sand at the repair sites.

More footsteps. Aaron raised his head, adjusting some internal antenna, feeling the blood pulsing in his ears. If this were a forest, he'd be listening for a twig to snap, the click of a gun lock, but here there seemed no sound at all, the city traffic a faint hum beyond the high walls, distant. Nothing to smell, just dust and heated stone, the occasional dying flower. Only sight mattered, picking out any movement, a change in the light, everything sharp and clear, survival vision.

At the end of the street, a few alleys down, Otto suddenly came into view, following the other man, but before Aaron could raise his gun, he was gone. Aaron tried to remember the map of the cemetery from his earlier visit, the Haussmann angles, the labyrinth at the west end, but it was guesswork. Now that Otto had passed, he could retreat back to the gate, try to raise some alarm, get out. But that wasn't what they were doing here. And Otto would move faster than the guard, trapping him. The problem was that there were two of them. No matter what, he needed to take out the other one, wound him, to level the odds. But could he do it? Everyone at the Agency had been trained to handle a gun, but he'd never shot anyone, had never hunted anything. Still, what choice was there? He thought of Fritz, the necklace of purple bruises around his neck.

He moved out from behind the tomb, still crouching, and

made his way to the next street, parallel to Otto's. It was easier to hear the footsteps now, shoe leather on pavement, and he followed behind the sounds. He had thought Otto and the other man would split up, fan out through the streets, but they seemed to be moving together, careful as they passed down a block of tombs, then scurrying across when they reached an intersection. He imagined them all from above, figures moving through a hedge maze, unable to see each other. A whisper, the other two consulting. Aaron came to a cross street and peeked around the corner, then jumped back, some flash of movement in the corner of his eye. He waited, then looked again. Not Otto, a shadow, another Mary looking down, this one with a halo. A few other shadows, urns and saints and little domes, all reflecting down on the street. Aaron tiptoed across, huddling against the base of a two-story tomb rising to a circle of columns. The Ortiz family, presumably not the doctor's. He listened. Still heading toward the cul-de-sacs, hoping to seal him off. Another extravagant tomb with bronze doors. A broader street now, darting across, closing in.

He heard the shot before he felt the slap against his upper arm, pushing him back against the wall. But no bullet, a miss, just the force of it enough to make him whirl backward. He gulped some air, panting. He'd been running, a moving target, or he'd be lying in the alley now, shoulder burning, blood welling up. Not tracking them, their prey. They knew where he was. Move. He raced back across the street, away from the cul-de-sacs. Another shot, after him, as loud as an explosion. Wouldn't the guard hear? Unless he wasn't there. People in the street? But he could barely hear the traffic. Outside the walls it might simply be a distant backfiring. He retraced his path, running hard, no longer worried about making noise, then veered off toward the avenues, the trees in the distance. He could hear them running behind him. A zigzag now, not staying in any street long enough to give them another shot. Head for the gates, get help somehow. But there were two of them. If he could only see the plan of the place, which streets led where, not run blind. He flattened himself against another bronze doorway, listening for them. Still running. Closer? The feet hard on the pavement.

He ran into the next street. More elaborate than the last, miniature churches with crosses, baroque statues, big enough to hide in, but every door locked, one even surrounded by a wrought iron fence. Footsteps louder. He was midway up the block, an easy target if one of them reached the corner. He looked to his side. A mausoleum with wedding cake setbacks. He climbed onto the first level, almost leaping, feeling a sharp ache in his shoulder, another near his elbow, still tender from the fall at the café. Never mind. Go. Another level, then one more climb onto the roof, finally above the maze, looking down, a sniper's advantage. He looked to either side. If it came to it, he could jump from one roof to the other, the tombs nearly abutting, a cat burglar. Until the impassable dome a few tombs down.

He looked down into the street. At the far end, the other man was walking in a crouch, signaling to Otto behind him, neither of them looking up. Aaron ducked, his foot slipping backward, dislodging a loose tile. He grabbed it at the edge, just before it could slip away, gripping it. He looked around. The whole roof was a mess, tiles battered and loose, so overdue for repair that it might not hold his weight. He looked over to the next tomb. A flat roof with an angel jutting out over the street, like a ship's prow.

He put the tile back gently and started for the edge, trying not to dislodge another one. One step over to the next roof. Now the other leg. He stopped. Someone below in the street. No, his shadow, moving with him. Something they'd see. Given away by the sun. He looked around the open roof, no cover, then down in the street again. His shadow still there, closer now to the other one, the angel spreading her wings. His guardian angel, the only shadow Otto would see. If she could hold him. The angel was lifting a figure in swirling robes, rising to the roof, maybe some version of the Assumption or just the tomb's occupant being taken to heaven. Real stone or just plaster? Maybe as neglected and fragile as the tile on the next tomb. Below, Otto and the other man were near the corner. Aaron lunged for the angel and lay down on its uncarved back, his arms extending along the wings, ready for flight. No creaks, no crumbling plaster, solid stone. He looked down. One shadow, wings stretched, and two men creeping along the walls. Aaron took a breath, holding it.

They were almost past his tomb when the tile slid down from the next roof, smashing on the ground, a startling noise, followed by a feral cat, who jumped after it and with a screech went streaking down the street. A nervous exhaling, embarrassed by their own shock, then a look up to see where the cat had come from, the unnoticed roofscape. Now. Aaron moved the gun to the edge of the wing, a clear aim at the man's shoulder, and fired. A deafening sound, close up, the man jerking back away from it, like the cat, only a second, but long enough for the bullet to catch him full in the throat instead. A spurt of blood. He fell over backward, a crunch as he hit the pavement, blood still gushing. Aaron looked down, stunned. Not a shooting game, real, blood in the street, and then the jerking stopped, everything. And Otto still there, crouching, ready to shoot back.

Aaron swept his hand left, aiming for Otto's leg, and fired again. A hit, throwing Otto back against the wall with a scream of pain or surprise, clutching his side, his gun clattering as it fell. But how many seconds before he could pick it up? Aaron leaped across to the tiles, dislodging a few more, jumping down to the next level, then the street, his mind not registering anything but the distance to Otto, the second it would take before he could reach down for the gun. A sprint, what felt like his whole body in the air, then shoving Otto back against the wall, his face wincing in pain, Aaron's gun at his chest.

"Leave it."

Both of them breathing fast, staring at each other. Then, keeping his gun aimed, Aaron bent down and picked up Otto's.

"Finish it," Otto said, breath still ragged, head drooping.

"Not yet."

Another moment, adjusting, his mind darting in several directions. The other man dead. But no sounds of footsteps running toward them. Still on their own. Otto groaned, looking down at his side, seeping blood. No hope of getting out through the gates now, visitors accidentally locked in. Some other way.

"Don't move. I mean it."

Aaron walked over to the other man and crouched down, one eye on Otto, and went through his pockets.

"Don't bother," Otto said, almost a taunt. "He didn't have a—"

Aaron stopped for a second, a twisting in his stomach. In cold blood.

"Who is he?"

"Nobody. A messenger."

Aaron finished rifling the pockets, pulling out an envelope. "Your ticket?" He glanced inside. "Let me guess. Herr Bildener?"

"Just finish it," Otto said, weary.

Aaron put the ticket in his pocket and looked down at the man, the torn hole in his neck. "Nobody," he said, Otto's tone. "Anybody going to miss him?"

"I don't know. We just meet at the café." He looked over. "He wasn't armed." An accusation, using it.

"But you were. With Fritz's gun," he said, holding it up.

"So now you have both. What are you going to do?" Not really curious, poking him.

What? Aaron looked around, as if an idea might be hanging in the air.

"Kill me? Go ahead. No. Max's boy," he said, an edge of contempt. "You can't."

"I won't have to," Aaron said, emptying the bullets out of his gun and flinging them up over the tiled roof.

"What are you doing?"

"In case you get any ideas. It's a murder weapon now. The bullet will match exactly. I'll leave the gun with you so the police will know who used it. Make it easy for them. Unless you bleed out during the night. That doesn't look good." He nodded toward the wound.

"Don't leave me here," Otto said, blurting it out, unguarded, suddenly childlike. "Not here."

"We can't walk out the door now, not after this," Aaron said, looking toward the dead man. "And I don't think you're in any shape to go over the walls. So—"

"Don't," Otto said, sliding down the wall, slumping on the ground.

Aaron raised the gun. "I said don't move."

"I'm dizzy. I don't feel well."

"That's not good. It's a long night."

Otto looked at him for a minute, just breathing. "And you? You can't let them see you either."

"No. I'll have to climb out."

Otto shook his head. "Too high. You notice, no broken glass on the top. They don't need it. Nobody can get up that high. You climb out, it's too long a drop. You'd break your legs."

"Not by the entrance. Only after you go down the hill. But nobody's going to break in by the entrance. You'd have the guard all over you. Too many people. But getting out? Nobody's inside to notice. And once you're over, it's a quick drop. Maybe somebody sees you, maybe they don't. It's a chance."

Otto looked down for a moment, thinking this through. "If you leave me here, it's the same as putting a bullet in my head." He nodded toward the body. "Like him." He moved his hand away from his side to check the blood.

"And you think I wouldn't want that on my conscience?" Aaron shook his head. "It would be like squashing a bug."

"Then why don't you do it?" Otto said, voice weaker, not

really expecting an answer. He closed his eyes, a minute's rest, face haggard.

Aaron looked up and down the street, an unexpected panic. One dead man, another fading. Too heavy to move if he was unconscious. Aaron would have to leave him, the end of it. And how long before they were found? Unless they were hidden. Where? He caught the irony—a cemetery with nowhere to put a dead man. But Otto wasn't dead, couldn't be. That was the point. He had to get him out. There'd been some tarp covers at one of the repair sites. He could put the other man there, at least buy time. But Otto would have to help, not try to turn on him. Use anything. Jamie's voice: You make the approach. Why not a convenient lie? Meanwhile, the shadows were lengthening in the street, the sun dropping. How long did they have? Recoleta in the dark, listening for rustlings, ghosts.

"Because we'd rather have you alive," he said, his Agency voice, only a minute later, all the rest of it a flash through his mind.

"Israelis? Another glass box and then you kill me. Do it now."

"I'm not Israeli. I don't work for them. I let them find you, that's all."

Otto looked over at him, weighing every part of this.

"Why?"

"To put you on the front page. Then we had a better idea. Since you're already dead. Erich Kruger goes to Brazil," he said, tapping the pocket with the envelope. "Then flies on to Madrid. A new life. With old friends. Some of your oldest friends. Happy to see you again. Exile being what it is. And you're happy to see them. Be of assistance, any way you can. And then talk to us about all the happy things you're doing."

Otto said nothing for a moment. "You're lying. But why?"

"Then don't do it. I didn't say it was my idea. I'd rather see you dead. But I don't run the Agency."

"Spy for you? Why would I do that?"

"Consider your options."

"And that's why you lock me in that place. In handcuffs."

Aaron nodded. "The Israelis. They can be a little heavy-handed. Especially with people like you. But here we are. And it's getting late."

"And I'm supposed to believe this? Someone who shoots me?" He glanced down at his side.

"After you missed."

Otto took this in, then grunted.

"We need to move him. We can't let him be found. Not yet. We need time." He paused. "Unless you're planning to spend the night."

Otto looked up, still uneasy.

"Or I get us out of here."

"I'm supposed to trust you."

Aaron shrugged. "That cuts two ways. But I have this," he said, waving the gun. "I'm not Fritz. I won't turn my back. Even for a second. I saw what you did to him. I didn't know you still had the strength. Big man. He must have—"

"*Dummkopf*."

"We can go back to the original plan if you like. Otto Schramm exposed. You don't have to be alive for that story. You can stay here and bleed out. Messy for the others. Bildener. Martínez. The police in Mar del Plata. And Hanna."

Otto looked up. "She had nothing to do with it. She didn't know."

"Or Otto Schramm died a few years ago. Everybody says so. And Erich Kruger's been a great help to us."

"Huh. Your lackey."

"I don't like it either. I think you should hang. But I'm just a messenger. Like him." He pointed to the body. "Putting a package on a plane."

"I don't believe you. It's a trap."

Aaron looked around. "And what's this? You want out, it's a chance you'll have to take."

"*Hola! Hola! El cementerio está cerrado!*" The guard, a few streets away.

Otto looked up, then at Aaron, neither of them moving. Drawn by the noise or just making rounds?

"*El cementerio está cerrado!*" No closer, a touch of bravado, another way of asking, Is anyone here? Then more Spanish, lower pitched, talking to himself. Aaron's eyes darted to the body, then to Otto, both of them staring at each other, waiting for a move. One shout and the guard would have to respond, look for whoever was there. Aaron took in the street again—a body, a gun, no time to move either, a crime scene. What explanation could there be? If the guard moved deeper into the cemetery, turned in to their street, they'd have to kill him. Another murder. He looked at Otto, their eyes meeting. One shout. No sound now, shallow breathing, listening for footsteps. A chance you'll have to take. If he took it. Aaron gripped the gun, waiting.

"*Alguien?*" The guard's voice again, a hollow appeal, just going through the motions, then the murmur again, grumbling to himself, the sounds getting fainter, heading back to the gate. Another look at Otto, his last chance to give them away. Otto looked back, the silence itself an agreement, both of them in it now.

Aaron waited a few more minutes.

"So," he said, then looked away, everything already said. "Help me move him."

At first they tried to carry the body by its hands and feet, but the weight was too much for Otto, weakened by the bullet.

"Wrap his head," he said, and then when Aaron looked puzzled, "For the blood. Use the jacket."

Aaron struggled getting it off, then cradled the man's head and wound the jacket around it. They each took a foot, Otto straining, and began to drag the body down the street. There was still a stain of blood on the pavement where he'd been shot, but no trail out, as if the angel had lifted him up too. Aaron guided them to the repair site near the Junin wall, the body making a scraping noise with each yank, another sound to unnerve the guard, some spirit movement among the tombs. Shadows longer now, dark enough for him to need a flashlight if he came back, a warning.

There was a ladder at the building site, tall enough to get a man to the roof of the tomb but not over the cemetery wall, at least twice Aaron's height. No steps or protruding handholds, smooth stucco.

"Now what?" Otto said.

"First, deal with him."

He pulled the tarp back. Stacks of bricks, half of them gone. He moved the remaining stacks closer together, creating a space for the body, then nodded to the man's feet.

"Can you do it? One heave. On three."

Otto winced, but the man went up and over, falling on the other side of the bricks. Aaron covered him with the tarp, then took out the empty gun and wiped it, placing it dangling from the man's hand.

"Nobody's going to believe that," Otto said.

"It'll buy us some time." He looked over. "The other one's still loaded."

Otto ignored this, placing the ladder against the wall. "It's not tall enough."

"Not here. There's a place closer to the gate. I was hiding there while you and— What's his name?"

"Julio. Why?"

"I just wanted to know." Somebody. "It's somewhere along here."

"It'll be getting dark soon."

And then, just as he said it, streetlights went on, the timing so quirky and unexpected that Otto almost smiled, a face Aaron hadn't seen before. The lamps were for pedestrians outside, not the dead inside, but enough of their glow came over the wall to make it easier to see.

"Like a Roman temple," Aaron said, still trying to spot it, the search now something they were doing together, a way out.

The side alley that ended at the wall was narrow, all its tombs looking oversized for the space. More bank vaults, a chapel with an obelisk, and then the temple at the end against the wall, just as he'd remembered. Dusty, under repair, but rising in setbacks, each stage wide enough to hold the ladder. The last platform put them halfway up the wall. Aaron wedged the ladder against the temple and started climbing.

"Hold it steady," he said.

Otto gripped it with one hand, the other still at his side.

"You OK?"

Otto nodded.

When his hands reached the last rung, Aaron realized he would now have to hold them flat against the wall as his feet took the last few steps up. Nothing to hold on to. Would he be high enough to reach over the top? He looked down at Otto holding the ladder, face upturned, following the last steps, no support, no mat, a trapeze act. All Otto would have to do now was shake the ladder, make him lose his footing, a sudden fall, hands trying to hold on to something as he plunged to the ground. No effort at all, not the strength he'd needed to choke Fritz. Just a shake. But then how would he get out? A dash to the gate, some story. But what story? Two bodies to explain. He took another step.

His hands touched the edge of the rounded top. He'd been afraid of coming up short—the ladder was too unsteady to use as a springboard, taking the last few feet in a jump. He'd have to pull himself up. He slid his hands farther over the rim. Wider than he'd expected. A last step, top of the ladder. His arms reached across the wall, almost at the other rim. One push, feet no longer on the rung, kicking to find some leverage on the wall, the sudden weight pulling his arms down. Don't slide back, hang on. Another push, putting everything into a final heave, grunting out loud, his chest hitting the top now, the weight finally in his favor, on his stomach, straddling it and moving his legs up behind him, stretched out on the wall. He lay there for a second, taking deep breaths, then looked down at Otto.

"Come on."

Even the first steps were tentative, testing the ladder, nobody holding it now, and by the time he reached the last handhold he was sweating, looking down, then up, an impossible climb.

"I can't do it."

"I'll help you up. But you need to be at the top of the ladder."

"It makes me dizzy, to look."

"Then don't look. Come on." He positioned himself across the top and reached down with one arm, a visual encouragement, like a dangling rope. "Grab my hand."

"I'll fall." Only a whisper, panicking.

"Grab it."

Otto took another step, only looking up now, eyes frightened. He slid his hand up the wall. Another step, the last, within reach. Aaron grabbed him, holding tight as Otto left the ladder, a second of free fall, an involuntary whimper, his eyes almost pleading now. And for a second Aaron realized that he held Otto's life in his hands, and he wondered how it would feel to let go, to see in Otto's eyes that he had done it, not just looked on at some impersonal hanging, but had deliberately opened his hand and let Otto's life slide out of it. He pulled again.

"Grab the other side. Almost there."

Otto grunted and lifted his chest over, still clutching Aaron's hand.

"I need to rest," he said, gasping.

"First get your legs up. Like riding a horse. It's easier."

Otto looked down into the street. Across Junin, the strip of park and then the cafés, but the sidewalk beneath them empty, the cemetery visitors gone.

"It's too far to jump," Otto said, talking to himself.

"We use the lamps," Aaron said. Large wrought iron street lamps were bolted into the walls, another nostalgic piece of Europe, the gaslight making yellow pools of light all the way down Junin. The bottom of the lamp, a decorative swirl of iron, was several feet down the wall, a body dangling from it would be another six feet down, the rest of the drop manageable. If the lamp could hold their weight.

"I'll go first," Aaron said, sliding backward toward the nearest lamp.

"It's too far."

"If it is, you're stuck," Aaron said, then more gently, a parent to a child, "If I can do it, you can do it. Watch."

He grabbed onto an ornamental crown near the top of the lamp and swung over, working his way down to the wall brace, finally to the bottom, holding on as he dangled. How far from here? Not quite his height. He tried to remember the Agency training about jumps, how to land, spring back after you touch down, but all he could see was the sidewalk a few feet below. Not grass, a hard landing.

He let go of the lamp and hit the ground in a crouch, absorbing the shock, and pushed up with his knees. Staggering a little, not used to it, but nothing broken. No one near, only a few cars. He looked up. Otto had started down the wall, gripping the brace, then dangling from the underside of the lamp, legs scissoring in the air. He was groaning, gravity pulling on his wound, obviously in pain.

"It's too far. I'll break—"

Aaron stood beneath him. "I'll catch you. Just drop. Let go."

"Catch me?"

"Quick. Before anyone comes." He looked up and down the street to check, then back up at Otto. "Trust me."

Otto looked at him with an expression Aaron couldn't read. But hanging was its own agony. He nodded. "Now?"

"Now," Aaron said, opening his arms, then suddenly knocked over as Otto fell on him, both of them down, piling on each other and rolling over, tangled together. Otto made a gasping sound.

"You OK?"

His answer was to clutch his side again and groan. Aaron got to his feet and pulled Otto after him, holding him upright, a kind of buttress, steadying him. Otto's head had begun to dip, a drunk's swaying, his body limp.

"Don't pass out on me."

Otto just nodded, speech too much of an effort.

"Lean on me. Here, on my shoulder. If anyone comes, I'm getting you home from a party. OK?"

Another nod.

They started up Junin, in a few minutes passing the entrance portico, a single light burning inside, probably the guard still listening for sounds. They kept to the park side, away from the cafés. Two women came out of Our Lady of Pilar, avoiding them as they passed, their faces clouded with disapproval. Otto slumped more heavily against him, as if the effort he'd put into the climb had drained him, his feet moving with an old man's shuffle.

"I never checked his pockets for any ID," Aaron said, just to say something, keep him awake. They were almost at the sloped plaza. "Just the ticket. How's the side? You still bleeding?"

Some neutral sound, which Aaron took as "no."

"Lucky about the lamps. If they used ordinary streetlights, we'd still be up on the wall."

A man coming toward them, wary in the dark. Otto leaned into Aaron, hiding his face. "*Noches,*" the man mumbled.

Another antique gas lamp with its yellow pool. "Not far now," Aaron said. He could see the dark ombu trees down the hill.

And then he felt it, the blunt metal in his pocket pushed up against him, Otto's hand holding it. He jerked his head around and saw Otto's blue eyes, steel, untamed, a wolf's eyes. I won't turn my back. But he had. So it would end now. In a second. Otto shoved the gun closer, Aaron holding still, any movement another trigger. In his mind he could see Otto's finger, tightening.

"Jew," Otto said, almost spitting it.

Aaron felt a tremor go through him, an actual shaking, then a numbness. All he was. Steel eyes, unforgiving. To the left.

"Jew," Otto said again, fainter this time, his eyes closing, then pitched forward, sliding down, his knees at Aaron's feet.

For a minute Aaron couldn't move, as if he had actually died and needed time to come back. Then he reached down and took Otto's hand out of his pocket, slowly, still afraid of any trigger movement, relieved when he felt the hand had gone slack, the gun slipping away from it as it came out of the pocket. He looked down. Never forget what you're hunting.

He knelt down. "Otto," he said, shaking his shoulder. "Get up." Too heavy to carry. Deadweight.

Otto opened his eyes, the steel gone. A groan.

"Get up," Aaron said again, trying to lift Otto to his feet. "It's not far." Otto closed his eyes again, drifting. "She's waiting."

A second's delay, taking this in, then opening his eyes. "Who?"

"Hanna. She's waiting. Get up."

"Hanna's waiting?" Confused, but making an effort now, finding his feet.

Aaron held him under the arms, helping him stand. Don't turn your back. But something had changed, a shift of power. He had survived, in charge now, Otto suddenly feeble, done.

"*Señor?*"

Two men, seeing Otto slump, some street emergency.

Aaron moved Otto's body, putting the wounded side next to him, obscured. Think.

"*Ivre,*" Aaron said. No, that was French. What was Spanish for drunk? *Ivro*?

Otto raised his head. One last chance to sound an alarm.

But Aaron was looking at him, eyes steady, holding him closer, snapping on a leash.

"*Borracho*," he said, then, acting it out, "*borracho*."

The two men giggled and Aaron saw that they were half-drunk themselves. A burst of Spanish, then one of them took Otto's other side, throwing an arm over his shoulder, helping Aaron move him. "*Dónde?*" He nodded toward the corner of Alvear and started walking.

"*Borracho*," Otto said to the ground, playing. More giggling from the other men, a running conversation in Spanish, turning it into an adventure, getting a drunk home, the wound still unnoticed. Otto heavy, but easier to move with two of them, feet shuffling, dragging from time to time.

When they reached the corner, Otto pulled himself up. "*Muchas gracias*," he said, dismissing them, leaning on Aaron, all he needed now to get home. To Aaron's surprise, the men nodded, oddly formal, some Castilian point of honor, then laughed.

"We'll be OK," Aaron said, but they were already moving off, back toward the lights of the cafés. "Can you make it? It's just here."

Otto looked at him, disconcerted. Some missing piece of the puzzle, Aaron knowing where.

Aaron used his passkey at the downstairs door. No noisy buzzers. Another look from Otto. In the elevator he slumped against the rail, weak again.

Aaron used the doorbell this time, afraid she'd think someone was breaking in if he used the key.

"*Sí?*"

The door opening a crack, then wider, all the way. She looked from one to the other, her face changing expressions, shock, fear, mouth open, unable to speak, and then back at Aaron, dismayed, as if she were trying to make up a story to explain things and none would work.

"Oh," she said, just a sound, then couldn't find the next word, looking from one to the other again.

"He's been shot."

"Shot?" Nothing making sense.

Aaron moved Otto in. "Close the blinds."

She looked at him, surprised at his tone, then did what he said. Easier to act than think.

Aaron got him into the bedroom, a final heave to lay him on the bed. He looked around, everything the way he remembered it, the bureau, the closets of clothes. He got a towel from the bathroom, wet it, and came back to wash the bullet wound, blotting it. Otto winced.

"Hanna," Otto said, voice still weak. "I'm sorry for this. There's nowhere else—"

"We have to get him a doctor," Aaron said.

"A doctor?" Some impossible idea.

"Who won't call the police. Who knows." He looked at her. "Bildener was a doctor. Could he handle this?"

"Call an ambulance," she said. "If he's dying—"

"He's not dying. We can't go to a hospital. Can Bildener do it?"

"Yes, I think so. It's serious?"

"It's a bullet wound. It will be if we don't get it taken care of. Call him."

"Now?" she said, a sleepwalker's voice, still trying to wake.

"Now. Wait. Your phone's tapped. Can you get him over here without anyone suspecting? Some story?"

"Tapped? You knew this?"

"We'll talk later."

She stood for a second, not moving, some light dimming in her eyes. "No," she said finally. "What's the difference?" She nodded to the bed. "I know how it ends."

"Sorry about the mess." The towel red from blood. "Will you call? We don't want sepsis. The bullet has to come out. Bildener will need his bag, if he still has one."

She nodded. "Who shot him?"

"I did."

Another moment of silence. "Oh," she said. "You did." Her voice falling, a disappointment so unguarded that he had to look away, back to the wound.

"I'll explain everything. But first call Bildener."

"Explain," she said. "More lies. Every man I've ever known lied to me."

"We can't stay here long. They're bound to check again."

"Who?"

"The Israelis."

Her eyes opened wider, alarmed. "Israelis. You're with them?"

"No. They think I am. Did you close the blinds?"

"Who, then? Tell me."

"I'm not with anybody. Not now. That's why I need your help."

"My help? What, to kill my father?"

"No, to get him out of Buenos Aires. Before they kill him."

"Hanna," Otto said from the bed.

She glanced over, but didn't go any closer. "And now this," she said, then to Otto, "I'll be right there. Let me call the doctor first."

"Be careful what you say," Aaron said.

"Oh, careful." She started to go, then turned back to Aaron. "So it was all lies? Everything you said?"

"No. Not everything," he said, looking at her.

"What a little friend you are. Tell me your story for my book."

"My father's death. How about that one?"

Her eyes flashed, another piece in place. "You knew."

"That you were protecting him?"

"You don't understand."

"Which part?"

"Did you enjoy that? Watching me say those things—knowing."

"It wasn't like that."

"No? How was it? Was there ever a book? Did that even exist? Your friend?"

Aaron nodded. "Until today. Otto killed him."

"Otto killed—" she said, thrown by this, looking over to the bed, Otto's eyes closed again. "Is that true?" A girl's voice.

Aaron nodded again.

"And now you want to save him."

"I want to get him out of Buenos Aires. I want him to stand trial."

Her head came up. "Trial. That would kill him. And you want me to help you? Why would—?"

"Because it's the right thing to do."

She looked at him, at a loss. "The right thing to do. You think you know what that is. You."

"Right now, it's get the doctor. Then we'll talk."

"You talk," she said. "I don't want to listen." She stopped, eyes softening. "I thought it was different. What happened."

"It was."

She looked away. "Get another towel. I'll call."

Otto drifted, not really unconscious but not wanting to talk, waiting for Hanna. Aaron dabbed at the wound, beginning to crust, looking around, the room the same, but everything else different. He thought of the afternoon light, the lingerie drawer, the charm bracelet laid out and ready, Otto close, just follow her to him, everything simple, and now knotted and tangled. The look on her face. I thought it was different.

When she came back, she brought a nursing pan.

"I'll do it," she said, shooing him aside. "He's a mess. So dusty. Where have you been?"

"The cemetery. We had to climb out."

"What?" she said.

He took out the ticket and handed it to her. "I assume you have the passport? For Kruger."

She held it for a second, then put it on the night table. "Where's Julio?"

"He's dead." He took a breath. "Bildener doesn't have to know that yet."

"Did Otto kill him too?"

"No."

She looked up at him, then let it go, pretending to concentrate on the wound, keeping her hand steady.

"Is he coming?"

She nodded.

"What did you tell him?"

"I said I was thinking about him because I'd seen a movie on television about a doctor. How he would come to the house with his black bag, just like you when I was a little girl. In the movie a friend had been shot and he had to rush to save him. And how is Trude? It's been so long since I've seen you."

"He get it?"

"I think so. We'll know soon."

"A movie. That was good," he said.

"I can do it too, make things up. We're well suited."

"Hanna—"

She glanced around the room. "Is the apartment bugged or just the phone?"

"Just the phone."

"And you know that because you arranged it?"

"Yes."

"And am I allowed to know? Who's listening? Besides you."

"The Agency."

"Jamie?"

"Somebody there."

"What did I say? Anything interesting?"

"You never mentioned him," he said, gesturing toward Otto. "You never made a mistake."

She looked up. "Not then," she said, then, before he could answer, "There's a clothes brush in the bathroom."

In the living room he moved the blind a crack and looked down. A few people in the street, all of them moving, probably returning to the hotel. The ombu tree dark under its thick cover. Too soon for Bildener. Where did he live? Some grand house out near the park, a formal dining room, a good brandy while he waited for the Fourth Reich. Nobody standing in the street. Where Aaron was supposed to be, Nathan's eyes on her apartment. Meet back at Goldfarb's. Ari out at Ezeiza. How to do this?

She stayed with Otto awhile, then finally came out and lit a cigarette, standing in Aaron's place at the window, looking down.

"If you sit here, anybody watching will see you alone."

"I thought you did desk work," she said, but took the seat, the light behind her. "What's all this business about Madrid? He's rambling. What does it mean?"

"The Agency thinks he could work there. An old friend of Perón. Keep his eyes and ears open and report back."

"They know he's alive?"

"They know I think he is. But I could be wrong. Mistaken."

"Let me understand. Erich Kruger spies for—your people. And Otto Schramm stays dead."

Aaron nodded.

"But you don't want that to happen."

"I want him to go to trial."

"That's right. The sword of justice. Hanging over us all. So you lied to him too. He thinks he's going to Madrid?"

"We can't drag him out. He has to be part of it."

"And now you want me to lie to him."

"We have to get him out."

"For his day in court. The Agency will never forgive you. They'll know you lied to them."

"They're going to know anyway, one way or the other." He stopped. "Maybe I don't like what they're doing anymore."

"With my father?"

"With a lot of things."

"Your wife would be pleased. Maybe you should get back together."

"I don't want to get back together. I found somebody else."

She looked at him through a wisp of smoke, the cigarette stopped in midair, then busied herself putting it out, moving on.

"You'd be throwing away your job."

"I'll get another one."

"With the Israelis?"

"No. Not after this. I'm supposed to be telling them where Otto is."

"You're popular with everybody."

"They're going to kill him. I never wanted that."

"Just the trial."

"My uncle was Max Weill," he said, watching for her reaction, the wary recognition. "I want to do this for him. No, that's not right. I want to do it for all of them. Otto killed my mother. Him, or someone like him. I want him to say it happened."

"He killed my mother too. I know," she said, holding up her

hand. "It's not the same. But there are lots of ways to do it. And what will he say? That he's sorry?"

"No. He's not. He'll say it happened. He'll be evidence. So we'll always know it happened. He'll answer for it."

"With his life."

"We don't know that. But what if he's killed without answering for it? The Israelis think that's enough. More efficient, anyway. A message to the others. But then nobody answers. Nobody's guilty."

"It won't change anything."

"Maybe. But we have to think it will. Or then what? There's only—who has the gun."

She took out another cigarette and lit it, taking a minute.

"Let me ask you something. How did you find him? Me?"

"I followed you."

"Yes? I never knew. You must be good at it. Or maybe—maybe I wasn't looking for that." She drew on the cigarette. "So you—got close to me."

"That was something else."

"A bonus."

"Stop. That's not the way it was."

"The way it was," she said, an exaggerated wryness. "My lover. A man who just shot my father. Who wants to bring him to justice. Whatever that is."

"You know what it is."

"No, you know. It's all you think about. I'm thinking about him. You don't know what he's like."

"Yes, I do."

"I don't mean that. Those days. Or now that he's so crazy. Since Eichmann, a crazy man. All that business with the accident, then living like a hermit. Afraid of everything. You want justice, there's some kind of justice there. To be afraid of everything. No," she said, slowing. "I meant what he was like to me. He would do anything for me in those days. There's a debt there."

Aaron said nothing, absorbing this, then met her eyes. "Now you can pay it. Help me. If I don't get him out of Buenos Aires, they're going to kill him."

"So we save his life. So you can make an example out of him. Shame him. That's my choice."

"Hanna, he tortured children. Not just killed them, tortured them."

A silence, everything in a dead stop, her eyes filling with tears. "I know," she said, then raised her head. "My father."

Another silence, broken by the buzzer from the downstairs door. Aaron jumped up, startled, and went over to the window.

"There's a car out front. It must be him."

Hanna wiped her face, then stood up, smoothing out her skirt.

"What do I say to him?"

"The Israelis. He was lucky to get away."

"More lies."

"We need his help. Hanna, it's the right thing."

"I don't know what that is anymore."

"Yes, you do. I know you. We know each other." He looked at her. "I never lied to you. Not about that."

She held his look for a second. "And that makes everything all right."

She had the door open before Bildener got off the elevator, waving him in. Hurry.

"I came as soon as I could. Where—?" He stopped, seeing Aaron.

Hanna and Aaron looked at each other.

"He knows," Hanna said finally.

"He knows? Him?" Not saying more, the surprise and contempt in his face enough. "You told him?"

Another glance at Aaron, then a turn to Bildener. "He's helping for me," she said, dropping it, taking Bildener's arm. "He's in here. You brought instruments? He's been raving, some nonsense about Madrid."

"Madrid."

"Pay no attention. Some foolishness. I thought, maybe a fever, but I don't know. You'll see. I'm so grateful. You know that, yes? Who else could I call? Who knows."

He looked back at Aaron. "It's not good. Telling people. Something comes out and—"

"He's all right, don't worry. He's here for me."

"Another—"

She cut him off. "You can take out a bullet?"

"That depends where it is. Who shot him?"

"The Israelis."

Bildener stopped, disturbed. "They know? They're here?"

"We have to get him away. As soon as— I don't mean to hurry you."

"No, no. Did he meet Julio?"

"He must have. He has the ticket."

"Markus," Otto said, trying to sit up.

"So, where did they get you? Ah. You're lucky. A few more inches here," he said, touching his stomach, "and it's real trouble. How many of them were there?"

"It wasn't like that."

"Well, tell me later. This will hurt."

Otto clutched his hand. "*Mein Freund.*"

"What do they think? A bullet's going to stop you? After everything. A little sting now. We have to cleanse the wound. It's OK, not too much?"

Otto nodded, gritting his teeth against the pain, not making a sound.

"I'm sorry we can't put you out. If you have to leave—" He turned to Hanna. "They know he's here?"

"No."

"But they know he's alive. They'll come to you."

She moved her head toward Aaron. "They sent him. So we have a little time."

Bildener blinked, working this out, then reached into his bag. "Hold him down," he said.

Aaron went behind Otto's head and pushed on his shoulders.

"Ready?" Bildener said to Otto. "Try not to move. I know it's difficult." He adjusted what looked like an elongated pair of pliers and leaned over Otto's wound. "I can see it. It's not deep." The instrument now touching the wound.

Otto's body jumped, a violent jackknife twitching, startling Aaron.

"Hold him," Bildener said, impatient.

A sharp intake of air, Otto closing his eyes, clenching his fists, willing himself through it. And then suddenly Aaron felt the resistance in his shoulders go slack, no longer fighting. No.

"Is he OK?" Hearing himself, worried, wanting Otto alive.

Bildener touched the side of Otto's neck. "He's out, that's all. A mercy. A man his age." He looked at Aaron. "Such pain. Even a superman would feel it." Implying somehow that Aaron wouldn't have lasted as long. The master race. "You can let go."

Aaron moved his hands away.

"I can finish here," Bildener said, dismissing him, turning his back. "Hanna, some gauze, tape?"

Aaron waited in the living room. How much longer before Nathan sent someone else to look? They couldn't move Otto if he was unconscious. Unless they went back to the driving plan, the bridge up beyond the delta. Hours.

Hanna came back, taking her seat by the window again.

"I couldn't watch. He got the bullet, but the wound looks He says it's the antiseptic that makes it look like that."

"But he'll be OK?"

"You mean, will he be able to stand up in court? I suppose."

"I meant, will he be OK."

She shrugged, letting it go, and reached for a cigarette. "He gave him a pill for the pain. So he's woozy. But maybe that's better for you. He'll think he's going to Madrid. That's what you want, isn't it? To trick him. So he walks into the trap. After his daughter tells him to go. Tells him it's all right."

Aaron looked over, saying nothing.

"How are you going to do it? You have a plan?"

"More or less."

"Mm. More, I think. I can see it in your face. That look you get."

"What look?"

"Moving the pieces into place. Working things out."

"I didn't know I was that easy to read."

"You weren't. I thought it was something else." She lit the cigarette. "So. You have a place to move him? He can't stay here."

"He can't stay anywhere in Buenos Aires. Either Bildener and his friends hide him again. Or the Israelis get him. Either way, I lose. And the Argentines will never extradite him. So we can't go to them."

"So he goes to Brazil? That's why you wanted the ticket from Julio?"

He shook his head. "The ticket was just a way to find him. He goes to Uruguay."

"Uruguay."

"It's close and they have no reason to say no when the Germans ask for him. No friends in high places."

"If the Germans ask for him."

"We take him to the West German Embassy in Montevideo. I alert the prosecutor in Frankfurt—a friend of my uncle's. There's already a warrant for Otto's arrest. If they don't put him on a plane home, I make a fuss until they do. The Israelis can't touch him in the embassy. They'll make a formal announcement congratulating the Germans and go home."

"And Markus?"

"Markus will lose a friend. Or do you mean all that business about identifying the body? I don't think anyone wants to lift up that rock. Too embarrassing. The Argentines will keep it all filed away somewhere. Bildener's friends will make sure."

"And when does my father know? That he's not going to Madrid?"

"At the embassy. He'll have to know then."

"If you can get him there."

Aaron nodded. "If they think he's going to Brazil, they'll be out at Ezeiza. But the Uruguayan flights are short—they leave from Aeroparque. We just need somebody to get a new ticket, somebody the Israelis aren't going to recognize if they do have someone watching. They can't cover all the gates, so they'll be at the counter. If he avoids that, we can get him out."

"With you."

"That's right. Tickets for both of us. We won't be able to order them from the travel agent on Anchorena this time."

She looked up, caught off guard by this.

"You were there? You know what this feels like? Someone taking your clothes off. But you did that too, didn't you?" She drew on the cigarette. "So you want me to buy the tickets."

"No. Nathan's men have been tailing you. So you might be recognized. Better not chance it."

"You're looking out for me," she said, a theatrical archness.

He ignored this. "And I was thinking we might pass the tickets in the men's room. It's the easiest place. Then straight to the gate."

"Who, then? You can't do it. They know you."

"But they don't know Bildener."

"Markus? Are you crazy? You think he would help you do this?"

"He won't know what we're doing. Just saving Otto from the Israelis." He looked at her. "He'd do it if you asked him. He'd believe you."

"He'd never forgive me."

"No."

She put out the cigarette, waving the smoke away from her face. "My head's spinning with all this. Now trick Markus. And when did you have this idea? While you were following me?"

"Tonight. I'm making this up as we go. I didn't know—it would happen like this. It just did. But now we have to get him out."

"And I'm left here to explain. What else? I might as well know the rest. What else do you want me to do?"

"Talk to Markus. He'll do it for you."

"No, for Otto. For his daughter. They're like— I don't know, brothers. Family."

"He ordered the experiments. From the Institute. That's who we're talking about."

She got up, about to leave, then stood there for a minute, arms folded over her chest, as if she were holding herself in.

"But there's no trial for him," she said.

"No. He was clever. He never left his desk. Otto was at the camp. Where the evidence was."

She said nothing for a moment. "But you can do a lot from a desk." And then, before he could say anything, she turned toward the bedroom. "I'll talk to him. And then it's finished."

13

AARON WENT OVER TO the window, the crack at the edge of the blind. No one in the street. What else? Think it through. Once they were on the plane they were safe. Then a taxi to the embassy, Otto still dreaming of Madrid. But first the plane. The tree below still a dark canopy. Car lights turning in to Casares at the foot of the park, climbing the hill. In a second, they'd turn on Alvear, maybe head for the hotel. Instead the car pulled into the curb, catty-corner to Hanna's building, and parked, killing the lights. Aaron waited to see who got out, but no one did. A few more minutes, still nobody. Who parked and sat in a dark car? He made his eyes into slits, peering, trying to see inside the car, but there wasn't enough street light to make out the driver. Or anyone else. How many? His mind clicked over, shuffling. Jamie didn't need to find Otto—he had Aaron doing it for him. No reason to think otherwise. Nathan may have got restless at

Goldfarb's, waiting for Aaron to check in, and sent another man to have a look. Or come himself, suspicious. But he wouldn't have sent a full car, a team. They were down a man, with a few locations to cover. So someone alone, maybe two. Or no one at all, Aaron's imagination running away. But no one got out of the car.

"Hanna tells me you want to move him," Bildener said, coming in. "He's in no condition for that."

"Is he awake? Can he walk?"

"With help, maybe. But he's—"

"I think the Israelis are outside."

"What?" Hanna said.

Bildener had gone pale. "The Israelis? You understand, I can't be involved in—"

"You're already involved. Now help us save him. Nobody's after you."

"How do you know? Any of this." He turned to Hanna. "Israelis outside and you trust him?"

Hanna looked at Aaron. "What do you want to do?"

"We have to change the plan." He looked down, absorbed in his own thoughts, then back out the window. "There's probably only one. If they had a full car, they'd already be up here searching the apartment."

"I'm sorry, I have to go," Bildener said, skittish.

"They'll kill him," Hanna said. "Markus."

"And if there's only one?" Bildener said. "So what?"

"It means we have a chance. But I can't carry him. So, can he walk?"

"If he has to. A strong man. But he's lost some blood. I can't guarantee—"

"Is there a back way out?" Aaron said to Hanna.

Hanna nodded. "To an alley. Behind the building."

"Where does it come out?"

"Around the corner. On Ayacucho. Near the middle of the block."

"Get a suitcase. Something Otto would use." He turned to Bildener. "You have a hat, right? If you keep your head down—"

"What?"

"You could pass. You're about the same size."

"What are you talking about?"

"Look, nobody knows who's here. If Hanna's alone. But they see her coming out with an old man and a suitcase—what are they going to think? You're taking him to the airport." He looked at Bildener. "You're the decoy."

"Decoy?" Bildener said, apprehensive.

"Don't worry, not the kind they shoot at. Not on Alvear. If nobody follows you, it's a false alarm. Maybe some kids necking in the car. But if he does follow, then we know."

"And what if it's more than one?" Hanna said.

"They could try to take you in the street."

"And get Markus. And then?"

"I'll get to the airport some other way. We have to chance it."

"But when he sees you—" Hanna said.

"They don't. They see you and Bildener coming out. I'll be with Otto in the alley. You pick us up. They can't tail you that closely around the corner, so they don't see it. We keep down and it's still just you and Otto on your way to the airport." He stopped. "If we can get the real Otto moving. You want to give me a hand?" he said to Bildener.

Bildener, dazed, looked to Hanna, a child asking permission. She nodded, then said, "I'll pack."

"Don't bother. Just the suitcase. It's a prop. You'd better bring your gun, though. Just in case," he said, motioning toward the drawer where she kept it.

Hanna stopped, staring at him. Only one way to have known that. A silent exchange, surprised and then refusing to be surprised, undressed again.

"A gun?" Bildener said, a tremor in his voice.

Hanna touched his arm. "He's just being careful," she said, shooting a look at Aaron. "We'd better hurry. Is the car still there?"

Aaron moved the blind. "Yes."

She reached into the desk drawer and pulled out a passport. "Here, you keep it. In case we're separated." She handed it to him. "Take care of him."

Otto was drowsy but awake, slightly confused by the activity around him. Bildener had covered the wound with a bandage, and now Otto had to be dressed again, shirt buttoned, the bloodstain dry, hidden by his jacket.

"Why can't I sleep?" he said to Hanna. "You don't want me here?"

"We don't want the Israelis to find you."

"No. They knew about Ortiz's. You were right. It didn't matter if I was dead. They found me anyway."

"Well, now we'll get you away."

"With him?" he said, pointing, as if Aaron had been out of focus and now was coming into view. "He's one of them."

"No. He's going to help you."

"Like at the cemetery," he said, vague, trying to remember.

"That's right. He's going to get you out. Can you stand? Walk a little?"

She helped him to his feet, bracing him as he found his balance.

"Can you walk? It's important."

"Markus gave me a pill. For the pain."

"I know. But you can do it. There, another step. Are you dizzy?"

"No. Where are we going?"

"The airport."

"Markus too?" he said, seeing the suitcase next to him.

"All of us. You go down with Aaron and we'll pick you up. Then the Israelis won't see."

"We outsmart them."

"That's right," she said, looking at Aaron.

"And we go to São Paulo."

"No, a change. Montevideo."

"Montevideo."

Another glance to Aaron. Now this. "For Madrid, remember? We were talking before."

"Yes, Madrid. Erich Kruger. I remember. A new place. You can come and see me. We'll be safe there. With the Americans. You could come. No one would know."

Hanna said nothing, deliberately not reacting to this.

"Now try it with Aaron," she said, slipping his arm through Aaron's. "He'll get you down to the car. Lean on him if you have to. Then it's easy."

"You know he's Max Weill's boy," Otto said.

Bildener looked up.

"Yes," Hanna said. "That doesn't matter now."

"So why does he help me?"

"He works for the Americans. He wants you in Madrid." Looking away as she said it.

"I said he was with the Americans," Bildener said, vindicated. "Bariloche. Such nonsense."

"They protect you, the Americans. Look at Barbie. The way he lives—out in the open. Gehlen, after the war. Now me. It's better than Brazil."

"Brazil would be safer," Bildener said.

"My old friend. So careful," Otto said, putting his hand on Bildener's arm, a good-bye. "We did good work together. Good science," he said, believing it. "Someday they'll use the research. If we live to see it." He turned to Aaron, another good-bye. "I saved his life. Max. He didn't understand that. How I saved his life."

"It's a long time ago now," Hanna said. "Here, put on this coat." She smoothed the back of his shoulders.

"It's too warm for a coat."

"I know, but it's winter there," she said quickly. "Markus and I will get the car. What do you think? Can you do it?"

"You're leaving me with him?"

"He'll get you to the car." She touched his hand, an encouragement. "He'll get you to Madrid."

Otto smiled faintly. "Then you come. No one will know. You know, with your hair like that, you look so like your mother. When I met her."

Hanna stopped, hand still on his, eyes not moving.

"It's the medicine," Bildener said. "It has an emotional effect."

Aaron looked at him, disconcerted. Bildener science. But now Hanna was moving again.

"You go first," she said to Aaron. "It'll take you longer."

"Let them get a good look. So they know it's you. And the suitcase."

"Take the service elevator. The stairs are too hard for him like this. Go left out the back door and follow the alley. Wait for us."

"What's in the alley?"

"Garbage. Rats. Stamp your feet. Go, go." She shooed them to the door

"Hanna—" Otto said.

"Go," Hanna said, not looking at him, all business.

In the elevator Otto leaned back against the wall, looking at the mop and bucket in the corner. "So now I'm the janitor," he said, amused, and then, his mind jumping, "You know all the money is at Ortiz's. There was no time—"

"I have money."

"Dollars. The rich American. And who pays you, I wonder."

"The same people who are going to pay you," Aaron said, playing with it, another twist.

"And make me rich?"

"No, just enough to keep you on a leash. That's how they do it."

"But my money. Not my daughter's. I won't have to ask."

Aaron said nothing.

"And you're taking me there? You're the delivery boy?"

"That's the idea."

"And Hanna says to go. She trusts you. I don't. You believe all those things. Max's stories. Exaggerations."

Aaron looked at him, about to speak, then dropped it.

"Here we go," he said, as the elevator door opened. "If we run into anybody, let me do the talking. You're not feeling well and I'm getting you to the hospital."

"Through the service alley. With no Spanish. Wonderful. To be in such good hands."

"Take my arm. And stay out of the pockets. That only works once."

The alley was dim, most of the light secondhand, coming in from the street. Big metal trash collectors, the backs of apartment buildings.

"You all right? Am I going too fast?"

"No, it's fine," Otto said, but short of breath, making an effort. More steps, Otto's shuffle scaring off anything scurrying in the dark. "It's useful that I learned."

"What?"

"Spanish," Otto said, somewhere else.

Lights now, closer to the street.

"I don't think she'll come to Madrid," Otto said, mostly to himself. "Maybe it's better. But you know, your child. The love for a child—"

Waving his hand at Daniel. You'll see him later.

"You could bring her," Otto said.

"Me?"

"She has a fondness for—" A clanging, tripping on a garbage can top. "Ouf."

Aaron held him closer, hand on his chest to prevent him from pitching forward. "Almost there."

"For your people," he finished. "So you make allowances. Your child. And it's another world now. What happened in the war, that was a political situation. Not personal."

"Not personal," Aaron said, as if he hadn't heard correctly.

"Not for me, no. A political situation. Of course, also racial. It was a serious problem then, at that time. Now it's different."

"How?"

"We were threatened then, the German people. By the Jews. Like a cancer. You have to cut it out to survive."

"And you did," Aaron said, hearing him on the stand, unrepentant, not Eichmann mumbling about orders, a doctor operating.

"But the numbers, that's an exaggeration. There weren't so many."

"How many, then?" Leading the witness.

"I don't know, but not what they say. It wouldn't have been possible, so many. Anyway, it was wartime."

Sterilizing with X-rays, burned scrotums, children. The war effort.

They had reached the end of the alley.

"OK, wait here." A quiet street, no cars. "It shouldn't be long."

Hanna would be coming out the door with Markus, solicitous, carrying his bag, getting him into the car. Now behind the wheel, putting the car in gear. Then what? Looking in the rear-view mirror. But if the other car was any good, he wouldn't pull out right away. He'd wait for Hanna to turn the corner.

"The Israelis are waiting for us?"

"We're not sure."

"But you're with them."

"They think I am."

"You were there. Where they kept me," he said, still trying to work it out.

"Here we go," Aaron said as the car stopped at the alley. "Quick."

He pulled Otto into the street, one arm around his shoulders, flinging open the back door, a push, then throwing himself in after, bumping up against the suitcase, lifting it out of the way, the car beginning to move before he could close the door.

"Keep down," he said to Otto. "Did they follow?"

"I don't know yet." She looked up into the mirror. "Yes. That's the car."

She kept going down the hill, residential streets, then turned onto Las Heras, a wide avenue with buses, where it would be harder to follow.

"More than one?" Aaron said.

"I can't tell. Maybe two. Does it matter?"

"Two and they might think about cutting you off. Jump you at a light or something. One, you've just got a tail."

"Jump us?" Bildener said.

They passed the turnoff for the cemetery, where Julio's body was lying under a tarp, waiting to be found. After Aaron had gone. If they made the plane.

"They're not coming any closer," Hanna said.

"Where are we going?" Otto said vaguely.

Aaron looked at him. "The airport. For the plane."

"That's right," Otto said, as if a name had slipped his mind and then come back. He lifted his head slightly, looking to see where they were. "This way?"

"The old airport. Aeroparque."

"And then Brazil," Otto said, going over an itinerary in his mind.

Bildener turned around, concerned. "It's the medicine."

"How much did you give him?"

"Enough to dull the pain," Bildener said, defensive, not used to being questioned.

"He going to make it through passport control?"

"I can do it," Otto said, trying to sit up.

"Keep your head down."

"Erich Kruger's first stamp. My new life."

"Are they still there?" Aaron said to Hanna.

"Yes, same distance."

She turned right into Castilla and a minute later was at Libertador, waiting at the light, then shooting past the stopped traffic, lined up like horses at a starting gate.

"Look where we are," Otto said, the quiet winding street of mansions instantly familiar. "You wanted to see the house, one last time. Calle Aguado."

"They're still behind," Hanna said, heading into a dark curving road, a spoke off a circle.

"It was a beautiful house," Otto said to Aaron. "An embassy now."

"A nice life," Aaron said.

"Yes, it was," Otto said, not hearing any irony.

"Don't try to lose them."

"Why not?"

"They'll go to the airport anyway, now that they see where we're going. But this way we know where they are. No surprises."

"There's the house," Otto said. "See the lights?"

"Such happy times there," Bildener said.

"It's a shortcut to Alcorta," Hanna said. "They won't suspect anything."

"OK. How many? Can you see now?"

"Two."

"Don't go near the docks, then. That's asking for trouble."

"No, through the park. The way a taxi would go." She glanced back at Otto, still peeking out the window. "How is he?"

Aaron made a so-so gesture.

"I don't think I'll come back here," Otto said.

"You knew that when you started all this," Hanna said. "Go to Brazil, be someone else."

Otto nodded. "So they'd leave me alone. Who looks for a dead man? But they found me anyway. At Ortiz's. How? They must have people everywhere." Hanna glanced at Aaron in the mirror. "Look how they found Eichmann. All those years."

"Did you ever meet him?" Aaron said.

"Once," Bildener said. "At the ABC restaurant." Aaron thought of Fritz, attacking his wurst, the *Gasthaus* wood paneling. "Not a very impressive man. Ordinary. Lower class, even. You could see it in the table manners."

"But if they could find him," Otto said, "a nobody, then it was dangerous for the rest."

"Maybe they just got lucky. A tip."

"No," Otto said. "They're methodical. Dangerous." Something he needed to believe, the worthy adversary.

"They're still behind," Hanna said. "One car away." She turned right on Sarmiento, heading toward the river. An arrowed sign for Aeroparque Jorge Newberry.

"Who was he? Newberry," Aaron said.

"An aviator. Argentine. His father was American." Making conversation, their eyes meeting in the mirror, wanting to say something else, but not saying it, focused on the drive now, the car racing around a traffic circle.

"Almost there," Hanna said. "What should I—?"

"Just do what you'd normally do. If you weren't being followed. Drop him at Departures. He takes his suitcase and goes in. You pull out, as if you were leaving, then farther up, get back into the drop-off area. They'll have to go after him, not you, so they won't see you, with all the taxis and everything. By the time they realize he's not Otto, they come out and you're gone. You're still their only lead to Otto, so I'm betting they'll want to go after you, try to pick up the car again before you leave the airport."

"And meanwhile what am I supposed to do?" Bildener said. "If they don't shoot me."

"Nobody's shooting anybody. Not at the airport. You just go about your business while they panic because you're not Otto, and now what do they do?"

"My business."

"Buy two tickets. Get the gate number. When they leave, come back out to where Hanna's waiting and Otto and I scram."

"And if they don't leave?"

"They will. They have to." He paused, thinking. "But if they don't, then find the men's room. If you're not back in ten minutes, we'll have to come to you."

There were parking lots on the left now, the terminal up ahead. On the right, the riverfront, restaurants and yacht clubs, and stretches of park, the dark water beyond, the industrial port somewhere behind them.

"You have to access the terminal from the other direction," Hanna said as they flew by it, bright with lights, all the traffic turning at a circle up ahead.

"Everything is mixed up," Otto said. "Why are you helping me?"

"We've told you that," Hanna said, impatient, cars cutting in on both sides as they fed into the circle.

"Why are they chasing you? You're with them."

"I should be," Aaron said. "Things got mixed up."

They followed a line of taxis to the drop-off area, a curving sweep of pavement.

"Pull up here. Before it gets too crowded. That's what you want later. Are they behind?"

"Yes."

"OK, Bildener, say good-bye and grab your suitcase. Come back out down there. The far doors."

"If I come out."

"You will. They don't want you."

Bildener turned and said something to Otto in German, his voice affectionate.

"*Viel Glück*," Otto said, reaching up to put his hand on Bildener's shoulder, the hand speckled with age, frail, like Max's at the end. No, not frail. Strong enough to hold the chain against Fritz's throat while he'd kicked the coffee table, thrashing, gasping. A few hours ago.

Bildener looked at Hanna. "I suppose if they're watching. A father's good-bye." He leaned over and kissed her cheek, then opened the door and took a breath, willing himself outside. Aaron handed him the suitcase from the back. An overnight bag, a short trip. Bildener started for the terminal doors. Luggage trolleys and porters and passengers saying good-byes. And then, like a flash, Nathan's bald head, darting out from behind and moving into Bildener's path, cutting him off, easier to do this outside, calling out a name, a quick stop as he saw the face, a look over Bildener's shoulder to the car, eyes on Hanna, then to the backseat. He stopped, confused, something out of place, not where it should be. Aaron in the back, not getting out, maybe being held there, maybe a gun in his ribs. He lunged toward the curb.

"Pull out. Fast."

Hanna jerked the wheel and screeched into the line of traffic, just missing another car. A blare of horns. Behind them, Nathan was racing back to his car.

"Move," Aaron said. "We have to lose him."

"What about Markus?"

"We can't worry about him now. Can you go any faster?"

"There's traffic." Hanna gripped the wheel. "I can't do this."

"Yes, you can. You're fine."

"Like a gangster. The getaway car. Are they going to shoot at me?"

"They don't want you. They want me. They think I'm in trouble. Why else would I be here?"

"With the Nazis. My god, I'm a Nazi now. With the Israelis after me. I can't—" Shaking a little, eyes fixed on the road.

"Israelis," Otto said. "*Schwein.*"

"And if we stop?" she said, her voice rising, an edge of hysteria.

"They take him," Aaron said simply, deflating the moment. "Here's the exit."

She turned onto the waterfront road. "Now where?"

"Circle back to the airport. They won't be expecting that."

"We have to go to the end to turn around."

"If they don't see us, it might work. Might. What happens if you keep going straight?"

"The port. This hour, you'd be out of the traffic at least."

"Like sitting ducks. Better to keep some cars around us."

"The port?" Otto said. "For an airplane?"

"Ferries," Aaron said, looking up. "They go to Montevideo, right? What is it, about an hour?"

"Three," she said, her voice calmer, caught up in the logistics. "There's a town straight across. Colonia del Sacramento. You can get to Montevideo from there. But the ferry leaves from the old port downtown. I don't think I can outrun them. A drive that far."

"You're doing fine."

But they couldn't just keep driving. Aaron turned and looked out the back window. The gleam of Nathan's head. Someone else at the wheel. After him. His people. Everything mixed up.

"A boat we could rent?" he said, throwing it out.

"At this hour?" Hanna said, then, half to herself, "A boat."

"You know one?"

"I know one we could steal."

Aaron looked at her in the mirror.

"Mine. Well, Tommy's. One of his toys. I got it in the settlement. I keep meaning to sell it."

"Where is it?"

"Back at the Pescadores. The yacht club."

"Where you had lunch," Aaron said.

Another look in the mirror.

"If it's yours, why do we have to steal it?"

"I don't have the keys. Carlos, at the club, takes care of it. But I can't ask him to—"

"It's what, a sailboat?"

"No, a motorboat. Tommy used to take it up to Tigre. Go around the islands. We could get across if it has gas. Decide. The traffic circle's coming up. Turn around or back through the park?"

"Without the keys—"

"We can hot-wire it."

Aaron looked at her, surprised.

"An old boyfriend taught me. He liked to steal cars."

"In your wild days."

"We always brought them back. It wasn't really stealing."

Up ahead cars and taxis were leaving the traffic circle at Sarmiento, back to town.

"OK," Aaron said. "If we can lose them."

They entered the circle, passing the exit branch for Sarmiento, then the road to the port, sweeping around until they were pointing back up the waterfront. Hanna turned left, doing the circle again, merging with new traffic from the airport.

"What are you doing?"

"Who goes around twice? They'll think I'm back on the airport road. See anybody?"

"No."

"That means we'll be behind them now," she said, pleased with herself.

"For a minute or two."

"That's all we need. The club's right up here."

A boathouse outlined in lights, a long dock with street lamps.

Hanna turned sharply into the driveway and went past a few parked cars before stopping and turning out the lights, her hands still on the wheel, taking short breaths.

"Give it a minute," Aaron said. "Just in case."

"No, now. They have to go up past the airport to turn around. That's our minute." She turned to Otto. "Ready?" In charge now.

The marina was on the other side of the clubhouse.

"Which one is it?"

There were several walkways of wooden planks, boats bobbing next to them, tied and covered for the night, asleep.

"Oh god, I don't know. Let me think. Down here maybe—unless Carlos put it somewhere else. Do they do that?"

"Not usually. You pay for your spot. Like a garage. Does it have a name?"

She looked at him. "*Hanna I.*" Then she took Otto's arm. "*Vati*, come away from the light. You don't want them to see. Here, put this on." She took a life jacket from a pile on a bench.

"We're taking a boat? To Brazil?"

"No, just across. No one will see. Here it is—I think. Help me with the tarp."

The *Hanna I* had gas, a spare tank in the hold, and bench seats on either side, a boat designed for short excursions, fun, not the endless stretch of black water in front of them, with ships hidden in the dark, waiting their turn at the port.

"It's nicer at night," Hanna said, looking out. "The water. In the day, it's brown. All the mud."

She was attacking the wiring under the controls while Aaron watched, fascinated. A spark, the engine turning over, surprisingly loud in the empty marina. Two headlights appeared in the parking lot.

"It might be them. Come on. No lights."

He threw the tie-up rope onto the planks.

"We have to have lights," Hanna said. "We'll run into something."

"Get out past the dock first."

"It's probably just someone late for dinner," Hanna said, backing the boat away and then heading out to open water, some moonlight catching the small waves, the reflective sheen of ink.

"Can you go faster?"

She was standing at the wheel, peering over the windshield, the marina lights behind them now.

"Not in the dark."

"We don't want anybody to see a light. Not yet."

She shrugged. "I should be used to it with you. Not knowing where I'm going. And then it's too late."

"What are you talking about?"

"Nothing." She switched on a lamp at the front of the boat, lighting up the water ahead. "I'm not going to drive into a freighter. It's pitch dark out here."

But in fact the city behind them was filling the sky with the milky haze of a million lights, the waterfront ribboned with them, the massive cranes at the port outlined in bright bulbs, like rides at a fair.

"Do you know how to get there?"

"It's a straight shot across. We'll see the shore lights." She jerked her head back. "How's he doing?"

Otto was sitting on the side bench, looking out at the city, his head tilted up, almost military, an admiral.

"All right. How are you doing?"

"I'm here, aren't I?"

He stood closer to her, putting his hand on her shoulder. "When this is over—"

She stiffened, backing away from his touch, retreating.

"What? We'll be lovers again? Kiss and make up? What a little boy you are."

"You know I—"

"Don't say it." She looked at him. "I think you do. Whatever that means to you. But it doesn't matter. Now it's never going to be over, all this. Not for me. I know," she said, waving off any interruption. "It's the right thing. Don't tell me again. So, the right thing. But what about me? What do I do during the trial? Sit there and watch? And they're watching me. Hide? All you see is him. But think what it means for me."

They were going more slowly now, away from the shore, the motor a softer purring than before.

"I can't change what happened," Aaron said. "What he did."

"No. Or forget it. You're going to make sure we don't do that."

"We can't forget it. We owe it to them."

She looked over at him. "The trial won't be the end for you either."

"What trial?" Otto said from the stern, suddenly alert. "What are you talking about?"

"Nothing," Hanna said. "Just talk. Are you warm enough?"

Otto touched his sleeve. "You were right about the coat. It gets chilly on the water." He looked up. "But how did you know we'd be on the water? We were going to the airport."

"The Israelis found us. We had to go a different way."

Otto thought about this for a second. "How do they know everything? They must have someone working for them. One of us."

"Don't talk crazy. Who? Markus?"

"No, not Markus. I don't know. Maybe Julio. Except you killed him," he said, looking at Aaron. "And you were with them at that place where they kept me."

"*Vati*, enough."

"How do you know who he is? You trust people. And look where we are," he said, turning his head. "In the middle of the ocean. He could kill me here and no one would know."

"Don't talk like that."

"One shot and over the side. Mission accomplished."

"Then why didn't I kill you in the cemetery?"

"I don't know. It's confusing."

"That's not who he is," Hanna said.

"No. Max's boy," Otto said, vague again. "I sent him to the gas. Did you escape? But that's not possible. Nobody could. We made sure of that. The times for the gas were exact. And then the capos checked—that everyone was dead. It didn't take long. And it was easier for them. A few minutes and—"

"Stop," Hanna said, staring at him.

"Yes, I know, nobody wants to hear now. But how else to do it? We couldn't afford to be sentimental. Max," he said, looking at Aaron, Max's boy again. "I made him do it. The experiments. I saved him to do it. He thought he was too good for that, our work. But you have to do it, like the rest of us. What could he do? Object? Nobody objected there. That's why it worked so well. But he never understood about you." He looked up at Aaron. "How I made it easier for you."

"That's what you want?" Hanna said to Aaron. "For everybody to hear him talking like this?"

"And now he's sent you to kill me. He said he would find me someday, but he died. So he sent you. And you," he said to Hanna. "You believe him. He tricked you, just like your husband, if you call him that. They're all alike. Their pound of flesh. Of course he blamed me. From university even, he was jealous. My fault, my fault, that he wanted to save his own skin. Did he say no? He did it."

"Stop," Hanna said softly, her body tense, a clock winding tighter. She put her hand on the control, idling the engine, and they began to drift, the motor less audible, as if calming the boat would slow down the flow of words.

"Why are we stopping?" Otto said, getting up, his voice frantic. "Is this where you plan to do it? Out here? And you, my own child. But weak, like your mother."

"Enough."

"To listen to a man like this. Max's boy. Why else would he be here, except to kill me? So Max has his revenge. Years it took him. I was too clever for him. But now—"

"He's taking you to Uruguay. And then to Germany."

"No, Madrid," Otto said, correcting a minor error.

"No, Germany. No more lies. To Germany. To stand trial."

Otto drew himself up, an admiral again.

"And you knew this?"

"Yes."

"He made you do this?"

"The Israelis will kill you if you don't get away. There's no choice. Now sit. Calm down."

"You did this," Otto said to Aaron. "Assassin. Why didn't you die in the gas? How did you escape? One of the capos must have—" He stopped, losing the thread, waiting for his thought to catch up.

Hanna looked at him, her eyes darting, dismayed.

"I was making it easier for you," Otto said, a plea. "Don't you understand that?" And then he blinked, back on the boat, taking Aaron in, and ran toward him, knocking him back against the control panel.

"Stop!" Hanna yelled, backing out of the way.

Aaron felt the hands on his throat, holding the chain on Fritz. Suddenly tighter. Not even another second. Now. He punched at Otto's bullet wound, hearing the scream of pain tear out of the boat and over the water. Otto doubled over, holding his side.

"Stop! Now. I'll shoot," Hanna said, a gun in her hand.

Aaron and Otto went still, both staring at her.

"What are you doing?" Aaron said quietly.

"What has to be done. You said to bring it. You were right. I need it."

"What for?"

"You didn't think I could let you do this, did you? Put him on trial. Put me on trial. Go through that all over again. Never an end. He's dead once, let him stay dead." She lowered her voice. "He's my father. The same blood."

"That's right," Otto said. "German blood."

"Oh, German," she said, her voice weary. "Again with that. It never ends. Not here. Not in Madrid."

"Blood doesn't mean anything," Aaron said.

"Then why do you look at me like that? You think I'm weak?" she said to Otto. "No. Strong. Like you."

She raised the gun. Aaron felt a tingling in his hands, some fragment of reflex to hold them up, but they stayed at his sides, locked in place, his whole body unable to move.

The sound exploded in his ear, booming on the water. He waited for the thud in his chest, the searing pain that would knock him over, but it was Otto who was pitching forward, mouth open in surprise, crashing down onto the deck in a heap. The boat rocked back and forth, then steadied, but Hanna's shoulders kept moving, the winding mechanism finally snapping.

"My god," she said, still shaking, dropping the hand with the gun to her side.

Aaron looked at her, too startled to speak.

"Is he dead?" she said finally.

Aaron stooped down and turned Otto over, checking his neck for a pulse. "Yes."

"So now I've done this. What kind of person does this? My god."

"Hanna—" he said, getting up, turning to her, but she was shaking her head, shoulders still heaving. She drew a breath, some audible sign of control.

"Take off the life jacket. We don't want him to float."

"What?"

"The life jacket." She looked up. "Help me. Do you think this is easy for me?"

He nodded to the gun, still in her hand. "Were you planning to do this?"

"No. Yes. I don't know. He kept talking. Talking. That's what it's like now. Imagine in court." She looked up. "I couldn't. So he's killed by his own child. Can you think of anything worse? Is that enough revenge for you? To be killed by your own?" Her voice breaking now. She looked down at the gun, surprised to see it, then lifted her hand and tossed it over the side, the splash like a starting sound, bringing her back. "Help me. Check his pockets."

"You can't just—"

"What? Put him in the water? Why not? He's dead."

"They'll find him. The body."

"No, the currents will take him. And if they do, who do they find? Otto Schramm died two years ago. The police say so. Everybody says so. So who is this?"

She knelt, taking papers out of his breast pocket and tearing them, then tossing them into the water.

"You have to help me with him. He's too heavy for me."

Aaron looked down at Otto's face, gray and inert, his mouth still open in surprise. What had he seen at the end? Hanna with a gun or some phantom in his mind, still tracking him all the way from Poland, finally here.

"I'll take his feet," Hanna said, the words waking him, tapping him on the shoulder.

He hooked his arms under Otto's and lifted him from behind. "Put his legs over."

And then the body was sliding, Otto's weight doing the work, Aaron spreading his legs apart to steady the boat as he heaved, waiting for the splash, oddly muffled, the water closing over the gray head.

Hanna stood for a minute looking at the water, until the ripples had gone.

"I don't know why I feel so bad. Somebody had to do it. You wanted to make a spectacle, show everybody how crazy he was."

"I never—"

"So somebody had to. You could see that tonight—he wasn't himself anymore. It's just—you don't expect to feel like this. You put a dog down. It's time. It's better for him. For everybody. But it's your dog." She turned to Aaron. "He was good to me. But he did those things. How do you make sense of that? How do you live with that?" Her mouth turned up, a wry gesture. "And now look. I didn't think I could do it. And then, when I had the gun, it wasn't hard. So, the father's daughter."

"You're not—"

"I saw your face and I knew. You thought I would do it. Kill you. Like him. Another Nazi. You change your name and you're still Otto Schramm's daughter. The same blood." She stopped, reminded of something, suddenly practical. "We have to clean up. Is there blood?"

"I'll look."

"We should get the boat back before anyone sees it's gone."

"What about Markus?"

"Well, Markus," she said, thinking out loud. "The Israelis. He'll believe that—he's afraid of them."

"And Julio? He worked for—"

"More Israelis. And now a case for the police. He won't want to go near that. Was anyone there besides you and my father?"

"No."

"Then no one knows."

"Except you."

She looked down, nodding to the water where Otto had disappeared.

"Or you with him. So that's useful." She stopped, looking away. "Isn't that what we do? Use each other."

"No."

"And now more lies. Worse."

"I didn't want this to happen."

"No? I did. And now he's dead and I'm still his daughter."

"The trial would have—"

"Oh, the famous trial. With all the world watching. And after? You think it would be over? For you?" She shook her head. "You think you're him. That boy. The one he kept seeing."

"Max's son."

"Yes, him. You think you're him. But he's dead."

"So we just forget about him?"

"I don't know. The way he died—what would be enough for that? But this business—you found my father, but look what you did to do it. Now what, another Otto? Then another? So many others."

"Otto was different."

"Maybe not." She looked at the water. "Or maybe it just seemed that way to me. My father. So now what?" She turned to face him. "Would you do something for me?"

He waited.

"Talk to Jamie."

"What?"

"I can't stay here now," she said, moving her hand toward the water. "It's finished for me. Markus, whatever I say to him, he'll be suspicious. It's better to go."

"Back to New York?" he said, not following.

"No. You gave me an idea."

"Me?"

"I can't get rid of the name, who I am, so where would I be welcome? Not here anymore. Not Germany. But Otto Schramm's daughter would be welcome in Madrid. Perón always liked him. And the others? A new face. And if I work for Jamie, I'm protected. Markus wouldn't dare make trouble for me. Or your Israelis. I'd be safe. Jamie wanted my father, but he gets something better. I'm a woman. I can do things my father couldn't do."

"Sleep with someone."

"If I have to. I'm easy. You ought to know."

"Hanna—"

"All you have to do is be nice to me. Don't look so shocked. Madrid's not bad. For once I'd be doing the right thing. Helping Uncle Sam. We'd be on the same side."

"No, we wouldn't."

"But we never have been, have we?"

He stared at her for a second, then took her by the shoulders. "You don't mean this. I won't—"

"Oh, and what? Save me for a better life? With you? It's too late for that. He ruined that for me too. I killed him but he's still in my head. And yours now. You'd only make it worse. Just seeing you. Both of us knowing. This way, sometimes I'll forget." She moved away from his hands, turning to the control knob to increase their speed, heading back to the club. "If you really want to help me, talk to Jamie. Soon."

"What do I say about this? He thinks Otto's alive."

"Because you did. But you were wrong. Otto died two years ago. You've been chasing a ghost."

Nathan was waiting at the marina, leaning against one of the dock lights, smoking, his head shining under the lamp. When Hanna steered the boat in and cut the engine, he moved toward them slowly, tossing the cigarette into the water, a forced casualness.

"Good trip?" he said.

"You've been waiting all this time?"

Nathan shrugged. "Nobody leaves a car out in Buenos Aires. They disappear. So I figured you'd be back." He nodded to Hanna. "You're quite a driver. Boats too?" He turned to Aaron. "Where is he?"

"He's dead." Aaron looked over at him. "I wanted to do it. For Max."

Hanna turned to him, staring.

"You shouldn't have done that. People think they know what they're doing and they make a mess of it."

"I didn't. He's gone. In the water."

"Bodies wash up."

"John Does. Otto's already dead."

"They're going to think we did it. All his pals."

"Then you get your message out anyway."

Nathan looked at Hanna. "And you?"

"She was lucky to get away," Aaron said. "When you snatched him. She thought you'd take her too, but you only wanted Otto, so she got away. In the car. It's Bildener's car." He looked at her. "You'll need something to tell him when you take it back. You don't know where they took Otto. You can only imagine the worst. What you've always been afraid of. And now you're frightened to stay here. Who's next? Can you do it?"

She nodded, her eyes on him.

Nathan looked at both of them, assessing, trying to piece this together, then turned to Hanna. "You'd better get going, then. It's late." He jerked his thumb toward Aaron. "I assume you disappeared when we snatched Otto? Or are you one of us?"

"You don't want any trouble with the Americans," Aaron said. "You threw me out of the car. I had to walk to the airport to get a cab home. But I saw you. Your face. So the sooner I get out of Buenos Aires the better."

"OK," Nathan said. "Someday tell me another story. The one that explains you," he said to Hanna.

"I would like to hear that one. That explains me." She waited a minute. "Tell me something. Would you have killed him?"

"In a heartbeat," Nathan said, his voice even.

"Then maybe it's better. He always thought Max would get him. This is the way it made sense to him." She looked at her watch. "I'll cover the boat. Carlos will never know."

She began to snap the tarp into place. Aaron had turned to help, but Nathan touched his arm, drawing him away, head close, private.

"Don't do that again. I thought something had happened to you."

"It was personal. For Max."

"There's no room for personal—"

"What's the difference? Somebody was going to do it."

"The difference is, now there's a witness."

"She's not—"

"Don't be an idiot. A roll in the hay and you think she's—? She's his daughter. She's a witness."

Aaron looked at him, alarmed, Hanna now in Nathan's cross-hairs, the hunt never over.

"Don't go near her," he said flatly.

"I've got the others to think about. Something starts unravel-ing and—"

"She works for us. The Agency. Leave it."

Nathan stopped. "You want to explain that to me?"

"Some other time. Right now, I just want to get out of here."

Nathan looked up at him. "Your first time?"

Aaron said nothing.

"You need anything cleaned up? Goldfarb's good at that."

Aaron shook his head. "It's done. He's gone."

Nathan was quiet for a moment. "It's not easy. You think it's going to be—" He took a breath. "But then it gets better. And you make them afraid. Every day they think, Is this the day? The day they come for me? It's not justice, but it's something." He took out a cigarette and lit it. "Not everybody can do this work. It takes a certain—"

"What?"

Nathan looked at him, not answering for a second, as if he was thinking this over. "Outrage, I think," he said finally. "A sense of outrage. That people help them. Hide them. Somebody went into business with Mengele when he was here. Somebody protected him in Paraguay. Now they say Brazil, but who knows? Only the protectors. And these are people who have seen what it was like. All the pictures. The corpses. In piles. And still they protect them. So, what do you think, do you have this outrage?"

"Why? Are you trying to recruit me?"

"Recruit you? You're already in it. You killed a man. I thought, at first—but I was wrong. You found him. You acted. Max would have been proud."

"No. It's not what he wanted."

"Max had no life. He ate soup every night alone, reading those files. Over and over. To catch a few guards. You caught Otto."

"But he got away. For good. He'll never answer now."

"So he answered to you."

Aaron looked down to the marina. "In a way."

"Don't beat yourself up. You'll feel better tomorrow."

"Do you? Every time you do it? Just curious."

Nathan met his eyes, then looked away, toward the boats. "You don't want to start anything there. She's a witness."

"Let me worry about that."

"Good. Worry. Keep your eyes open. And when any of this

makes sense, let me know. Meanwhile, you'd better say good-bye to Buenos Aires. Go sort out the files."

"You can have the files. I'm out. I don't want to feel better the next day. What does that make me? Like them, maybe."

"Then who does it?"

"I don't know. Somebody tough." Looking at him.

"You want to know something? The first time, I threw up."

Aaron smiled. "But you got over it."

"So will you." Nathan hesitated. "It's something you don't walk away from. Not now. There are other people to consider." Staring at him. "You're a witness too."

Aaron stared back, seeing the rest of it, the door closing, everything that didn't need to be said.

"Here's your girlfriend."

She was coming down the marina walkway, shoes clicking on the planks, the dock light behind her.

"That should do it," she said. "Did you work things out? Am I free to go?" Brisk, the sarcasm a kind of poke.

Nathan, surprised, waved his arm in a maître d' gesture.

"Walk me to the car," she said to Aaron.

He followed her up the short flight of steps to the parking lot, dark, only a few security lights left on, a pale patch at the back of her neck, the first thing he had noticed.

"So thank you for that," she said when they were out of earshot. "You didn't have to say you did it."

"I know. He'd never understand it. This way—"

"You're protecting me again. You like that."

"We both did it. I started. You just—finished it."

She looked at him again. "Your accomplice. Or maybe you were mine. Isn't it funny. After everything, all the lies—" She put her hand up to the side of his face. "Still. From that first night. At the Alvear." Her hand stopped. "If it means anything to you, I wish it had been different. That we'd both been—somebody else."

"But we weren't."

No," she said, dropping the hand. "So here we are." She looked up, eyes fixing on his.

"It's not too late," he said, wanting to stick out his hand, to catch something.

"Shh," she said, hushing a child. "Do you know what I think, though? I'm the last. So that's something. You'll be like him now." She nodded to Nathan. "Chasing Ottos. And missing—"

"Missing what?" he said quietly, stung, the words stopping his breathing.

She looked away. "But maybe I'm just imagining it. People do, when it's over. The love of my life. Like a song. And was it?"

"Was it?"

She leaned up and kissed him on the cheek. "Let's pretend it was. So what do you think?" she said, a wry cheerfulness. "Will Perón tell me his secrets?" Her voice low with the old intimacy, speaking a language only they knew, and he looked at her, light-headed, suddenly feeling it slip away, the only thing that had ever happened to him, irretrievable, gone.

He nodded, trying to find the same voice. "Anybody would."

She hesitated for a second, then she smiled, a last smile, and got in the car.

"What was that all about?" Nathan said, at his side.

"Good-bye," Aaron said, watching her drive away, her voice still in his head.

"She looks like him. Imagine looking at him every day. After you—" He stopped. "Come on, let's get you packed. Somebody's going to start missing Fritz soon and you don't want to be around to answer any questions." In charge, taking care of his team.

"Fritz," Aaron said, seeing him again, the splayed legs, the welts on his neck.

"Don't forget who he was, Papa Schramm," Nathan said, still following the car. He turned to Aaron. "You did the right thing."

The words hung between them for a second. "Yes," Aaron said, just to say something, not answering, his hand on the open car door, listening for her voice, head turned up as if the sound were really outside him, some private conversation in the air. But Nathan was talking again, his gravelly voice drowning out the whispering one, which grew fainter, more distant, until Aaron didn't hear it anymore.